Christmas at the Beach House

Diamond Beach Book 7

MAGGIE MILLER

CHRISTMAS AT THE BEACH HOUSE: Diamond Beach, book 7
Copyright © 2023 Maggie Miller

It's Christmastime in Diamond Beach!

With the holidays fast approaching, Claire, Roxie, and their families are all anticipating the big day. There are gifts to buy, parties to attend, trees to decorate, and festivities to prepare for. There is so much to do, so much to get ready for, and so many exciting events going on in their lives. Not to mention the new homes, new proposals, and new promises.

Catch up with the families and all the changes that have taken place in lives in the past months. Join the fun as they celebrate Christmas at the beach house!

Chapter One

If there was one season Claire loved more than any other, it was Christmas. No other time of year, not even Thanksgiving or Easter, although those came close, lent itself to being celebrated through baking the way Christmas did. Being part-owner of a bakery at Christmastime just supercharged her desire to bake everything.

People gave tins of cookies as gifts, which was how she'd come up with the idea of offering tins of cookies ready to go. What other time of year did that happen? No other time, that's when.

Those tins were selling well, too, making her proud that she'd come up with the idea.

She brushed a little flour off her apron and went to have a peek at the gingerbread Santas baking in Oven Number One. The phone rang but she let it go. It was the job of those working on the retail side to answer it. The cookies looked good. They smelled even better. In fact, the whole bakery was perfumed with the sweet, spicy aroma.

For this particular batch of gingerbread, she'd hand-selected the best-quality cinnamon, ginger, and cloves. She'd chosen molasses from a company that made it in small batches, producing a syrup known for its depth of flavor. All the ingredients were top notch. It was too bad the molasses was back-ordered and had only just arrived. She would have loved to have these Santas available much sooner in the season, but there wasn't anything she could do about that.

She couldn't wait to see how this first tray turned out.

Raul, one of the bakers she and Danny had hired as part of their opening team, smiled at her from across the worktable, where he was filling loaf pans with fruitcake batter. "The cookies smell great."

"They really do, don't they?" She went over to check his work—not that she had any real concerns. Hiring Raul had been a great decision. He was skilled in the kitchen, as well as quick and neat. And he knew his Puerto Rican flavors. "I hope our customers are as happy with these as I am."

"How could they not be?"

"Let's hope." She smiled. The fruitcakes were available by special order only and she'd limited the run to a hundred cakes. Originally, it had been fifty, but demand had been greater than she'd expected. These would all be boxed for pickup once they were done, all of them spoken for.

There couldn't be any more made, because there wasn't time. Soaking the dried fruits in brandy took nearly four weeks. Her recipe was developed from several very old recipes, and it had taken her a while to perfect it. She wasn't going to shortcut anything just to suit someone's needs.

Raul laughed. "There's enough brandy in these cakes to make anyone happy. I bet next year, the demand doubles."

"Wouldn't that be something?"

The oven timer went off. She put mitts on and got the cookies out, transferring them to a cooling rack. She leaned over them and inhaled. They'd still need to be decorated, but she'd taste one without icing as soon as they were cool enough.

Danny came into the kitchen. "Is that gingerbread I smell?"

"It is." He'd known she was making them. He'd undoubtedly come in to do his own taste test. "But they're not cool enough to taste yet."

He took a closer look at the cookies on the baking rack.

"You'll burn your fingers," she warned, laughing.

He shook his head. "It's hard to wait."

"Is that what you came back here for? To test a cookie?"

He grinned. "Not entirely. We just got a call requesting a special Christmas cake." His brows lifted. "It's for the mayor's Christmas party."

"Christmas is in something like a week and a half. He's just calling now?"

"It wasn't him, it was his office. And apparently, the girl who called thought the other girl in the office had ordered it, but she hadn't, because she thought the girl who called had ordered it. There was a big misunderstanding and now the mayor has no cake for his party. It would be great if we could help them out. Be good for our reputation, you know?"

"I do know." Claire exhaled. "I need to look at the job board and see if I can find room. How big of a cake do they need? And how fancy?"

Danny made a face. "Big enough for a hundred and fifty people. As for the decorations, they don't care, as long as it's Christmasy."

That was a big cake. And she was taking half the

day off tomorrow, something she wasn't about to change. "Any special flavors?"

He shook his head. "Again, so long as it's seasonally appropriate, they don't care. They're more concerned about actually having a cake than what that cake is."

"I can understand that. Give me a couple minutes to figure out if I can do it and I'll let you know."

His gaze went to the cookies again.

She laughed. "I'll bring you a cookie when I come to give you my answer."

"Deal." He returned to the front of the shop.

She went to study the jobs board. It was filled with special orders. Every day had at least one job to be done. Most days had two or three. This close to Christmas, they were hustling like mad. She crossed her arms as she stared at the board. Making a cake for the mayor's party would mean working a late night or two.

It wasn't something she could just cobble together. This was for the mayor's party. A lot of influential people would be there. People who could give the bakery more business with their own functions.

She didn't want to lose out on this job, but it was going to be tricky.

Raul came to stand beside her. "Whatever you need to get that cake done, I'll help."

She glanced at him. "You're sure? What about your daughter? Isn't she on winter break already?" Raul had a nine-year-old daughter he was raising alone. He'd lost his wife in a car accident not long after their daughter was born. His sister lived with him and helped out where she could.

He nodded. "She is. But if it's okay with you, she could come in with me when I'd normally be home with her or when Teresa can't watch her. Louisa won't be in the way. She'll just sit and read or play on her tablet."

Claire smiled. "I'm not worried about Louisa being in the way. She's a sweet kid. I'm more worried about her being bored."

He grinned. "Give her a cookie now and then and she'll be perfectly happy, I promise." He shrugged. "And I wouldn't mind the extra hours. The older she gets, the more expensive her wish list is."

"I hear you on that. Okay, you can help me, then. We'll need to figure out pretty quick what we're doing so we know we have what we need."

"We should stick with something we can do in our sleep."

She nodded. "I was thinking red velvet with a vanilla cream cheese frosting."

"Red is festive." He shrugged, amusement on his face. "You're the boss. I think they'll be happy with anything."

"Maybe." She shook her head. "But I don't want to risk that. If they want us to make the cake, they need to pick the flavors. I don't want to hear back that no one liked it because we chose something the mayor wasn't a fan of. Not to mention, we have enough to worry about without adding to it."

"I agree. Good thinking."

She gave him a smile, then grabbed a gingerbread Santa and headed out to the front of the store to let Danny know her decision. He was ringing up a customer who was buying a sour orange pie. Thanks to the article in the *Gulf Gazette* that Conrad, her mom's fiancé, had written, those pies were doing great. On the weekends, it was hard to keep them in stock.

She broke the head off the Santa and ate it while thinking about her mom and Conrad. The cookie was even better than she'd hoped. After tomorrow's

Justice of the Peace ceremony, her mom and Conrad would be married. Wouldn't that be something?

Claire was tempted to eat more of the cookie, but things were busy out front. Amy, the young woman they'd hired to work the retail side of things, was making coffee for someone. There were people waiting at the counter, too.

Claire set the cookie down and jumped in to help. "Who's next?"

A woman raised her hand. "I am."

"What can I get you?"

"These two tins, plus two dozen assorted cookies and a dozen assorted cupcakes."

Claire grabbed a box for the cookies first. "You got it." She filled the order and took the boxes to the register for Danny to ring up, then she helped the next customer. It took fifteen minutes for things to slow down long enough for her to talk to him.

She blew out a breath. "We need more help."

He was eating the gingerbread cookie she'd left on the counter. "This is really good. And I was just thinking the same thing. It's a little too late to put an ad in the paper with Christmas so close, though."

"I know. I guess we're just going to have to do the best we can. Next year, though? We're hiring holiday help."

"Agreed. Did you decide about the mayor's cake?"

"I did. I'll do it, but they have to pick out the flavors. I don't want to guess and be wrong."

"You sure you can handle an extra order that's this substantial? You're not going to skip your mom's wedding, are you?"

"Not a chance. Raul said he'd help me so long as we don't mind Louisa coming in with him when necessary. Which I don't. She's off for winter break, so he doesn't have a choice."

"Fine with me. So long as she's not bored to death."

"I said the same thing. He assures me she won't be."

"Then we're set." He pulled a piece of paper from his apron pocket. "This number is Regina at the mayor's office. You want to talk to her?"

Claire took the paper. "I do."

More customers came in.

"And now I'm leaving before I never make it back to the kitchen."

He smiled. "I've asked Ivelisse to let all the Mrs. Butter's Popcorn crews know that we have hours available at the bakery if any of them want to make some extra Christmas money." He held a finger up. "Still doing things differently next year, however."

"For sure." She gave him a thumbs-up as she went back through the kitchen door. She went straight to the office and called the number.

"Mayor Griffin Tate's office, this is Regina speaking. How can the mayor help you today?"

"Hi, Regina. This is Claire Thompson from Mrs. Butter's Bakery, calling you back about the cake?"

"Oh, thank you, Lord. Are you able to make a cake for us? Please say yes."

Claire smiled. "We don't really have room in our schedule, but we're going to make room. On one condition."

"Anything. Name it. You want to charge extra? Totally understand. You need tickets to something? Want the mayor to visit the shop? A street named after you? I can arrange all sorts of things. Well, maybe not that last one. But I can definitely work with you."

Claire laughed. "I just need you to tell me what flavor cake and buttercream the mayor would like."

"Oh." Regina went silent. "He loves chocolate and orange. Can you do something with that?"

"Sure." Chocolate and orange was a great combination. And a classic for Christmas. "Dark chocolate or milk chocolate?"

"He doesn't care. He just loves chocolate. Honestly, as long as the cake looks like Christmas and tastes good, he'll be happy."

Claire was happy, too. She already had chocolate blanks, which were pre-baked sheet cakes well-wrapped and ready to go, in the freezer. All she'd have to do would be to cut them to size, fill the layers, and decorate them. This was going to be easier than she'd thought.

Even easier than the simple cake she'd made for her mom and Conrad's wedding lunch tomorrow. "Consider it done."

Chapter Two

Roxie tossed a load of towels into the salon's dryer and set the machine to run. Walter, her daughter's little white terrier, was in his bed, gnawing on one of his Nyla bones. Roxie scratched his head. "You're being such a good boy, Walter. I promise we'll go for a walk soon, okay?"

He wasn't fazed, too occupied with his bone to care about going for a walk at that moment.

She went back out onto the floor. The salon was jumping, with every chair filled and two more women in the waiting area. The phone had been ringing constantly with calls from people hoping to get their hair done before the holidays.

Amber, the salon assistant, was sweeping up. Keeping the salon tidy was a full-time job when it was this busy.

Roxie loved it when it was like this, high energy

and bustling with activity. Made the day fly by. And it made her feel super useful. That was so important.

She stopped by Trina's station, where she was giving the mayor's wife, Rebecca Tate, her now-signature caramel-blond highlights. "You need anything, Trina?"

Trina shook her head as she brushed bleach onto the hair within the foil. "I'm good, Ma. Becs, you want something?"

Rebecca looked up from her phone. "I'd love a bottle of water."

"Coming right up," Roxie said. Trina's miraculous salvation of Rebecca's self-inflicted hair disaster had done wonders for the shop. They'd been busy almost since Day One. Word, when it came from the right people, spread like crazy.

They'd even had a little writeup in the *Gulf Gazette*'s social column.

She went back to the breakroom, got a bottle of water, dropped it off with Rebecca, then headed for the reception desk. She arrived in time to answer the phone. "A Cut Above hair salon, this is Roxie speaking. How can I help?"

"Hi. Do you guys do waxing?"

"No, I'm sorry, we don't offer that at this time."

"Okay, thanks."

Roxie hung up. Waxing was something Trina had talked about but had yet to hire anyone to do. They'd definitely had requests for it, but adding the service would mean dedicating some space for the setup and, right now, they were too busy to think about it.

Maybe she'd talk to Trina about it again tonight. From here, they were going over to Willie's for the very first dinner at the new house. Roxie was so excited. Not just to see the place, but to celebrate with her mom and Miguel.

Ethan, Roxie's boyfriend, was a big reason why Willie and Miguel had gotten into their house before Christmas. Once he'd finished the shopping center renovations, Willie had hired him and his crew to oversee the finishing of the house.

The extra hands had meant the house had been done almost a month early. And while it had cost Willie and Miguel some money, they said it had been worth it.

Now they were in and getting ready to celebrate Christmas in their new place. Roxie was thrilled for them.

She smiled. She knew that Miguel was presenting Willie with her Christmas gift tonight, even though Christmas wasn't for another week. With a gift like this, there was no waiting.

She had a feeling her mom was going to cry when she saw it.

A customer came in.

"Hi," Roxie said. She glanced at the schedule on the computer. "Are you Jane?"

The woman smiled. "I am. Jane Simmons. I have a three o'clock with Ginger."

"She's just finishing up. Have a seat and I'll let her know you're here."

Roxie went back to Ginger's station, where she was polishing her blowout. "Looks great." Roxie smiled at the woman in the chair before speaking to Ginger. "Your three o'clock is here. Jane Simmons."

"Two minutes. Thanks." Ginger turned off the hair dryer and gave her client a big smile. "You look like a million bucks, Mrs. Zimbalist."

Roxie took a quick look around before she returned to the reception desk, just to see if anyone needed anything. Jacques, the newest hire and the only man on staff, gave her a communicating glance.

She went to see what was up. "Did you need me?"

He nodded. "Lynn needs an appointment for an

updo on the twenty-third. Can you see if I'm available at three for that?"

"Sure thing. Be right back."

Amber was at the desk now, so Roxie didn't have to be as concerned about walk-ins. She pulled up Jacques' schedule. He had an opening at the right time on the right day, so she typed Lynn Crawford's name into the spot. Then she wrote the appointment down on a card and went back to his station.

"Here you go, Lynn. You're all booked."

"Thank you." Lynn took the card with a smile.

With that done, Roxie went back to check on Walter. She got his leash off the hook on the wall. "Okay, buddy. Let's go out for a quick walk. See if you need to do anything."

She took him out the back door and past the dumpsters to where a small strip of grass separated the paved area from a retention pond. A chain-link fence surrounded it, making sure no one wandered in. Or, as was sometimes the case in Florida, no gators wandered out.

Even so, Roxie kept a close eye on the water. Never hurt to be careful. She imagined Walter might look like a tasty snack to a gator. Walter paid the retention pond no mind. He did what he needed to do, scratched up some grass, sniffed a flowering weed, then trotted toward the dumpsters.

"Oh, no, you don't." Roxie took him back in.

By six o'clock, she was ready to go. The salon would be open for three more hours, but Ginger, who'd been promoted to assistant manager a month ago, would lock up.

Roxie and Trina were off to Willie's with Walter securely in his car seat for safe traveling.

Trina let out big exhale. "Man, I can't believe how busy we've been. I'm seriously amazed."

"You shouldn't be," Roxie said. "It's all your doing. All your great hair and hard work. People love you."

Trina smiled. "It's been a team effort. And let's be honest—me getting to fix Becs' hair was huge. I mean, *huge*. And I had nothing to do with her calling me. That was just chance."

Roxie nodded as she turned toward Dunes West, the retirement community where Willie and Miguel now lived. "First of all, it wasn't chance. It was God." Going to church with Ethan had really changed her perspective on a lot of things. "Secondly, if you hadn't made her happy with the results, it wouldn't have mattered."

"That's true." Trina glanced out the window. "I wish Miles could make it tonight."

"I know, honey. I wish he could, too." Roxie felt a little guilty that Ethan would be at dinner. She knew how much Trina would be missing Miles, but he was a paramedic and he worked different shifts from most people.

"It's okay," Trina said. "I'll have Walter." She glanced into the backseat. "Won't I, baby? You're such a good boy."

"He really is," Roxie said. "He does so good at the shop."

"Which I'm very glad for. I don't know what I'd do if I had to leave him home."

"We'd figure something out. But thankfully, we don't have to."

"Oh!" Trina sat up straighter. "I totally forgot to tell you. Becs invited us to the mayor's Christmas party."

Roxie blinked, mouth open. "Seriously? You mean 'us,' as in I'm invited, too?"

Trina nodded. "And you can bring a guest, so Ethan, obviously. It's kind of crazy, right? I've never been to a party like that before. She said it's really more of a Christmas open house, but the fact that she invited us is very cool. I don't think it's something you can just show up to, even if it is sort of an open house."

"I'm sure you can't, unless you're already friends with them. Wow." Roxie smiled. "We're moving up in the world, kid."

Trina laughed. "Who'd have thought, huh?"

Roxie went through the gate at the Preserve, the high-end section of Dunes West where Willie lived, and a few minutes later, she was pulling into her mom's new driveway. Ethan's truck was currently parked there. "Look at this place, will you? Gorgeous. I can't believe your grandmother lives here."

"It's like Barbie's Dreamhouse. If Barbie hit it big as a senior."

Roxie laughed. "Come on. Let's go in. I can't wait to see the inside."

Trina unbuckled her seatbelt. "Are Walter's feet clean? I don't want him tracking anything on the floors."

"They should be. He was in the salon most of the day."

Trina carried Walter to the front door, maybe to make sure he didn't step in anything, though Roxie wasn't sure what he could have gotten into. Everything, landscaping included, was brand new and pristine.

Willie opened the door before Roxie could push the bell. "There's my girls! And my great-granddog! Come on in."

"Ma," Roxie said. "This place is..." She shook her head at the white marble tiles, deep teal walls, and crystal accents. "There aren't words. Except for gorgeous."

Willie beamed. "I keep pinching myself but it's real. Ain't it something?"

"I almost feel bad bringing Walter in," Trina said. "I don't want him to mess anything up."

"Oh, nonsense. You let that baby down. He can run around and do anything he wants."

"Okay," Trina said. "If you say so." She put Walter down, but he stayed by her side.

"Where's Ethan?" Roxie asked.

"Out back with Miguel. He's grilling some chicken for dinner. You want the tour?"

"I thought you'd never ask," Roxie said.

Willie took them on a walk through the downstairs, pointing out all the little touches and fancy things. She'd hired a decorator to help with making the place look the way she wanted it, and Roxie thought it was money well spent. The house could have been straight out of a magazine.

She especially loved the quirky touches, like the enormous multicolor painting of a fantastical fish in the dining room, complete with large, sequin scales, and the mirrored accent pieces, reminiscent of a disco ball. The fruit bowl in the kitchen held fake fruit: three blue bananas, a yellow and blue polka-dotted apple, a bunch of hot pink grapes, and a green orange.

There was still a coastal vibe, but not in an over-the-top way that so many vacation homes had. This was unique and personal and very much Willie.

"It's a really happy house, Ma. I love that it's not so serious, too. It feels like a place where fun is had."

Willie grinned. "That's what I wanted. Fancy but not stuffy. A place anyone could feel welcome."

Walter let out a little bark and ran toward the sliding doors that led outside. Miguel and Ethan were at the grill, their backs to the women. The lights were on, as it was already dark, and there were three tall propane heaters running to make the dining area more comfortable. December in the panhandle of Florida meant cooler temps and it was in the low sixties at the moment, although it would probably drop a little more as the night went on.

Willie went to the doors. "He's got the right idea. Come on and see the pool area."

She led them outside. The pool was lit up red and green for Christmas and there were lights strung along the back of the property. The cool air felt nice, but Roxie could see how sitting outside in this would feel chilly after a while. The heaters were a good idea.

Ethan touched Miguel's shoulder. "Be right back."

He came up to Roxie. "Hello, there."

"Hi," she said softly.

He greeted her with a kiss. "How was your day?"

"Long." She smiled. She was so ready to spend some time with him. "But it's looking pretty good right now."

Chapter Three

Kat settled in next to Alex on the couch. She'd come to his place straight after work and changed into clothes she'd brought with her, jeans and a Chauncy's Surf Shop sweatshirt. "I can't believe you have to work on Christmas."

"I know. But I'll be off for New Year's. That's something. And at least I'll be with you tomorrow for your grandmother's wedding."

"I'm glad about that." She stared at the television as he selected a streaming channel, her thoughts turning to her grandmother. She'd insisted on a small civil ceremony. No fuss. There would be a reception afterwards at the Brighton Arms Hotel for a much larger number of people. But the only guests at the wedding would be Kat, Alex, Dinah, and Kat's mom. Although Aunt Jules and Cash would have obviously been included if they hadn't been on tour.

Alex kissed the side of her head. "But it's not Christmas. Not the same thing as being home with family. Trust me, I get it."

She nodded, but she also didn't want to make him feel worse than he already did. "We'll make the best of it. Just part of being involved with a first responder, right?"

"Right."

She changed the subject. "Have you finished your Christmas shopping?" They'd decided to keep their gifts really minimal. No more than twenty dollars. Trina and Miles weren't doing presents at all, since they were saving up for their wedding.

"I'm almost there." He laughed. "Most guys don't really finish until Christmas Eve anyway."

She shook her head. "I'd be a stress ball if I did that."

He aimed the remote and started scrolling through the movie options on the screen. "You know you're welcome to come by the firehouse. If you're not too busy with family stuff. If you are and you can't, I understand. No hard feelings, either. Seriously. Holidays are hard when you work the kind of schedule I do."

"I'm going to be there, I promise."

He gestured at the screen. "What do you want? Action and adventure? Comedy? Or a good old-fashioned Christmas movie?"

She smiled. "I could really go for some *Home Alone.*"

"Classic," he said, making the selection. "Irresponsible parents and a precocious eight-year-old it is."

Ten minutes later, there was a knock on his door.

"Pizza's here," he announced. He paused the movie and got up to answer the door while Kat went into the kitchen and got plates, napkins, and sodas for both of them.

She took them out to the living room, setting them up on the coffee table.

He brought the pizza in and set it on the table, opening the box to reveal their dinner. "Sausage, caramelized onions, mushrooms, and extra cheese. Mm-mmm, that looks good."

"Yes, it does," Kat said. She put a slice on each of their plates, the gooey cheese stretching out.

He started the movie going again before picking up his pizza. They ate and laughed and enjoyed the evening. Alex polished off four slices to Kat's two. They finished the meal with some cookies and ice cream that Alex had on hand, then they shared the cleaning up duties.

By the end of the movie, Kat could feel herself drifting toward sleep. No surprise there. Things had been incredibly busy at Future Florida. The holidays were a big giving season and it had been her idea to give out fancy certificates to people that could be used as gifts. Basically, someone could donate to Future Florida in someone else's name. In return, they'd get a certificate highlighting that donation, which could be given to that person.

Those certificates, according to Tom and Molly, the bosses, had brought in an extra eight thousand dollars so far this year. In comparison to what the charity brought in normally, it wasn't such a big amount. But it also wasn't nothing. Eight thousand dollars could go a long way toward helping someone.

Tom and Molly had acted like it was a big deal. Kat wondered if that was more for her benefit. To make her feel good about her idea.

If so, it wasn't necessary. She didn't need any kind of recognition. She was just happy to be contributing. Something she'd already done by getting her Aunt Jules to team up with Future Florida. Not only had she done the Fourth of July concert, but she was donating a percentage of her album sales to the charity.

Kat sighed as her thoughts turned to her aunt and cousin.

"What was that for?" Alex asked.

"Just thinking about how Aunt Jules and Cash won't be here for Christmas, either."

"I know they're on tour, but can't they come home for a few days?"

"Not now. One of the special guests for the Grand Ole Opry's Christmas show had to drop out and they asked Aunt Jules to fill in last-minute. It worked with her tour schedule, so she's doing it. She's pushing hard to make this album a huge success."

"Isn't it one already?"

"Yes, but I think she's a little afraid of backing off just yet. Anyway, on December 23rd, she'll be on stage performing at the Grand Ole Opry. And December 26th, she's supposed to be in Kansas City for the next stop on her tour. That means there's no time for them to come home in between."

"That's a bummer, but she must be thrilled. The Grand Ole Opry is a pretty big deal, isn't it?"

"Oh, definitely. She's already a member, but being asked to be the special guest for one of their

Christmas shows has to really make her feel like she's reached a new level, you know? I'm just being selfish and wanting her home."

He hugged her close. "It's okay to be selfish. This is your first Christmas without your dad. Your life has changed so much this year. It's understandable that you'd want your family around you."

Kat took a deep breath. "I hadn't really thought about it that way, but you're right. So much is different. My grandmother moved out a month ago, but I still expect to see her in the house. Just like I still expect to see Toby come trotting into the kitchen."

"You could get a dog, you know."

"I know. I've thought a lot about it. Just doesn't seem fair to get a dog then leave him home by himself all day. It's not even like my mom would be there. She works longer hours than I do sometimes."

"How's the bakery doing?"

"Amazing," Kat answered. "They're killing it. I couldn't be happier for her. She deserves this."

"That's awesome. It's no surprise to me they're doing well. I tasted all those delicious things your mom sent to the firehouse. She's a baking genius."

Kat grinned. "Maybe we should do some baking."

"Us?" His brows went up. "What would we bake?"

"Christmas cookies for the firehouse."

He laughed. "I hate to tell you this, but Larry's already been making cookies for us. He's got a new one at dinner just about every night."

Larry was the firehouse's cook. He definitely knew his way around the kitchen. "What kinds has he made so far?"

"He did some kind of oatmeal jam bar the other night. Before that there was an M&M cookie made with red and green M&Ms. He did some gingerbread ones, and something called a snowball."

"Oh, I love those. Those are hands down my favorite of all the cookies my mom makes. They melt in your mouth. So good. Although, I don't know if there will be any this year. She's so busy at the bakery that she probably won't have time to make cookies for us."

"You could make them."

She shot him a look. "I'm not sure. I was only kidding when I suggested we make some for the firehouse. I didn't really inherit my mom's kitchen skills."

"They're cookies. How hard can they be?" He got a twinkle in his eyes. "Tell you what—why don't we make them together? If you want. I'll come to your place, and we'll make whatever kinds of cookies you like. We could do it for New Year's Eve. Unless you think that's too boring. What do you say?"

She liked being in the kitchen with Alex. She liked doing anything with him, really, but working in the kitchen together was a lot of fun. Honestly, *everything* with him was a lot of fun. "I think that sounds like a great New Year's Eve. We can watch the ball drop on TV. Hey, why don't we invite Miles and Trina, too? They'll be downstairs anyway. And we'll share the cookies with them. If they're edible."

"If they're edible?" He snorted. "You don't have a lot of faith in us."

"I just know my own limitations. But you're right. They're cookies. Definitely easier to make than a lot of other things. I'll run to the store next week and make sure we have all the right ingredients." Kat scooted forward. "Now, I should get going. I don't want to, but I have work tomorrow and I'm already getting sleepy."

"I hate being away from you."

She sighed. "I hate being away from you."

"Someday, I'm going to do something about that. When we're ready." He leaned in and kissed her.

She closed her eyes. They'd talked about marriage a few times. Kat knew it was a huge step, but she'd never been so happy in her life as she was currently. Marriage was definitely what they were moving toward. They'd been seeing each other for almost nine months. Everything about being with Alex felt right. But it was still a big step, and she wasn't sure he was as close to that decision as she was.

When the kiss ended, she nodded. "I'm ready. If you are. But, you know, in your own time."

"I'm getting close." He got up and offered her a hand, helping her to her feet. "I do think about it."

"That's good." She wasn't going to push him. They had to both want to be married or there was no point in even talking about it. She got up and walked with him to the door, where the bag with her work clothes was sitting.

He carried her bag down to her car, making sure she got in all right. "Text me when you get home, so I know you got there safe."

She smiled. He was so sweet. So perfect. He was going to make an amazing husband. And father. Someday. "I will. See you tomorrow."

He nodded, a sparkle in his eyes. "Can't wait."

She drove home thinking about what it would be

like to be married to Alex. To have him sharing the beach house with her.

There was more than enough space. Certainly, more than at his little apartment. Especially now that it was just her and her mom. She missed her aunt and her cousin. And her grandmother, even though she wasn't that far away.

Eventually, Kat knew her mom was going to marry Danny. It was inevitable. They were probably closer to that decision than Kat and Alex were.

That would mean her mom would move out, too. It wouldn't be so bad. Her mom would only be next door, because that's where Danny lived.

But then Kat would be all alone.

What was she waiting for? When Alex asked her to marry him, she was going to say yes. But she couldn't give him that answer until he asked the question. And she was starting to think it might not happen soon enough for her.

Chapter Four

Trina helped herself to a piece of grilled chicken, a spoonful of yellow rice, and two spoonfuls of grilled veggies as the serving plates were passed around. "This place really is stunning, Mimi. And this backyard...I feel like I'm at a resort. A really fancy, expensive resort."

Roxie nodded. "Being on the water like this is something special. It's so peaceful here."

Her grandmother smiled. "Thank you, my girls. I couldn't be happier." She looked at Miguel. "We couldn't be happier, right?"

He smiled back at her. "I am as happy as a man could be, my love."

Ethan took a sip of his water. "Happy wife, happy life."

Willie was cutting a piece of chicken. "Happy spouse, happy house."

"That's a good one, too," Roxie said. She looked across the table at Ethan, giving him an affectionate glance that almost made Trina blush.

It wouldn't be long before those two were hitched. She slipped a piece of chicken to Walter. She just had a feeling they weren't going to wait much longer. And it was giving her another feeling. The kind where she wanted that for herself. She'd talked to Kat about it, because Kat was feeling the same way.

Ready for the next thing in her life. The next big step.

Trina was right there with her, but unlike Kat and Alex, Trina and Miles were at least already engaged. At the moment, what Trina was really feeling was Miles's absence. Not his fault, of course. He had to work the hours that came with his job.

It was a job she was super proud of him for doing, too. But being proud didn't keep her from missing him.

Walter seemed content to sleep under her chair after his bite of chicken. She ate her dinner and joined in the conversation a little, but her mind was elsewhere. On Miles. And the future. And when that was all going to get started. They really needed to set a date and start planning.

"You're awfully quiet, my girl."

Trina looked at her grandmother. "Sorry, Mimi. Long day."

"Busy day," Roxie added. "The salon is doing great."

Trina nodded. "It is. Better than I thought. I know I have Rebecca, the mayor's wife, to thank for that. Which reminds me—she invited me and Ma to the mayor's Christmas party."

"How about that?" Ethan said. "Fancy stuff. You're going to be Diamond Beach society girls, huh?"

Roxie laughed. "I don't know about all that. By the way, you're my date for that party, so..."

He snorted. "I am not wearing an ugly Christmas sweater."

"No, you're not," Roxie said. "It's not that kind of party." She looked at Trina. "Is it?"

Trina shook her head. "No, it's more dressed up."

Ethan made a face. "I'm not wearing a tie, either."

"We'll talk later," Roxie said.

Miguel gestured with his fork. "Your mother and I will be there, too. As will Danny and Claire, I'm sure. The Rojas have been invited every year for quite some time."

Ethan nodded. "My parents get invited. I suppose I could have gone with them if I'd wanted to but I'm more of a low-profile guy."

Roxie let out a little laugh. "Not anymore you aren't."

"Apparently." He winked at her, smiling in a way that said he was just fine with the change to his life. He pushed his plate away. "That was a great dinner, Miguel. Thank you, Willie, for the invite."

"You're very welcome," Willie said.

Miguel nodded and took out his phone, looking at the screen briefly before putting it away again. "Anytime, Ethan. You're practically family."

"About that," Willie said. "When are you going to make an honest woman out of my daughter?"

"Ma!"

"Mimi!" Trina couldn't believe her grandmother sometimes.

Ethan laughed, stood up, and pulled a small box from his pocket. "I'm glad you asked." He walked over to Roxie's chair and got down on one knee.

Roxie clapped her hands over her mouth.

"Roxie, what do you say?" He opened the box, revealing a gorgeous sparkler of a ring. "Would you do me the honor of marrying me?"

Happy tears trickled down Trina's cheeks as Roxie nodded.

"Yes," she said. "I will."

With a grin that spread from ear to ear, Ethan took the ring from the box and slipped it onto Roxie's finger, then he pulled her into his arms.

Trina sniffed. "You guys. I'm so happy." She glanced down at Walter. "Your grandmother is getting married, Walter."

Mimi was crying and Miguel's eyes looked damp. He got up from the table. "This calls for champagne."

"I agree," Willie said. She went inside with him.

Trina felt a little like she was intruding, but then her mom and Ethan broke apart.

"Congratulations," Trina said. "I love you both. I couldn't be happier for you."

"Thanks," Ethan said. His arm was around Roxie's waist. "I never thought I'd find a woman as wonderful as your mom." He looked at Roxie, smiling. "Isn't life something?"

"It sure is," Roxie said, smiling back at him.

"You two are really making me miss Miles."

Roxie laughed. "Aw, honey, I'm sorry. I wish he could be here with us tonight, too."

Trina nodded as Willie and Miguel came back

out. She was carrying four champagne glasses while Miguel had the fifth one and the bottle of bubbly.

"Here we go," he said.

They put the glasses on the table and Miguel handed Ethan the bottle. He quickly popped the cork and poured. Glasses were handed out and lifted.

Miguel offered the toast. "To love and commitment and a lifetime of happiness."

"Hear, hear," Ethan said.

They all took a sip, but Miguel set his glass down to look at his phone. He gave a quick nod, a brief smile on his lips. The smile remained, along with a mysterious glint in his eyes.

Trina didn't know what to make of it.

Mimi finished her glass of champagne, then clapped her hands. "All right, time for dessert. Coconut cake from the bakery. Who wants a slice?"

The doorbell rang.

"I'll get it," Miguel said, already headed toward the front of the house.

Roxie looked at Willie. "Ma, why don't we sit a minute and have some more champagne? Then I'll help you get dessert."

Trina nodded. "I might see if Walter needs a

quick trip to the grass, too." But he was passed out under her chair, looking very content.

Miguel returned in a minute, a young woman with him. She was holding a white cardboard box with holes in it. Miguel remained standing. "Willie, my love, your Christmas present has arrived a little early."

Willie's brows bent as her gaze went from Miguel to the young woman to the box. "What have you done, Miguel?"

He smiled. "I know we talked about it, and we both decided a dog would be too much for us."

She nodded. "We did." She looked at Trina. "Although we love Walter, you know that."

"I do," Trina said. Her gaze went to the box. What was in there? Then she caught a glimpse of a little pink nose.

"I thought we should still have a little extra company in the house." Miguel took a deep breath. "I hope you approve. I picked her out just for you." He gestured to the young woman. "This is Cindy from Family Friends Rescue."

Roxie was grinning. "That's where I got Walter."

Miguel nodded. "Roxie helped me with this."

"I can't take it anymore," Willie said. "What's in the box?"

Trina nodded. "I can't take it, either." She had no idea her mother had been up to something like this.

Cindy brought the box over and set it on Miguel's chair, then carefully opened it. Miguel reached in and lifted out a fluffy white kitten wearing a sparkly pink halter and leash.

Willie sucked in a breath, her hand going to her heart. "Oh, no, that can't be for me. Is that real?" She started to cry. "Oh, she's so beautiful. Oh, Miggy. I love her already."

She reached for the kitten and Miguel, now sniffly, handed the little cat over. Willie held her close, kissing her on the head.

Trina felt herself get weepy. It was all so precious.

Willie just shook her head and sniffled while petting the cat and kissing her. "What's her name?"

Cindy answered. "She doesn't have one yet. She's eight weeks and three days old. Mr. Rojas reserved her for you a month ago but she's only now just old enough to be adopted."

Miguel cleared his throat. "And I didn't want her to have to stay at the rescue any longer than necessary."

"I love her," Willie said. "She's perfect." She smiled at Miguel. "So are you."

"I'm glad you like her. What are you going to name her?"

"Something over the top." Willie lifted the kitten to get a better look at her. "I think her name is... Princess Snowball. Snowy for short."

"Snowy it is." Roxie laughed and clapped her hands. "She's beautiful, Ma."

"She's gorgeous, Mimi." Trina couldn't believe what Miguel had done. But she was thrilled he'd done it. She loved that her grandmother would have an animal to keep her company. Trina picked up Walter and showed him Snowball. "Look, Walter. You have a cousin."

Willie laughed, then looked at Cindy. "Does she walk on the leash? Or do I need to train her to do that?"

"We've gotten her started with leash training, but you'll need to work with her a little more on that. She'll get there. She's comfortable in the halter, though, as you can see," Cindy answered. "She's up to date on all of her shots and she's scheduled for a spay in two weeks. I have her folder in the car. I'll run out and get it, then let you folks get acquainted with her."

As Cindy left, Miguel moved the cardboard

carrier to the floor and took his seat. "You're really happy with her, my love?"

Willie hadn't let go of the kitten yet. "I am madly in love with her. Thank you. This is the best Christmas present I've ever gotten."

He smiled.

Trina did, too. What a dinner this had been. An engagement and a new kitten! And they hadn't even had dessert yet. She pulled out her phone to send Miles a text and give him all the news. She snapped a quick picture of Snowy and sent that along as well.

She still missed him, but her heart was happy. Hard to be anything else while surrounded by this much joy.

Chapter Five

E reader in hand, Jules stretched out on her bunk on the tour bus, leaving the privacy screen open. She only closed it when she intended to sleep or needed some alone time. The accordion-style screen had some sound-deadening qualities, but she used earplugs if she was after serious silence.

Right now, she just wanted to rest and read a bit, enjoying the brief window of downtime before they arrived at their stop for their next show. She was trying not to think too much about missing her mom's wedding tomorrow. Even if it was only a civil ceremony, Jules wanted to be there, but it wasn't possible.

She stared at the wall at the end of her bunk, not really seeing it so much as she was her own thoughts. She'd chosen a middle bunk so that the older band members could have the ones on the bottom. It was just easier for them.

Although, as much fun as this tour was, it was also reminding her that she wasn't twenty anymore, that was for sure. But the rush of performing and the appreciation of the fans, along with the incredible boost it was giving her career, made up for the extra time it took her to bounce back after a show.

It was nothing major. She just had to make sure she got enough sleep, ate right, and got some exercise when she could. She'd also cut way back on alcohol. She'd seen firsthand how that could destroy a person's health. Among other things. Her ex-husband and the father of her two boys, Lars, was a perfect example of that.

Since leaving his most recent stint in rehab, he'd stayed clean and on track. She was happy he'd been able to do that. Cash, her son, had enough going on without worrying about his dad. Both her sons did. And she didn't really have the time to deal with more Lars drama, either. Nor did her boys.

This tour, all she wanted to focus on was giving her audiences the best possible show, staying in the best shape she could, and making core memories with Cash and Jesse. It was quite an adventure to be on tour with two of the three men she cared most about.

Well, that wasn't right. It was more like three of the four men, if she included Toby, her dachshund, who was snoring softly by her feet. He would have needed help getting in even if she'd gotten a bottom bunk. Those little legs weren't built for heights. She didn't mind helping him in and out, though.

Jesse's dog, a beautiful golden retriever named Shiloh, tended to sleep on the couch at the back of the bus. There was no way she and Jesse could fit in one bunk. Not for long. Once in a while, Toby would fuss to get up on the couch with her.

Toby was unabashedly in love with Shiloh. She was pretty fond of him, too. It was too cute for words.

Jules glanced across the aisle at Jesse's bunk and smiled, even though he wasn't in it. She knew how Toby felt. Having Jesse along on the tour was pretty amazing. She missed her other son, her sister, her niece, and her mom, too, of course, but having Jesse and Cash with her really made everything much more bearable.

They were only a month into the tour and, thankfully, there hadn't been a fight or an argument yet. Among anyone. All the band members were getting on great. She thought it helped that they were older and more seasoned. They all seemed to really be enjoying the experience.

It was a real blessing to have that kind of peace during the tour. She hoped it stayed that way. She'd had tours, smaller ones, to be sure, that hadn't gone as smoothly as this one was.

And now they had the performance at the Grand Ole Opry to look forward to. It was a real honor to be asked, even if it was to fill in for the original headliner who'd had to cancel.

Her star was on the rise. She wasn't getting a big head about it. Fame and fortune were fleeting things in this business. But it did feel like the new album had elevated her career in a way no previous album had.

Reviews of *Dixie's Got Her Boots On* had started referring to Jules in some pretty glowing terms. Saying things like she was "a solid fixture in the country folk music scene." "A reliable source of great entertainment." "A true wordsmith as a songwriter." One review had even said she was fast becoming an icon alongside the likes of Dolly, Reba, Emmy, and Martina.

It was heady stuff. And a little hard to take in when it was so extravagant. But Jules wasn't about to let it change her.

She was the same person she'd always been. And no matter what kind of success she had, there was always going to be a part of her that would rather be home with family for Christmas than on the road.

She smiled wistfully. She'd have Cash and Jesse on the holiday, though. And Sierra, Cash's girlfriend, and all the other band members. Christmas would still be good. Even if she was missing Fender, her mom, Claire, and Kat.

They'd FaceTime, so she'd get to visit with them in the loosest interpretation of that word. Wasn't the same. But it was better than nothing.

Jesse came down the hall, stopping next to her bunk. "Are you trying to nap? If so, I'll leave you alone."

"No. I was going to read but I ended up lost in my own thoughts."

He nodded. "Hard to be away from family this time of year, isn't it? Especially with your mom about to tie the knot."

She would have asked how he'd known that was what she was thinking about, but Jesse was pretty intuitive. "It is. I'm so glad you and Cash are here with me. That helps a lot."

He grinned. "Performing at the Opry will probably help some, too."

She laughed. "I still can't believe they asked me."

"It's a big deal, but then, so are you these days."

"Who'd have thought?" She snorted softly. "Well, you did. You thought *Dixie* was going to be big. So did Cash and Billy. Pretty much everyone did but me. I just wasn't sure."

"It was such a new sound for you. You had every reason to be skeptical." He reached over and scratched Toby under the chin. "I'm going to check in at the club, just so they know I still exist, then I was thinking about watching a movie in the lounge. You interested?"

She nodded and put her ereader away. "While you make your call, I think I'll check in with Fen. Then I'll meet you in the back."

"See you in a few."

She closed her privacy curtain, then called her son. There was no answer and his voicemail picked up. She hadn't been prepared to leave a message, thinking they were just going to chat, so she hesitated. "Hey, it's your mom. Just called to check in. We're about six hours from our next stop. I love you and miss you. Give my best to Anna. Talk to you soon."

She hung up and held her phone to her chest for

a moment, a little melancholy at not getting to hear his voice.

Then her phone vibrated.

She looked at the screen and smiled. Fen was calling her back. "Hi, honey."

"Hi, Mom. I saw I missed your call. Sorry about that. I was fixing the kitchen faucet. It's been leaking. Anyway, you didn't call to hear about that."

"No, I love hearing about that. I love hearing what you've been up to. I don't care how mundane it is. I miss you."

"I miss you, too. How's the tour going?"

"Pretty amazing, that's how."

"So I understand." He laughed softly. "You're not going to believe this but a club downtown called me two days ago to see if Steel Trap would be interested in playing there." Steel Trap was Fen's band. "I said sure. Then they asked if I could bring you along as a special guest. They wanted my mother."

Jules pursed her lips and tried not to laugh. "You poor, poor boys. All your lives you've grown up under the shadow of your father, and now your mother suddenly becomes popular."

"I know, right?" He chuckled. "Nah, it's all good. I'm proud of you, Mom. I can't go online without seeing a mention of you. It's pretty cool to have famous parents. But it's also really nice to have a mother who's famous for only good things."

"Thanks, sweetheart." She knew what he meant. Too often Lars had been in the news because of his inebriated exploits.

"I heard about how part of your profits are going to help battered women through that charity in Florida. That was a really good thing you did."

"I appreciate you saying that. Thank you. Now, enough about me. Tell me how you're doing. How's Anna?"

"She's good." He let out a little sigh that sounded both happy and nervous. "She's, uh, she's pregnant, Mom."

Jules sucked in a breath. "I'm going to be a grandmother?"

"Yeah, you are. In about seven months."

Jules couldn't talk for a moment. The idea of her first grandchild had struck her dumb with joy.

"Listen, we were supposed to keep it a secret until Christmas because she wants to surprise her parents with the news, so don't say anything to anybody, okay?"

Jules nodded and found her voice. "Okay."

"Not Cash or Dad or Grandma or anyone."

"I won't. Not a word. How exciting! Give her my

best. But you should really tell your grandmother soon. She'll be thrilled."

"I will, promise. I'm going to call her tomorrow after the ceremony."

"That's good."

"Well, I should run, because that faucet still isn't right, and it needs to be before Anna gets home."

"Okay. You get that taken care of. I love you."

"I love you, too. Talk soon."

"Soon." She hung up, sniffed once, and ran her fingers under her eyes. A grandchild. That was a spectacular Christmas gift.

She blew out a breath. It was also going to be a hard secret to keep. But she'd promised, so she had to. Not telling Jesse and Cash was going to be tough. She had to keep things even or they'd know she was hiding something. Secrets didn't stay secrets long when you were in such close quarters.

She picked her phone up and used it to send a big bouquet of multicolored roses to Anna and Fen congratulating them on their news, then she got out of her bunk and went to the back of the bus, helping Toby down so he could follow. He wasn't one to be left out of anything if he could help it.

Jesse was there on the couch, waiting on her, Shiloh at his side. His brows lifted. "Good call?"

He had no idea. She nodded and quickly changed the subject, doing her best not to grin like an idiot. "How's the club?"

"Running smoothly, if reports are to be believed." He smiled. "Which I'm sure they are. What kind of movie are you in the mood for?"

"I'm not sure. As long as it's interesting, I'm in." She helped Toby up so he could sit by Shiloh, then Jules settled in beside Jesse.

"Interesting, huh? Are you willing to watch something you've already seen before?"

"Maybe."

He pulled up the old movie channel and started to scroll through the streamed offerings. "How about something funny?"

"Funny is good." Probably better than sentimental or sad. She'd cry too easily.

He glanced at her. "How about *Monty Python And The Holy Grail*?"

She shrugged. "I've actually never seen that."

He looked horrified. "You haven't?"

"Nope."

"It's silly and British."

It would be good to laugh. It would help her express some of the joy she was feeling. "Sounds like just the thing."

Chapter Six

After saying goodbye to Roxie, Trina, and Ethan, Willie arranged all of Snowy's new things. Miguel had a whole slew of accessories in the trunk of his car that Ethan had helped bring in.

She put one of the scratching posts at the end of the couch in the living room. Another went in the laundry room where the litter box was set up. There were two soft, fluffy cat beds. One of those went on the couch, another in the master bedroom under Willie's dressing chair in the corner of the room. Snowy's food and water got set up in the kitchen.

The catnip mice and crinkly foil balls were slowly being distributed throughout the house by Snowy.

Now, Willie sat in the living room with Snowy, who'd been relieved of her halter in favor of a hot pink collar with rhinestones. Willie was using the fishing pole toy, a long bendy stick with a length of fishing line that held a feathered toy, to play with the little cat.

Willie found Snowy fascinating. First of all, she was a beautiful creature. Sleek and gorgeous, with fur too soft to be believed. Secondly, she was graceful without even trying, even when she was being silly and playing. And she was very silly. Willie had never laughed so much. Every little thing she did was perfect. Thirdly, there was the way she purred.

Willie knew cats purred. But having never had a cat or really even been around cats, she'd had no experience with it. She hadn't realized the purr was something you could hear *and* feel.

Cats were something else. Snowy literally vibrated. And sometimes, the purring started up just because Willie had spoken to her. That made Willie feel like Snowy was happy in her new home. Willie hoped so.

Miguel came into the living room after making sure the front door was locked and the house secure before they turned in for the night. "You like her, eh?"

"I adore her. I think she's the most amazing gift I've ever been given." Outside of the millions Zippy had left her in his will, but that wasn't the same thing at all. This was a living, breathing creature.

Miguel smiled and sat next to her. "Just so long as you don't love her more than me."

Willie laughed. "Not possible. But I might love her as much."

"That's okay. I can live with that. Are you ready for bed?"

She nodded. "I am." Their new nightly ritual was to sit in bed and watch an episode or two of whatever show they were streaming before turning in. They were currently working their way through a cozy mystery series set in a small English village, *The Village Vicar*. She hesitated. "I'd like Snowy to sleep with us. If she wants. Is that okay with you?"

He nodded. "I figured you would." He shrugged. "So long as she doesn't take up too much room or try to steal the remote." He winked at Willie.

Willie smiled. Miguel was so easygoing, so willing to please her. "I don't think she will. You're sure you don't mind? She won't bother you?"

He shook his head. "I got her for you with the hope that she would become an important part of your life. I'd be bothered if you didn't want her with you."

"Thank you." Willie scooped Snowy up and kissed her on the head. "I love you both very much."

They went into the bedroom. Miguel went into the bathroom to get ready for bed. Willie put Snowy on the bed to see what she'd do.

She immediately spread her feet out and went into some kind of attack mode. There was nothing to attack, but Snowy didn't seem to know that. She did a little hop, zipped to one side of the bed, then the other, before finally sitting down, extending one foot over her head and licking the back of it.

Willie laughed and shook her head. "You are so silly."

She changed into her nightgown, then joined Miguel at the vanity to brush her teeth. The double sinks were so nice to have.

The master bath was one of her favorite rooms. It was bigger than her bedroom at the beach house had been. The driftwood-colored ceramic tile that looked like planks of hardwood continued from the bedroom into the bathroom. The walk-in shower was tiled in a mix of pale blue and green glass tiles on the walls with the same flooring as the rest of the room.

The walls were painted the same soft sea blue as the bedroom walls. The color palette had been designed to evoke the sea's serene calming effects, according to the designer. Willie had to agree that it worked.

Willie had used more of the pale blues and greens for the towels and bathmats. And the designer had found a big painting of a pair of sea turtles for the wall right before the room that held the toilet. The painting had been done by a local artist, which Willie really liked.

Having the toilet in its own room seemed pretty fancy to Willie at first, but now that she was sharing a house with Miguel, she realized how nice it was to have a little extra privacy. Didn't matter how much you loved someone, there were certain things you didn't need to see. That probably made her old-fashioned, but she didn't give a hoot.

Nothing wrong with a woman keeping a few secrets. Easier to keep the romance alive that way.

Miguel finished up before her and went to bed. It took Willie longer. She had face cream and eye cream to put on after brushing her teeth. By the time that was all done, and she returned to the bedroom, she was surprised by what she found.

Snowy was curled up against Miguel's side, eyes closed, looking very happy. Probably purring, too, although Willie couldn't hear her.

Willie put her hands on her hips and pretended to be upset. "What's this? You're stealing my cat already?"

Miguel laughed and patted Snowy's side. "What can I say? She loves me even though you're clearly her favorite. She is a dear little one, isn't she?"

"She is." Willie smiled and went around to her side of the bed. "And it's no wonder she loves you. You're the one who changed her life by bringing her into our family." She got under the covers, sitting with the pillows propped up behind her. Snowy was between them, eyes still closed. "Do you think she knows she's going to have a good life here?"

Miguel nodded as he used the remote to find their show. "I think animals can sense these things. They are smart in ways we'll never understand."

"I hope she knows she's safe and loved and has nothing to worry about anymore." She touched Snowy's side, completely amazed at how soft she was. "Did all of her littermates get adopted?"

Miguel nodded. "They did. And so did the mama cat."

"That's good." Willie liked a happy ending. She sat back to watch the show. "I can't believe Margo and Conrad are getting married tomorrow."

"About time," Miguel said. "But why City Hall? Why not a little ceremony like we did?"

"You know how Margo is. She doesn't like fuss. At least they're having a reception after. That will be nice." Willie had bought a new dress at Lady M's boutique just for the occasion.

"It will." He smiled at her. "And it's at our favorite place."

They'd spent a little time at the Brighton Arms after they'd gotten married, thanks to Roxie. "It is. Should be a great place for a wedding reception. We had such a nice stay there, didn't we?"

"We did. But we had an even better time in Puerto Rico."

She laughed. "That's for sure." They'd spent a month on the island, visiting all kinds of sights and seeing all of Miguel's extended family who still lived there. She'd gained eight pounds on the trip, despite all the walking they'd done. They'd even gone dancing one night with some of the younger relatives.

Those extra pounds weren't surprising, considering how much good food they'd eaten. Some days, it felt like all they'd done was eat. She wouldn't have changed a thing about that, though.

Miguel glanced over. "What would you think if

maybe next year we invited my cousin, Consuela, and her husband, Felix, to stay with us here for Christmas?"

"I think that would be great." They'd stayed with Consuela for a week and had the best time. Consuela was a lovely woman who worked for the Department of Tourism, and she knew all the best places to go, along with all the shady ones to avoid. Her husband, Felix, managed the bottling division of a local rum distillery. He had one of the best-stocked home bars Willie had ever seen. "We could have had them this year."

Miguel shook his head. "They both need to request the time off. But we'll plan it for next year, for sure."

"It'll be fun. And they can see Danny and Ivelisse and all the kids. We'll have a big Christmas dinner with all kinds of goodies, just like we're having this year. Maybe the weather will be nice enough that we can eat outside, too."

"There is a lot of planning to do," he said. "One thing I know is it won't be quiet around here, that's for sure."

"That's okay," Willie said. "My family's not exactly sedate."

He laughed. "I suppose not. And Snowy will be well settled in by then."

"She will be." Willie leaned over and kissed him. "I love our life."

"I love our life, too. We are blessed."

"Yes, we are." She settled back against the pillows again. "All right, let's see what the vicar is up to."

Miguel pressed the Play button. "I wonder who will die in this episode?"

"I can't imagine, but for a small village, Sparrow's Rise has an awful murder rate."

Miguel chuckled as the show's opening began. "If they were smart, they'd all move."

Snowy shifted and stretched her back feet out so that she was touching Miguel and Willie.

"You're right, they would. They must really love their little village." Willie knew the feeling. She was perfectly content right where she was.

Chapter Seven

"Do you take this man to be your lawfully wedded husband?"

Emotions whirled through Margo, all of them good. Without hesitation, she nodded. "I do."

The Justice of the Peace, Mr. Gershwin smiled at her and Conrad. He clasped his hands in front of him. "Then, by the power vested in me by the state of Florida, I now pronounce you husband and wife. You may kiss your bride."

Conrad leaned in and kissed her, lingering for a moment longer than he usually did. Finally, he pulled back. "How about that? We did it."

She smiled. "Yes, we did."

Their small audience of Dinah, Claire, Kat, and Alex all applauded.

"Congratulations," Claire said. "Mrs. Ballard."

"Thank you," Margo said. She took Conrad's arm

and glanced up at her husband. Today was a very good day.

Alex was filming and Kat was taking pictures. Dinah looked weepy, which was about what Margo had expected. Conrad's sister might have done a lot of changing lately, but she was still very sentimental about her brother. Margo wasn't about to try to change that about her.

"All right," Conrad said. "Get a picture of us now that we're official."

Kat obliged them as they posed with the Justice of the Peace. After a second, she nodded. "I got a few."

"Good," he said. "Time to head off to the reception and have some lunch with our friends."

When they got outside, there was a beautiful white Mercedes-Benz limousine sitting at the curb. The back window was artfully painted with the words, "Just Married," and standing by the driver's door was a middle-aged gentleman in a suit and cap. The sign he was holding said, "Mr. & Mrs. Ballard."

Margo gave Conrad's arm a squeeze. "Did you do that?"

He shook his head and looked surprised. "I wish I could say yes, but I didn't."

Claire was all smiles. "Jules arranged that for you."

Dinah had a pleased look on her face as well. "Wasn't that sweet? I'll drive your car to the hotel for the reception, Connie."

"Thanks," he said.

"We need more pictures," Kat said. "Stand by the car."

Margo and Conrad introduced themselves to the driver and then took a spot near the rear passenger door by the curb. Margo smoothed the skirt of her powder blue suit while Conrad buttoned his dusty blue sportscoat. They posed for a variety of shots as Kat called them out.

Finally, they were done. Jerry, the driver, opened the door for them.

Margo carefully made her way inside, Conrad following. There was champagne on ice.

Jerry stuck his head in. "You folks go ahead and enjoy that champagne. I've been instructed to take you for a little drive before the hotel."

"Sounds good to me," Conrad said. "We can make a grand entrance that way."

Jerry smiled. "That's the idea. Congratulations, by the way."

"Thank you," Margo said.

He nodded and shut the door.

"This is nice, isn't it?" She looked around. She hadn't been in a limousine in a long time. "Awfully considerate of Jules."

"Very nice." Conrad picked up the champagne and made short work of the cork. He filled the two glasses that were there and handed her one. "Our first drink as husband and wife." He lifted his glass. "To our new life."

Margo nodded. "To our new life. I love you."

"I love you." He kissed her before taking a sip, delaying hers as well. "And tonight will be our first night in the new place."

She smiled. "*Our* new place." She knew he was having a hard time thinking of the new house as his, too, but it was. "Just like the place Dinah's living in is technically our place, too. Now that we're married, they're both ours."

He nodded. "True. I'll get used to it. I promise."

"I hope so."

He took her hand. "I will. I'm looking forward to it being just you and me."

"That will be wonderful. I'm looking forward to our honeymoon, too." They'd decided, in lieu of a more traditional honeymoon, to go to a writer's conference in Atlanta at the end of January.

"So am I. You sure you're okay with our plans?"

"I'm not just okay, I'm excited about it. And I know we'll fit in some fun so that it isn't all work." They had plans to see a play and visit a museum once the conference was over. "But what I'd really like is to land an agent. Or an editor." She laughed. "Either one would be fine by me."

"Same here. This is a tough time of year, though. The big publishers are shut down for the holidays."

"I understand. Still, it would be nice to hear something. Our book has been making the rounds for about a month now. You'd think someone would have something to say."

"Better no news than a rejection." He sipped his champagne.

"I suppose." She glanced out the window as they drove down Main Street, watching the people smiling at the limousine. A few of them waved. There was no point in waving back. The tinted windows meant no one could see in.

"Do you think this is what most newlyweds talk about? How their book is doing?"

She laughed softly. "We might be the only ones. But it's kind of like having another child. You put so much of yourself into the book, then you send it out into the world, hoping everyone else thinks it's as smart and pretty as you do."

"Yep."

She exhaled. "But what if they all hate it?"

"No one said publishing was easy."

"No, and I didn't expect it to be. I just thought..." She shook her head. "I don't know what I thought."

"That our book would be different? That someone would fall desperately in love with it and make us a groundbreaking offer?"

One side of her mouth lifted in a smirk. "Maybe just a little."

"We can always self-publish, you know. There are people making great money in the world of independent publishing. It's nothing like it used to be."

"It's definitely something to keep in mind. And just so you know, I don't care so much about the money. I care about being read. About entertaining people. That's more important."

"I don't disagree, but the two usually go hand in hand."

She took a sip from her flute, then snuggled in closer to him. "In that case, I've changed my mind. I want to make a lot of money."

He laughed. "Mrs. Ballard, I couldn't agree more."

It would be nice to have some extra income. She could use it to help Kat with her wedding.

The ride lasted a few more minutes. When they arrived at the Brighton Arms, a small crowd was waiting on them. Dinah, Claire, Kat, Alex, Willie and Miguel, Danny, Roxie, Ethan, and a whole host of their friends. There were folks from the *Gazette*, some from the library book club, and a few from Conrad's church, which Margo had started attending.

She stared in amazement. "This is going to be a bigger reception than I'd realized."

"They did RSVP," Conrad said.

"I know, but I guess I still wasn't expecting them all to show up." There had to be fifty people.

The limousine rolled to a stop, Jerry got out, and opened the passenger door. "Ladies and gentlemen, it's my honor to present to you Mr. and Mrs. Ballard."

He gave Margo a hand out of the car. Conrad followed her and as he joined Margo on the sidewalk, everyone began to applaud.

Margo said nothing for a few seconds, then she motioned for the well-wishers to quiet down. "Thank you all for coming and for the warm reception. Let's go inside now, shall we? Some of you have got to be as hungry as we are."

Laughter answered her. Dinah gestured for Margo and Conrad to come with her. "The ballroom is ready and the buffet is hot. All we have to do is get people into the room."

Conrad nodded. "Then, by all means, lead the way."

They let her escort them, and the crowd followed.

The ballroom was tastefully decorated in white and blue with touches of golden yellow and metallic gold. Margo had thought it foolish to waste a lot of money on flowers, especially as this was her third wedding. Instead, she'd let the hotel decorate with what they had on hand and spent the bulk of the budget on food and music.

The band they'd hired played a nice mix of songs from the '50s and '60s as well as some jazz and big band. Perhaps not everyone's taste, but she'd only wanted to please herself and Conrad.

It was their day, after all.

And while the buffet had been a budget compromise, the food had not been. Salmon in dill sauce, chicken with wild mushrooms, and a carving station of prime rib, along with an assortment of side dishes such as rice, vegetables, and salad. Claire had made them a wedding cake, too.

Nothing quite as extravagant as the one she'd made for Willie and Miguel, this one was three round tiers of vanilla cake with chocolate ganache filling. The outside was all white, with simple piping and flowers. The topper was a pale blue cutout featuring their first initials.

The cake was elegant and understated, and Margo already knew it would taste fantastic. She approved of what her daughter had done for them.

The band leader also had the job of emceeing the reception. He gave Margo a look. She nodded back.

He leaned into the mic. "Welcome, everyone. Margo and Conrad are so pleased you could join them today and help them celebrate their marriage. How about we get things started by having our bride and groom make their trip through the buffet, then we'll get everyone fed. We'll keep you entertained in the meantime."

Conrad took Margo's hand. "All right, wife. Let's eat."

Chapter Eight

*E*than trailed Roxie in the buffet line. She helped herself to a piece of salmon.

He leaned in. "Pretty nice room, huh? You think we should have our reception here?"

She smiled and glanced back at him. "I don't know. A place like this has to be expensive."

"So?" He shrugged. "You only get married twice."

She laughed and added a spoonful of mixed vegetables to her plate. "I was thinking we'd keep it small. Just family and a few friends. Although I suppose you have more of both of those than I do. How many guests do you think you'll have?"

He took some veggies for his plate. "I don't know, but I can keep it down. Maybe forty? It doesn't need to be a big thing, but there are definitely a few people my mom will want to invite."

"I understand. I was sort of imagining we'd do the whole thing at the church."

He smiled. "Yeah?"

"Sure. The sanctuary is nice, and the fellowship hall can hold a hundred. We don't need more than that, do we?"

"No. I like the idea of having it all there. My parents will be thrilled."

"Good. We can talk to Pastor Tim after church on Sunday about it."

"I bet he'll be thrilled, too."

"Why's that?" Roxie asked.

Ethan's expression held some amusement. "I think he thinks I deserve a good woman after what happened."

"You mean with your ex and your brother." She continued on down the buffet line, adding a few more delicious-looking things to her plate.

Ethan did the same. "Right."

"Well, you do." Roxie grinned. "And I'm her."

"You most certainly are." He snuck a quick kiss to her cheek.

She smiled and glanced at her engagement ring. She loved looking at it. And not just because it was big and sparkly. It made her happy seeing that ring there. It was Ethan's promise that her future was going to be very different from her past.

He'd already done a lot to make her forget the past. She rarely thought about Bryan and his infidelities these days. Now she just considered Claire and her family as friends. Brought together by an odd, unimaginable situation, but none of that mattered anymore. It was water under the bridge.

The existence of Paulina, Bryan's third wife, and of Nico, his only son, no longer bothered Roxie like they once had. It helped that Paulina wasn't such a big part of their lives. Kat and Trina made an effort to see the little boy at least once a month, but he was their half-brother and they should have a relationship with him.

Roxie was proud of both girls for that. Nico deserved to know his sisters. The circumstances surrounding his life weren't his fault.

"You went quiet all of a sudden," Ethan said. "Something I said or just lost in thought about the wedding?"

Roxie faced him abruptly, plate in her hands. "I don't want to wait too long. I want to do it soon. My mom's not getting any younger."

He nodded with understanding. "I'm fine with that. And keeping it small will make things easier.

Tell you what—you pick a date that works for you, and we'll make it happen."

"Thanks." She took a breath as they walked back to their table. "There's so much to do."

"You basically planned Willie's wedding." He put his plate down, then pulled her chair out for her. "Won't this be just like that all over again? But in a church instead of on the beach?"

"Sort of. I guess." Her thoughts spun out as she sat down. "I need a dress and you need a suit. We need flowers and music for the reception, but a DJ would be just fine. And then there's the food and the cake. Of course, I'll ask Claire about that. And I'll talk to Thomas Plummer about the photography."

Ethan took his seat next to her. "He did take great pictures for your mom and Miguel. What can I do to help?"

"Get yourself a nice suit."

"I can handle that. What color?"

She opened her mouth to answer him, but she didn't have an answer. "I...don't know. I mean, I guess that depends on what our colors are, but it should be something you'll get some use out of. So... dark blue? Or maybe charcoal? Or maybe tan would be better. More usable year-round."

"Tan and aqua would be nice colors. Very beachy."

She nodded. "But maybe too much like my mom's."

"She had lavender with blue, though."

Roxie smiled at the fact that he'd remembered. "That's true, she did."

"And the tan and aqua would work with the church's existing color scheme."

"Also true." She exhaled. He was helping more than he knew. "Tan and aqua it is then."

"Really?" He seemed surprised.

"Sure, why not? We'll have Thomas do the photos, Claire will make us a nice cake, and the rest of it will fall into place." Somehow. She unrolled her napkin, taking out the silverware, and spread it over her lap.

He'd already done that. He picked up his fork but had yet to take a bite. "Are you going to wear white?"

She hadn't thought about that. "I was going to. Why? Do you think I shouldn't?"

He quickly shook his head. "I think you should wear whatever you want to." Then he smiled. "I'd love to see you in a white dress, but again, totally up to you."

There was a bridal shop in town. Anna Marie's Bridal Boutique. She hadn't thought about going there, but maybe she should. Just to see what they had. Couldn't hurt to look. She could look at Lady M's, too. They might have a white dress that would be suitable. "I honestly have no idea what I'll end up with at this point, but if it's going to happen soon, I don't think I'll have time to order something."

His brows bent. "It doesn't have to be soon. You're the one who wanted it right away."

"I know." She glanced across the table to where her mom and Miguel were seated. "I just feel like it should be. Don't worry, I'll find a dress. Are you sure you'll be able to find a suit?"

"Shouldn't be hard. I'll go to Portman's in town. The men's shop. I'm sure they can help me." He chuckled. "That's where my dad shops."

"Hey, your dad always looks nice."

"He does." Ethan ate some of the chicken on his plate. "This food is pretty good. What do you want to have at our reception?"

She shook her head. "I have no idea."

"You know, if you want, I could ask my mom to help you. She'd love to do it. And she's good at organizing big events. She helps with vacation bible school at the church every year."

That was a big event. But it was not a wedding. Then another question popped into her head. "Do your parents know you asked me to marry you?"

He grinned. "They do." He took a bite of his buttered roll. "What do you think about my mom helping with the wedding stuff? I promise she won't try to take over. She's not like that."

It would be a good chance to get closer to his mom. Brenda was a very sweet woman. Roxie didn't think she'd be hard to work with. She nodded. "I'd love for your mom to help. If she has the time and wants to."

"I already know the answer to both of those and it's yes."

Roxie smiled. "Then by all means, give her a call."

"I don't need to," Ethan said. "When I told my parents I was going to ask you, my mom offered. All you have to do is reach out to her and let her know what you need."

"It might be a lot of work."

"She won't care."

"Okay," Roxie said. "I'll call her when I get home."

"Speaking of..." He sipped his drink, a Coke, before finishing. "Are you okay moving into my place? Which would be our place, obviously. Or do you think it's too small? Should we look for somewhere else?"

She put her hand on his. "I love your place. It's the perfect size. And you're on the beach. Why on Earth would you want to give that up?"

"I don't. But I would for you."

She shook her head. "No, your place is perfect. I might want to do a little redecorating. Not much. Just a few things."

"You can do whatever you want. Seriously. Just tell me."

She hesitated for a second. There were some things she'd been thinking about. "Some paint and a new couch, to start with."

He nodded. "I agree with that. My couch isn't great. I should have replaced it years ago. A lot of my furniture could go, actually. Most of it was sort of cobbled together when I was going through the divorce and only meant to be temporary anyway. What else?"

She took a breath. "Seeing as how you're capable of doing the work yourself, there are a few other things..."

He put his hands on the table like he was bracing himself. "Yes?"

"Maybe the master bath could get a little update? And we could repaint the master bedroom? Also, some new linens."

He smiled. "Seeing your mom's new house has filled you with all kinds of ideas, hasn't it?"

She laughed, leaned in, and kissed him. "Maybe. Doesn't mean we need to do all of them. But a few things."

He nodded and kissed her back. "Anything for my bride."

Chapter Nine

Claire smiled, happy because her mom was happy, but also because Conrad was such a great guy and her mom deserved someone that wonderful. Someone who made her want to live life again, and he'd certainly done that.

Danny returned to her side, handing her a cup of punch that he'd just gone to get. He took his seat next to her. "They look good together."

"They do," Claire said. She sipped the punch, surprised to find a hint of rum in it. Obviously, Willie or Miguel had had something to do with that. "Even better is how happy they make each other."

Danny put his napkin on his lap and gave her a wink before picking up his fork. "You make me pretty happy."

Her smile widened a little. "You make me fantastically happy." She was thrilled he'd gotten Ivelisse to cover him for a few hours at the bakery so he could be here with Claire.

"We're well paired."

She nodded. "We are."

He stared into her eyes for a moment without saying anything. "Maybe we should do something about it."

He'd been hinting around at them getting married for a while. And although it wasn't like her to play dumb, she'd gotten used to this little game that had been going on between them. She pretended like she didn't know what he was talking about. "Something like what? We're already business partners."

He shrugged and cut a piece of prime rib. "I'm all alone in that house now, you know."

"I know. Do you get lonely?"

One side of his mouth hitched up. "Only for you."

"That's nice to hear."

"You'd be okay to live in that house, wouldn't you?"

"Sure. It's very convenient to where my daughter lives."

He laughed. "That it is."

She speared a piece of broccoli, smiling to

herself. "You already know what my answer will be."

He looked at her in mock surprise. "Claire Thompson. Are you saying you want to move in with me?"

She poked her finger into his side. "That's not what I was talking about, and you know it."

His barely suppressed grin said she was right. He nodded. "Rojas is a pretty good last name."

"Better than if you were actually Mr. Butters." She loved teasing him but, truthfully, "Claire Rojas" did sound nice to her ears.

He snorted, wiped his hands on his napkin, then took hers. "That we can definitely agree on. Are you going to dance with me later?"

"I am. Probably Conrad, too. But you're first on my list."

"Good to know."

"You'll always be first on my list."

"Maybe I should teach you to salsa."

"Maybe you should."

And just like all their other conversations, the subject changed and the hints about marriage were, at least temporarily, put to rest.

Claire tried not to let it bother her, but she was starting to wonder if Danny just wasn't ready. That was fine. She understood that losing his wife to cancer meant only that his wife was gone, not Danny's love for her.

Claire had had a much easier time moving on from Bryan. After all, he'd been royally unfaithful. Although now, she was grateful for the friendship of Roxie and her family. Claire was especially grateful for the way Kat and Trina had become very much like the sisters they were.

She had no complaints. Her life was great. She was busy with work at the bakery, where she saw Danny all the time, and when she wasn't at the bakery, she spent a lot of her free time with him, too. They had dinner together at least two nights a week, usually on the nights Kat went to Alex's.

If Danny didn't want to get married, she'd be okay with that. A little let down, sure. Maybe more than a little, in light of Roxie's recent engagement. But Claire would be able to understand. It was very possible Danny couldn't bring himself to commit to another woman the way he had to Maria.

Maybe this business partnership with Claire was all he could handle.

She turned to look at her mom and Conrad. Her mom had lost two husbands, both men she'd loved dearly, and yet, she'd married again.

Maybe Danny's issue wasn't being able to commit. Maybe he just didn't love Claire that way.

It hurt to think that. Claire would be lying to herself if she didn't admit that. But she was a grown woman. She'd get over it. Being married again wasn't something she needed to feel fulfilled.

As lunch wound down, the band started to play more danceable music. At least danceable by Conrad and Margo's standards. It was nice music, more suited to partner dancing than the sort of free-for-all that accompanied most modern tunes.

Danny held his hand out to Claire. "Want to cut a rug?"

"I'd love to." She took his hand and out to the dance floor they went, joining the other couples who'd already made their way there.

They took a few spins around, staying for the rest of the song and then the next one. Danny seemed distracted, though. He kept glancing at the band.

Claire wasn't sure what was going on. Maybe he wanted to request a song?

Then the band leader was on the microphone again. "Ladies and gentlemen, we're going to slow it down for just a moment. One of our guests has a very special question he'd like to ask someone."

The band leader took the mic off the stand, walked straight to Danny, and handed it over.

Danny took the mic and smiled at Claire.

Her spine started to tingle in the oddest way.

"Claire Thompson, you are an amazing woman. If you don't already know how I feel about you, let me make it clear. I am deeply in love with you. I love who you are. I love who I am when I'm with you. More than anything, I want us to be together for the rest of our lives."

He got down on one knee and, out of nowhere, there was a ring in his hand. "Would you do me the honor of becoming my wife?"

There was no breath in her lungs, no words in her mouth. She blinked, then quickly nodded, finally taking in air. "Yes," she said. "I was starting to think...never mind." She laughed. "Yes."

He got to his feet and pulled her into his arms, kissing her. All around them, applause went up. "Thank you," he whispered into her ear. "I love you."

"I love you, too."

Her mom, Conrad, Willie, and Miguel were standing there when Claire and Danny came apart. There were more hugs and lots of smiles and congratulations. So many congratulations.

Her mom looked unbelievably joyful, but then,

why wouldn't she be on this day? She took Claire's hands. "I'm so happy for you, Claire. For both of you. But especially for you. Danny is the sort of man you've always deserved."

"Thanks, Mom. Did you know about this?"

Her mother's smile grew wider. "I did. He wanted my blessing, not just to ask you but to ask you here, today. I thought it was a marvelous idea."

"That was kind of you."

Danny was suddenly beside her, holding something out to her. "Would you like to put this on?"

She looked at what he was offering her. The ring. She nodded. "I would."

She'd barely noticed it before. Now she took a real pause to give it the attention it deserved. The round center stone was flanked by two smaller marquises set lengthwise on an ornate filigree band of white gold.

Her eyes narrowed at the sight of it. The ring was gorgeous, no doubt about that, but there was something familiar about it, too. Then it struck her. "Mom, this was your ring."

Her mother nodded. "Your father gave that to me. I thought it was about time it went to you anyway. If you don't like it or you'd rather have something different—"

"No," Claire managed, her throat tight with so much emotion. "I love it." She hugged her mother. "Thank you."

"You're welcome." Margo cleared her throat softly. "Now put it on before you lose it."

"Yes, Mom." Claire laughed and slipped the ring on her finger.

Then she danced with her fiancé again.

Chapter Ten

For the first time since opening the salon, Trina wished she could have taken a day off. She loved weddings and she would have loved to have been at Margo and Conrad's, but there was no way she and her mom could be gone at the same time. Plus, she was so busy she didn't dare cancel appointments.

There was a small amount of fear in her about doing that. A tiny bit of worry that by not being here when she was supposed to be, she'd miss an important client. Or something else important. The shop was still so new, still building its clientele, and taking a day off didn't seem like a good idea. She did have scheduled days off, which she tried to coordinate with Miles's days off so they could hang out, but today hadn't been one of those.

She was probably overthinking it, but it was too

late to do anything different now. She'd see pictures. And she'd sent a gift with her mom. A beautiful silver picture frame engraved with the date.

She finished the blow dry and style she was working on, then sent her client off to the front desk to check out.

The upside of being so busy was not just the other stylists getting business, but Trina was making money. Enough so that she'd begun paying her grandmother back while still having enough left over to put a little bit away each month.

For a while, she wasn't sure Mimi was going to let her pay rent, but Trina had been adamant about doing that. Naturally, her grandmother had fussed about it and tried to say it wasn't necessary. Trina had argued that her grandmother might get into some kind of tax trouble if she had a renter who wasn't paying rent. That it might look like something shady was going on if she ever got audited.

Trina honestly wasn't sure about that, but apparently, her grandmother wasn't either, because she'd finally agreed to let Trina pay a reasonable sum.

Besides the rent and payroll, the shop had insurance and utilities, along with supplies that needed to be purchased. All of that was being handled, though.

And without too much effort. It felt good being able to do that.

It felt even better to be making the money required for all those things.

She cleaned up her station, then went to the desk to check on her next appointment. She'd finished a little early with the last client, so she had fifteen minutes until the next one came in. That would be Mrs. Bronson, who tended to be a few minutes late.

That didn't bother Trina. Renee Bronson was one of the first new clients she'd gotten after the shop had opened. Just walked in one day to check the place out and had been a repeat customer ever since. She'd sent many of her friends in, too.

Trina appreciated that kind of loyalty.

She waited until Amber was off the phone. "I have a few minutes, so I'm going to take Walter out."

"Oh, I just did that about twenty minutes ago."

"Thanks." Amber was good about taking care of Walter when Trina's mom wasn't here. "In that case, I'm going to grab a bite in the breakroom. If you need me."

"Okay, boss. You got it."

Trina smiled. She'd get to hang out with Walter that way. And she could use something more in her belly. She'd only had enough time to eat half of her lunch. Maybe she could finish the rest of it now.

She went to the breakroom, thankful to have a few minutes of breaktime. Walter was in his dog bed, snoozing. "Hiya, baby."

His ears perked up and he lifted his head. His tail started to wag. He was the cutest thing God had ever made.

"I know, I've missed you, too." Trina got her lunch out of the fridge. All that remained of it was half of a peanut butter and jam sandwich on whole wheat bread with a few carrot sticks. She took a can of Diet Pepsi from the case she had in the fridge, then she sat at the table and patted her knee. "Come on, baby. Come sit with Mama."

Walter came to her and put his front paws on her leg, doing the little hop he did when he wanted to get up on something. She lifted him onto her lap. He settled in, looking very happy to be near her.

She ate her lunch with one hand and petted him with the other. It was so nice having Walter in the shop. He made the bad days better. Not that there had really been any bad days. A few very hectic ones, but that was a good problem to have when you were running a new business.

It was nice to be off her feet for a bit, too. The

thick fatigue mats she'd bought for the shop worked great, but there was no substitute to sitting down once in a while.

With one eye on the time, she ate quickly. She saved a tiny piece of her sandwich for Walter, who gulped it down in one bite. When he was done, she kissed his head. "I have to go get ready for my next client. I love you, baby. Maybe we'll have a quick walk on the beach tonight. What do you think?"

He smiled, tongue lolling out at the mention of the word "beach."

She put him back down on the floor. He went to his bed and curled up with his stuffed bear. She threw away her trash, cleaned off the table, then grabbed her can of soda and some fresh towels for her station. "Bye, sweetums."

Walter put his head down on the bear.

"I know. Only a few more hours." Trina went back onto the floor.

Amber was sweeping and all the other stylists were in the midst of a service, except for Ginger, who was in between and headed for the breakroom. She looked at Trina. "You want a cup of coffee?"

"No, I'm all right, thanks. I still have some soda left."

Ginger had brought several clients with her,

which was great, and she was fast gaining more regulars as she became one of the most sought-after stylists in the shop. Making her the assistant manager had been a smart move.

Another smart move was possibly raising prices. Trina had begun thinking about doing that at the start of the new year. She'd priced the salon's services competitively at first because she didn't want to give anyone a reason not to try them. There were definitely more expensive salons in Diamond Beach. Some of them might offer a few more services, like nails or waxing, and facials, but A Cut Above delivered when it came to hair.

Now that they had a stable base of customers, Trina felt it was time. They were providing a nice environment, good-quality cuts and color services, and they had a decent number of walk-ins, a sure sign that people knew about them.

She wasn't going to go crazy. Just slightly bump prices up. Maybe fifteen percent. She could work on that tonight. Maybe even do some online research to see exactly what other places were charging.

Mrs. Bronson came in and waved at Trina. "Hello, there!"

Trina waved back. "Hello, Renee. Don't you look festive."

Renee did a little shimmy, making the bells on the Christmas tree on the front of her sweater jingle. "Tis the season!"

Trina laughed. "Yes, it is." She had little candy cane earrings on herself today. "Come on back. I'm ready for you."

"Great." Renee put her purse on Trina's station, keeping her phone out, and settled into the chair.

"What are we doing today?"

"Just touching up the color. Don't want to have roots in the Christmas pics. Maybe a little trim, if you think it needs it."

Trina finger-combed the woman's hair, looking at the roots and checking the shape of the cut. Renee had grays showing as her sandy blond grew out. "A trim would go a long way, since we're doing your color, too. Then you wouldn't need to come in again until February."

"Sounds good." Renee's phone chimed twice. She stared at the screen for a while, then finally sighed heavily.

Trina didn't like to intrude on her clients' personal business, but she was too empathetic not to ask. "Everything okay?"

Renee frowned. "I'm supposed to go visit my daughter in Pensacola for Christmas, but the kennel where I was going to board Tinkerbell just texted to say they've had an outbreak of kennel cough and can't take any new dogs. They cancelled my reservation. I'd love to take her with me, but my grandkids are allergic."

"Oh, no."

Her shoulders slumped. "I don't know what I'm going to do. I was really looking forward to this trip." She sniffed softly.

Renee's husband had passed away two years ago, and her daughter and grandchildren were important to her, which Trina totally understood. But Tinkerbell was important to Renee as well. Trina had seen the small brown dog once, after a grooming appointment next door. Tinkerbell and Walter had sniffed each other a lot. "Remind me what kind of dog Tinkerbell is?"

"She's a Yorkie. Just a little bit of a thing."

"I remember she was tiny. And very cute." Trina smiled as she came around to face Renee. She put her hand on Renee's arm. "How do you think Tinkerbell would like to spend Christmas with me and Walter?"

Renee looked up from her phone, eyes shining with unshed tears. Her brow furrowed. "Trina, you don't mean—"

Trina nodded. "Sure I do. I'll watch her. It'll be no trouble at all. She can come into work with us during the day and have the run of the house when we're home."

Renee inhaled, blinking in disbelief. "Would you really do that for me? That seems like such an imposition."

"It's not an imposition, I promise." It made Trina so happy to help. "And I wouldn't have offered otherwise."

Renee put her hand to her mouth. "I don't know what to say, except for thank you. That's so generous. I'll pay you, of course."

Trina shook her head. "You don't need to do that. Just make sure I have food for her and whatever else she likes. I think Walter would enjoy the company. He loves other dogs. And I know they get along, because they already met that day you had her groomed."

"They did seem to like each other, didn't they?" Renee smiled as a single tear fell. "I don't know how to thank you enough. I thought I was going to have to cancel my trip. You saved my Christmas."

Trina just grinned. "I'm happy to do it. I just have to make sure Walter knows he's not getting a permanent little sister."

Chapter Eleven

Kat couldn't believe her grandmother was married and her mother was engaged. She watched both couples slow dancing in the center of the reception room.

"Do you want to dance?" Alex asked.

She shook her head and smiled. "No, I'm happy just to sit here with you and watch them."

"Big day, huh?"

"Very big," she said. "I guess we'll have more weddings to go to in the future."

"As long as your mom makes the cake, I'm there." He lifted another forkful to his mouth.

Kat laughed. "You do like your cake."

"Your mom's is the best. What's not to like? Seriously, every flavor she makes is amazing."

"She makes at least two wedding cakes a month these days. Did you know that?"

"Doesn't surprise me." He ate the last bite, then wiped his mouth. "What flavors should we have for our wedding cake?"

Kat stared at him, mouth open. "*Our* wedding cake?"

He nodded. "You do want to get married, don't you?"

"I...yes, I do, but you haven't actually asked me yet."

He blinked. "Yeah, you're right. I haven't. I've been thinking about it so much that I guess I thought I had. Sorry. I don't want to take anything away from your mom and Danny, but..."

He reached into his pocket and pulled out a small black leather box. "As it happens, I've been carrying this around with me so that when the right time presented itself, I'd be ready."

Kat was speechless.

"What do you say, Kat?" He opened the box. "Will you marry me? The most forgetful firefighter in Diamond Beach?"

She covered her mouth with her hands, trying not to cry. All this time she'd thought he wasn't ready. Now she found out he'd been carrying the ring around with him the whole time? She nodded. "Yes, I will."

"Cool." He slipped the ring on her finger.

She looked at it. The round diamond had two small waves on either side that held two more smaller diamonds.

"I had it custom made. I hope you like it."

"I love it." She hugged him. "I love you."

"I love you, too. When do you want to have the ceremony?"

She tried to think. "How about late spring? On the beach. Something simple and fun?"

She could wear a white sundress and he'd be in white linen pants and a white shirt. That would work.

He nodded. "I love it. And what about our cake?"

She smiled. "How about lemon cake with a filling of vanilla buttercream and fresh raspberries? That seems springy."

He tipped his head, eyes narrowed. "No chocolate?"

She smiled. He loved his chocolate. "We could have chocolate cake with vanilla buttercream and fresh raspberries instead. How about that?"

He nodded. "I like that." His gaze wandered to the cake table.

"You want another piece, don't you."

"Do you think it would be okay?"

"You're practically family. Even more so now. I think my grandmother would be thrilled that you had another piece." And thrilled that he'd finally made things official. "At this point, we all pretty much expect you to have seconds anyway."

He laughed. "Okay, you talked me into it. You want anything?"

"Another Diet Coke?"

"Coming right up." He went to get the soda and cake.

While he was gone, her mom and Danny returned, both smiling, both looking so, so happy. Kat wanted to share her news, but not until she'd congratulated her mom and Danny first.

"Congratulations, you two," Kat said. "Let me see that ring."

"It was your grandmother's," Claire said as she held out her hand. "From when she married your grandfather."

"That is so cool." Kat took her mom's hand, studying the ring. "All of that history and love. That's really special." She let her mom's hand go. "I'm very happy for both of you."

"Thank you." Her mom looked at the ring, then at Danny. "I couldn't love it more."

Kat drank the last of her soda. "So, when are you thinking? To actually get married, I mean."

Danny looked at Claire, who looked at him. He shrugged. "Whenever your mom wants is fine with me."

"Soon," Claire said. "And it doesn't need to be a big deal."

"Why not?" Kat asked. "I mean, it doesn't have to be over the top, but I think you could do something bigger than the Justice of the Peace. That was fine for grandma, who didn't want a fuss, but..." She shrugged, not sure if she was making any sense.

"I don't think I'm a beach wedding sort of person," her mom said.

"What about church, then?"

Claire nodded. "Maybe."

Kat understood her mom's reluctance. They'd started going to church, but her mom had been so busy with the bakery she didn't always make it. Danny was the same way. In a touristy area like Diamond Beach, owning a business meant being open every day of the week. And sometimes, that meant you had to be at the business yourself.

Claire smiled. "We'll figure something out."

Alex returned with a large slice of cake and Kat's soda. "Hey, congrats, you guys." He sat down and handed Kat her drink. "I guess that means you're going to be my father-in-law, Danny."

Claire made a surprised face. "Did something happen that I don't know about?"

Kat held up her hand. "Yes. Just now."

Her mom sucked in a breath. "Oh, that's wonderful. That's just wonderful."

Danny smiled and shook Alex's hand. "I guess I *will* be your father-in-law."

"We should hang sometime," Alex said. "Go surfing, maybe."

Danny shrugged. "Sure, I'd be game for that. Or we could take the catamaran out."

"Cool," Alex said. "I've seen that little boat. Looks fun." He lifted his fork. "Great cake, Mrs. T." He laughed. "I'll have to change that to Mrs. R soon enough, huh?"

"Or..." Claire smiled demurely. "You could just call me Mom."

"Yeah?" Alex sat up a little straighter. He nodded. "Okay. I could call you Mom."

Kat felt a new warmth in her heart for Alex. He was such a good man.

Danny raised his brows and grinned. "You can keep on calling me Danny."

Alex laughed. "All right."

Her mom sipped her water. "What about you two? What kind of wedding are you thinking about?"

Kat glanced at Alex. "A beach wedding in the spring. We really liked what Willie and Miguel did, having it all right there at the house. That was nice and easy. That's what I want. Friends and family, nice and easy."

"And," Alex piped up. "We know what flavor of cake we want."

Claire smiled. "Already? What is it?"

"Chocolate with raspberries," Alex answered.

"I can do that."

Inspiration struck Kat. "And for the topper, two surfboards."

"Hey," Alex said. "That would be cool."

They went surfing whenever they could. During the colder months, that meant getting into a wetsuit, but Kat had all the necessary gear, including her board. Not only had the activity brought her and Alex closer together, but she'd toned up, building muscle and shedding some fat. She'd even had to buy some new clothes.

That gave her another idea. "You know, I think I might look at the thrift shop for a dress. I don't really need a fancy wedding dress to get married on the beach. I was really thinking a white sundress would work."

"It would," her mom said. "Maybe we can go look together on Saturday."

"I'd like that," Kat said. "We could ask Trina and Roxie, too. If you want."

"The more the merrier," her mom answered.

"Did I hear my name?" Roxie approached the table, Ethan at her side.

"Kat and I were talking about going to Classic Closet tomorrow. She wants to look for a white sundress she could get married in, since she and Alex are now officially engaged. Would you and Trina like to join us?"

"Congratulations, Kat."

"Thanks," Kat said.

"Trina and I both have to work, but that is sweet of you to ask." Roxie looked at Kat again. "That's a great idea to look there, though. I think I'll swing by the shop myself the next chance I get. I was going to go to the bridal boutique in town, but do you know how expensive wedding dresses are?"

"Very," Kat answered. She hadn't said anything to anyone, but she'd already gone by the bridal shop after work one day. Just to look.

The dress she'd liked best was three thousand

dollars. There was no way she was spending that much money on a dress she was going to wear once. She didn't want to spend that much on the whole wedding, although she knew that wasn't realistic.

"Do you guys want to come sit with us?" Kat asked. "We're all talking wedding stuff anyway."

Roxie and Ethan both smiled. Ethan slipped his arm around Roxie's waist. "We haven't had cake yet. We were about to do that. But then we could join you."

"Great," Danny said. "I could go for a piece myself."

"I'm good," Claire said. "I eat enough sweets and I already know what that cake tastes like."

Kat smiled as Ethan and Danny went to get cake. Roxie took a seat. "All the wedding talk is pretty exciting." She looked at Claire. "I need to get on your cake-making schedule as soon as we figure out a date. I would love to have you make our cake."

"I'd be happy to do it," Claire said.

"You're becoming the cake queen of Diamond Beach," Kat said.

Her mom laughed. "I'm all right with that." She glanced down at her phone on the table. The screen had just lit up. "Oh, that's your Aunt Jules Face-Timing me."

"I want to talk to her," Kat said.

"I'll let you, don't worry." Claire answered. "Hi, Jules. It's a little noisy in here. Can you hear us?"

Jules appeared on the screen, all made up for the stage and smiling. "I can. We're on in about an hour. I just tried to call Mom but got no answer. How did everything go?"

Kat leaned in. "Hi, Aunt Jules. Grandma and Conrad are on the dance floor. Everything went great. They loved the limo. That was super nice of you."

Jules smiled. "I'm so glad."

"How's the tour going?" Kat asked.

"It's going very well. There's some talk of adding a few more venues at the end, which would extend the tour by a week and a half."

Claire frowned. "We're never going to see you again. But I'm glad things are going so well."

Jules nodded. "Trust me, I want to be home with you guys very much."

"It's okay," Kat said. "This tour is important. We know that. Although you *did* just miss your sister getting engaged."

"And your niece," Claire added.

"What?" Jules shrieked. "Someone, please, tell me everything."

Kat smiled and sat back. It was great seeing her aunt. She missed Jules, but she understood how major this new rise in her aunt's career was. People all over the country were discovering just how amazing Jules and her music were and that was about as cool as cool could be.

Alex reached out and took her hand. "Come on." He tipped his head toward the dance floor. "One song."

Kat nodded. "Okay. Mom, tell Aunt Jules I'll call her later."

"I will," her mom answered.

Kat and Alex went out to the dance floor. It was a sweet song, slow and old-fashioned and very romantic. "This is nice." She smiled. "And we need to stay in shape for our wedding anyway."

Chapter Twelve

Willie groaned as she sat on the bed and worked on taking her shoes off. "Miguel, I don't know if you realize this, but I'm an old woman."

He laughed. "That's a good thing, since I am an old man."

She chuckled. "Yeah, but you're *my* old man."

He sat beside her on the bed, loosening his tie. "It was a nice affair. Beautiful room. And they look very happy."

"They sure do. I hope they're as happy as we are. Do you think that's possible?"

He kissed her. "No. No one can be as happy as we are."

Snowy, who'd been sleeping on the bed, walked over and stuck her face between them, then let out a loud meow.

Willie laughed. "I think the princess wants her dinner." She petted the cat on the head. "Hang on, little baby. I gotta get these shoes off before my feet swell up and I'm stuck in them."

Miguel, tie off, got up and brought Willie's orthopedic slippers to her.

She smiled at him. "You're a good man."

He bowed in response. "How about I fix us a nice cup of coffee with a little rum in it?"

Her smile got bigger. "I know it's a little early to turn in, but so long as we can drink it in bed while we're watching our show, I'm in." They might be old, but they didn't generally go to bed at seven p.m.

"Done. And just because we're in bed doesn't mean we have to go to sleep." He massaged his lower back. "I'm tired and ready to relax. Might as well do it in the most comfortable place in the house."

"Agreed."

They changed into their pajamas, then went out to the kitchen together. Willie got Snowy a can of food. Snowy ate a fancy brand that was packaged in small portions. It was expensive, but Willie didn't mind. Snowy liked it and it was supposed to be good quality. She planned to ask the vet about it when she took Snowy in for her visit tomorrow. She'd set it up right away. Not because there was anything wrong with Snowy, but because she just thought it was a good thing to do to get Snowy established at the vet. In case a need did arise someday.

Miguel made two cups of decaf with the Keurig and fixed them up with a little sugar, some creamer and a nice splash of dark rum. He also made a plate of cookies.

They'd eaten more than enough at the reception, but a small snack couldn't hurt.

Willie set Snowy's bowl down. Willie was going to sleep like a baby tonight. All that dancing and nice food had worn her out. The rum on top of that would be all she needed. She watched Snowy eat for a second. She knew the cat would come to bed when she was done with her dinner. "See you in there, baby cat."

She and Miguel went back to the bedroom, each with a cup in their hands, him with the plate of cookies. Willie set her coffee on her nightstand, then went to do her evening routine so that she wouldn't have to get up again.

Although she would. There was no such thing as sleeping through the night at her age. When your bladder decided it was time to get up, you got up. Usually, she had no issues going back to sleep afterwards. Thankfully.

Creams and potions applied, she got back into bed. Miguel had his reading glasses on and was looking at his phone. The plate of cookies rested on the bed between them. He turned the screen so she could see it. "Look what Danny sent me."

She put her reading glasses on to make sense of what he was showing her. It was a picture of her and Miguel dancing. She smiled. It was a nice picture. "We should print that out and frame it. We look good in that shot."

He nodded. "I will do it tomorrow."

"Tell him I said thank you for sending it."

"I will. He sent me a few. I'll forward them to your phone so you can have them."

"Very good." She didn't mind pictures on her phone, but she missed the days of photo albums. She still had some and now and then she loved to sit and go through them. It was so much simpler than trying to find things on her phone.

All those pictures they'd taken in Puerto Rico were just sitting on that silly device, not being enjoyed the way they should be.

She looked at Miguel. "I miss photo albums."

He nodded. "So do I." He shook his head. "Technology is a wonderful thing, but it's not always an improvement."

"I agree. I want to make a photo album of our trip to Puerto Rico. Do we have enough paper to print out the pictures?"

"Not really. That's a lot of pictures. We need special photo paper."

"Do you know what kind to get? Can you order it?"

"I do and I will. Do we have a photo album?"

"No, but I'll get one." There was a craft store in the Dunes West shopping center. Maybe she'd take a look around in there after Snowy's vet visit. She'd have to bring Snowy back first, but that wasn't a big deal. She'd gotten pretty good at driving the golf cart. It was all she needed to get around Dunes West.

She took a cookie off the plate. A rectangle of shortbread. She picked up her coffee and dunked it in, then bit off that part. It was delicious. "The cookies were a good idea," she mumbled through a mouthful of crumbs.

Miguel smiled and picked up the remote. "Ready to watch?"

She nodded. "I might not have more than an episode or two in me. That reception wore me out."

"Me, too." He turned on the television and navigated through the streaming channels to the one they watched their show on.

If she didn't like the selection of photo albums at the craft store, she'd look on Amazon. In fact, maybe she should look on there first, just to see what prices were like.

The idea of having a new project made her happy.

Snowy came strolling in. She jumped up onto the bed, sat down at the foot of it, and began to groom herself.

Willie watched her, admiring the cat's flexibility. "Can you imagine being able to put your foot over your head like that?"

Miguel snorted. "Just the idea makes my hips hurt."

"Mine, too. We should crank up the heater on the pool and have a swim tomorrow. We need to stay active, you know."

"I know. We could try pickleball. It's very popular at the sports center."

She made a face. "It sounds weird."

"What would you like to do then?"

"I don't know, but we should do something. Don't you think?"

"I'm game. Just tell me what you want to do."

"Maybe...yoga for seniors?" She'd seen the

poster advertising the class when she'd been in the grocery store.

"Yoga?" He shrugged. "Okay. We can give it a try."

"Really?"

"Why not? We won't know until we at least attempt it."

She smiled. "I'll find out when the next class is."

He picked up a cookie, a vanilla cream-filled. "We could also go for walks around the neighborhood. We could take Snowy with us."

She blinked at him. "I don't know why I didn't think about that."

He ate a bite of the cookie. He'd yet to start the show. "You want to try a walk in the morning? See how she does?"

"I do. Might not be a bad idea to try to wear her out a little before the vet visit. Just in case she wants to act up." Willie hoped Snowy wasn't scared by the visit. That would make things difficult in the future. "Not saying I think she's going to, but I have no idea how she'll react."

"Then after our coffee, we'll take her out and see how she does. It'll be good for all of us."

"Yes, it will."

Snowy finished grooming herself and walked toward them. She sniffed the plate of cookies, then lay down between Miguel and Willie, paying the sweets no mind. She had her back against Willie's leg and her feet on Miguel's. She liked to be touching both of them, that much Willie had noticed.

"She's such a good girl," Willie said. She patted Miguel's arm. "She really was the best gift ever. Thank you."

"You're welcome. I'm very glad we got her, too. She's good company."

"And she naps more than we do, which is saying something."

Miguel laughed. "Ready to watch the show?"

Willie nodded. "I am." She sipped her coffee, the warmth of the drink and the rum and Snowy's body against her leg making her drowsy in the most pleasant way. "I can't wait to see who gets murdered this time."

Chapter Thirteen

"Thank you! You've been wonderful!" Jules took a bow, waved goodnight to the crowd, and finally, after two encores, walked off the stage with the rest of the band behind her.

Jesse was there to greet her. "Great show, babe. Fantastic." He looked at the band. "You guys killed it up there tonight."

"Thanks, man," Cash said.

Bobby, the fiddle player, gave him a big smile. "We were hot tonight."

"Yes, you were," Jesse confirmed.

Jules smiled and handed her guitar to a roadie. "They were a great audience."

"You can say that again," Rita commented as she went past. "Boy, I've missed that. Nothing like the energy of a receptive crowd."

Jules nodded. "That's for sure. I can't believe how

many of them were singing along. It amazes me they know the words when the album's only been out a few months." She shook her head as she wiped sweat off the back of her neck.

"We've got dinner at Villa Roma in an hour," Jesse announced. "The bus is pulling out in forty-five minutes."

Nods, gestures, and a few words of thanks answered him.

He gave Jules his attention again. "And you have a meet-and-greet with two fans who won a radio contest."

"Right. I feel bad that they're going to get post-show me. I'm a little sweaty. Those lights are hot."

"I promise you, that's not going to matter to them. They are so jazzed up to meet you that you could be in a gorilla suit and they still wouldn't care."

She laughed. "I don't know about that. Give me five minutes to freshen up and I'll be there. Green room?"

He nodded. "I'll let them know you're on your way."

"Thank you." She went straight to her dressing room and changed her shirt, spritzed on some perfume, cleaned up her makeup as best she could, and then grabbed some gift bags she kept for such occasions.

Each bag held a signed copy of the new album, a *Dixie's Got Her Boots On* T-shirt, a tour poster signed by everyone in the band, and a Julia Bloom and the Road Dogs ballcap. The Road Dogs was what the band had decided to name themselves, mostly because of Toby and Shiloh coming on the tour with them. Rita's pooch had stayed home with her husband, but Jules didn't think one more dog on the bus would have made a difference.

She checked herself one more time in the mirror. Satisfied she looked decent, she headed for the green room.

Jesse was there, entertaining the two women who'd won. Jules smiled to herself. She wasn't so sure they even needed her, as Jesse had clearly charmed them. The women, who were probably around Claire's age, were gazing up at him with adoration in their eyes.

Jules almost laughed, but she'd become accustomed to Jesse's effect on women. She completely understood. He was a very good-looking man.

Still smiling, she walked in. The pair were wearing T-shirts from Jules's 2018 tour. Talk about a blast from the past. They were some serious fans. "Hello, there. I'm Julia Bloom."

The women looked at her, mouths open. Then the shorter one gasped. "Yes, you are."

Jules nodded. "That's me."

"Holy cow," the other woman exclaimed. "It really is you."

Jesse gestured to the shorter woman. "This is Francie Barker." Then to the other one. "And Maxine Wojak. And they are *big* fans."

"The biggest," Francie said. "We run the Bloomers."

"Get out of town," Jules said. "I know about the Bloomers." They were a very active online fan club. Maybe one of the biggest. Not that there were that many Julia Bloom fan clubs. But the Bloomers even put out a newsletter. "It's great to meet you both."

"It's great to meet you," Maxine said. "It's like a dream. I can't believe we're really here. I can't believe *you're* really here."

"Well, I am, I promise." Jules held out the gift bags. "Here's a little something for both of you."

They dug into the bags, squealing at the things inside. Jesse winked at Jules. She smiled back. The adoration and appreciation of fans was a strange thing.

On one hand, it amazed Jules that anyone felt that way about her. On the other, there were artists and musicians who made *her* feel that way, so she understood it.

It just seemed odd to know there were people who held her in that sort of esteem. She didn't think she'd ever get used to it, no matter how long she remained in this career.

"Thank you so much," Francie said. "Could we get some pictures with you?"

"Of course. Would you like to meet Cash? My son?"

"Heck, yes," Maxine said.

Jesse smiled. "I'll go get him."

"Thanks, honey."

Maxine and Francie looked at each other, then Francie spoke. "Is that tall drink of water your boyfriend?"

Jules laughed softly. "Actually, Jesse is my fiancé."

Maxine's brows shot up. "You go, girl."

Jules smiled, proud of Jesse. "Thanks."

Jesse returned with Cash and Sierra. Jules introduced them, although it probably wasn't necessary. "This is my son, Cash, and our number one backup singer and keyboardist, Sierra. Cash, Sierra, this is Maxine and Francie. They run the Bloomers fan club and won a radio contest to come backstage."

There was lots of handshaking and fangirling. Jules loved it. She knew neither Cash nor Sierra had experienced that sort of thing before and she could tell from their slightly dazed expressions that they didn't quite know what to make of it.

After a few minutes of that, Jesse took some group photos. Then the women had Cash and Sierra sign the album. After that was done, Cash and Sierra excused themselves, and Jesse took some more photos of Jules with both women, then each of them individually.

Finally, it was time for Jules to get to dinner. "I'm so honored to have met you both. Thank you for being fans and thank you for all the hard work you do in running the Bloomers. That's such an amazing thing you do."

"Do you think we could email you for a little interview for the next newsletter?" Maxine asked.

"You sure can. I need to get ready for dinner, but Jesse will make sure you have all the right contact information."

"You're so nice," Francie said. "You know, they say never meet your heroes, but you're even better in person than I'd hoped for."

Her words touched Jules deeply. That was such high praise. She put her hand to her chest. "That is very kind. But you know what? I'm really just a regular person like you."

Francie grinned. "No, you're not, but it's nice of you to say that. We love you."

"I love you guys right back. Have a wonderful evening." She gave them a wave and headed off to her dressing room to decompress.

She went in, closed the door, and just sat on the couch, eyes closed, head tipped back. She did her best to let the energy of the performance wash out of her so that she could relax and have a peaceful meal.

A few minutes later, the door opened.

She looked over to see Jesse had come in. "Cash and Sierra walked the dogs and everyone's on the bus. You ready to go?"

She picked her head up and nodded. "I am. Just taking a few minutes, but I'm starving. Those women were sweet."

"They were. But all your fans are pretty much like that."

"I'm just lucky that way." She smiled at him. "I'm lucky in a lot of ways." Her eyes narrowed. "That would make a great song title, wouldn't it? *Lucky In A Lot Of Ways.*"

He smiled. "You need a minute to make some notes?"

She was already digging in her bag for her notebook and pen. "Just a couple. Then we're going to eat some pasta. I burned enough calories on that stage. I've earned it."

She started writing down the ideas for the new song as they came to her. "Just take my elbow and guide me to the bus. I'll write as we walk."

Jesse laughed to himself but did as she asked, directing her through the labyrinth of the backstage area and out to the waiting bus.

By the time they got to the restaurant, she had the bones of the song down. She set her notebook aside. She'd done enough work for the night.

Now it was time to unwind and let herself chill, because tomorrow night, she was going to have to do it all over again.

Chapter Fourteen

Roxie kissed Ethan good night as he dropped her off at the beach house. "You sure you don't want to come up?"

He shook his head. "I know it's still early, and I'd love to, but I'm beat, and I have a meeting with the planning commission tomorrow about the addition to the shopping center. It's first thing in the morning. I can't be late."

"Definitely, not." Willie had decided to go forward with adding to the shopping center, going ahead with the plans that had been drawn up to add a block of three more stores. It wasn't going to be cheap, but the increase in revenue would be significant. "I'll see you later then."

He nodded. "Love you."

She smiled. She grabbed her purse and the little

box of cake she'd brought home for Trina. "Love you, too."

As he usually did, he waited until she'd gone up the steps and given him a wave from the door before he pulled away. She unlocked the door and went in. What a fun day. A long one, but a really good one.

"Trina, I'm home," she called out.

"Hi, Ma," Trina answered.

Walter came running to greet her. Along with a smaller tan and brown dog Roxie didn't recognize. "Um, since when do we have two dogs? I'm pretty sure I would have remembered such a cute little face as this." She smiled down at the new dog. "You are sweet, aren't you? Yes, you are."

The little dog wiggled with doggy excitement.

Trina came out from the living room, smiling. "Since I offered to watch Tinkerbell for Renee Bronson." She explained what had happened with the kennel reservation and how they were going to be dogsitting for Renee.

"That was a nice thing to do." Roxie shifted her purse into the same hand the cake box was in so she could crouch down and give the two pups some scratches. "Walter seems to be all right with having a friend over."

"For sure. The two of them have been playing a lot. Tug of war, a little wrestling, lots of general silliness. I think it'll be good for both of them. How was the reception?"

"Really nice." Roxie stood, slipping off her heels. She handed Trina the cake box. "Here you go. Wedding cake."

"Awesome, thank you. I want to hear all about it."

"I'll tell you one thing—that hotel is beautiful. It's got a very glamorous, Old Money kind of feeling to it. I can see why Conrad and Margo like it so much. It really suits them."

"Too fancy for you and Ethan?"

"Not necessarily." Roxie picked up her shoes, letting them dangle from her hand. "But I don't see any reason not to do the whole thing at the church. It'll be more convenient. Not to mention cheaper."

"Not as fancy, though."

Roxie smiled. "I don't need fancy. I just need Ethan."

"That's nice, Ma."

The dogs suddenly took off toward the living room, their nails scrabbling on the hardwood floor until they reached the rug, where they started a new wrestling match.

The playful woofs and obviously pretend growling made Trina laugh. "This has been going on since I got home with them."

Roxie shook her head. "You won't have to worry about either of them sleeping tonight."

"Speaking of sleeping, you're not going right to bed, are you?"

"No. I'm going to change, then make myself a cup of tea and relax a bit."

"Okay. Come watch something with me, then. If you want."

"What do you have on?"

"Nothing, really. We'll find something. There's a new episode of *Tiny House Makeover*."

"Perfect. Be out in a few minutes."

"What kind of tea do you want? I can get it started."

"That new berry blend I just got. The box is next to the coffeemaker."

"Oh, that sounds good. I think I'll have a cup, too. Might as well if I'm going to eat this cake."

With a smile, Trina went off to the kitchen. Roxie headed for her bedroom. She put her purse on the dresser, then unzipped her dress, happy to be out of it even though it had been nice to get dressed up.

She hung up the dress, put her shoes away, then got into her PJs and went into the bathroom to wash her face.

Once she was scrubbed clean and moisturized, she went out to the living room. There was a cup of tea and the box of cake, open with a fork in it, in front of Trina, who was tossing a ball for the dogs, and another cup on the table next to Roxie's chair.

The same chair that had once been Willie's spot.

Roxie settled into it, her mind on her mom. "It was nice to see your grandmother and Miguel today. They were on the dance floor more than Ethan and I were. Oh! I almost forgot. Danny and Claire officially got engaged today. He proposed to her in the middle of the dance floor with the same ring that Claire's father used to propose to Margo."

"That is so romantic," Trina said. "I love that. Please tell me you got pictures."

"I did. I have a bunch. You can scroll through my phone and look at them. But that's not all. Kat and Alex got engaged, too. Right there at the table! It was a big day."

"Wow, I'll say. How awesome! I'll have to text them my congrats. How was the food?"

"Really good. That hotel doesn't fool around.

And, of course, Claire's cake was amazing, as you'll see for yourself."

Trina tossed the ball one more time. "That's it, puppies. I'm going to have my cake now." She sat back on the couch. "Sounds like a perfect day. I'm happy for all of them. Dinah didn't cause any problems?"

"Nope. From what I understand, she helped with the planning."

"Boy, has she changed."

"That's for sure. Jules sent a gorgeous white Mercedes limousine to take Margo and Conrad from City Hall to the Brighton Arms. I got a picture of it, you'll see."

"That was nice of her." Trina picked up the box of cake and took a bite. "Mmm, this is good. Man, Claire can bake. I'm definitely having her make our cake."

Roxie nodded. "So are Ethan and I. I already talked to her about it at the reception."

"I need to get us on her schedule, too." Trina sighed. "Of course, to do that, we'd need to have a date for the wedding."

"When are you going to work on that?"

Trina shrugged. "Soon. We've both been so busy.

I'll see him tomorrow night, though. Maybe we can talk about it then."

"Does Miles know about Tinkerbell?"

Trina smiled. "He does. He can't wait to play with her."

Roxie smiled. There was something very sweet about a big guy who liked little dogs. "Claire and Kat are going to Classic Closet to do some wedding dress shopping. I was thinking we might do the same thing when we can both get some time off together. Probably not until after Christmas, but that's okay."

"That's a great idea."

Roxie nodded. "They invited us to go with them on Saturday, but I already knew we'd both be working."

"And we will be for a while. The salon has been so busy I can barely keep up. We had to turn away three walk-ins today. Three! We just didn't have any availability."

"That's a good problem to have."

"It is. I've tried to tell people they don't have to tip me, because I'm the owner, but they have been anyway. And not small tips, either. Christmas money tips." Trina found their show and got it set up to watch.

Roxie smiled. "If people want to give you money, Trina, let them."

Trina laughed. "I have been. I don't have much choice. No one yet has taken the money back when I tried to refuse it." She lifted one shoulder. "I've kind of given up. If nothing else, it'll help me finish my Christmas shopping."

"I thought you were done."

She shook her head. "Almost. I still haven't gotten anything for Mimi. She's not that easy to buy for. When she really wants something, she just gets it for herself."

Roxie sighed. "That does make it hard. Is there anything you could make for her?"

Trina made a face. "Ma, I'm not good at stuff like that. You know that. I mean, I can cut and color her hair all day long, but I already do that for her for free."

"Right." Roxie wracked her brain. "Is there anything cat-related you could get for her?"

"Maybe. But she already has a lot of stuff. You saw the bags Ethan helped bring in."

"I did."

"I mean, I guess I could get her some more but how much can one cat use?" She rolled her eyes. "This is a hard one."

"Have you talked to Miguel? He might know if there's something your grandmother wants."

"Ma, that is a great idea. That's exactly what I'm going to do. Thanks." She went back to the cake. "This is good. What else did they have to eat?"

Roxie drank her tea and told Trina all about the reception. What kind of food they'd had, what the room looked like, what Margo and Conrad had worn, what other people had worn. By the time she was done, so was Trina's cake.

"I really wish I could have gone," Trina said.

"I know. But you sent a gift, and they understood you had to work."

"I hope so."

"Even Danny had to leave early to get back to the bakery. Trust me. They get it."

"Good." Trina picked up the remote. "Ready to watch?"

Roxie sank back into the chair and opened up the footrest on the recliner. "Yep."

Even the dogs finally settled down, as if they knew the clock was winding toward bed.

Roxie yawned, already feeling sleep tugging at her, but she wanted to spend time with Trina. Soon they'd both be married and living their own lives and not seeing nearly as much of each other. They'd have work, of course. But that wasn't the same thing.

Roxie glanced at her beautiful daughter and a sense of pride filled her. It was a good feeling to have.

Chapter Fifteen

Margo woke up to the smell of coffee and the sound of Conrad whistling happily. She smiled as she listened to him. This was a new way to wake up for her. For a little over a month, she'd been living in her new house, renovations mostly finished, all by herself.

It had been far lonelier than she'd anticipated. As it turned out, having a newly renovated home was no substitute for company. Something she'd gotten used to, living at the beach house.

She tossed the covers back, pulled on her robe, then went to the bathroom to freshen up. She fluffed her hair and brushed her teeth before going out to see what all the whistling was about.

Conrad was in the kitchen working on breakfast. "There's my beautiful bride. How did you sleep?"

"Soundly," Margo answered. He was in striped pajama pants and a plain white T-shirt that nicely showed off the physique he worked so hard to maintain. "Have you been up long?"

"About twenty minutes." He was cracking eggs into a bowl. Nearby were diced onions, red and green bell peppers, and ham. There was a bag of shredded cheese on the counter, too.

She interrupted his breakfast efforts by sliding her arms around his waist and kissing him. "If this is married life, I like it."

He smiled, kissing her back, eggs momentarily forgotten. "It's *our* married life. I'm a big fan myself."

She laughed, moving away to get coffee. "Are we working today?"

"We can. A little. Nothing wrong with getting started on Book Two." He whipped the eggs with a fork.

They'd talked about the second book, even done some planning for it, but had yet to put words on paper. "I think that would be good. We should start it. See how it feels. I don't want to get out of the writing habit, either."

"Neither do I. I like the rhythm we had going." He added in the rest of the ingredients along with some salt and pepper, stirred it all together, then poured everything into a buttered glass dish. The dish went into the oven. He set the timer on the stove before turning around to face her.

She fixed a big mug of coffee for herself. "Me, too. We shouldn't lose that just because we're waiting to hear about Book One. And, I suppose, at some point we'll need to make a decision about whether or not we're going to wait on New York."

He looked at her, surprise brightening his eyes. "You mean you'd consider publishing the book ourselves?"

She leaned against the counter by the sink and sipped her coffee. "I already am, although it's not my preference. We'd have to do it right, of course. Find a great editor, a really exceptional cover artist, a reliable proofreader, all of those things. We can't put out something that looks self-published."

"I agree. And there's no reason to. There are incredible resources out there." He refilled his coffee cup. "We'd keep the lion's share of the profit if we went indie."

"True. But there'd be no advance, either."

"Advances aren't what they used to be these days. Granted, there are exceptions to every rule, but I don't think debut authors are raking in the big bucks."

"You really want to publish the book ourselves, don't you?"

He took a drink before answering. "I'm not opposed to it, that's for sure. There are a lot of upsides."

She was willing to hear him out. "Such as?"

"We could have the book out in a matter of months as opposed to a year or more with a traditional publisher."

She frowned. "Would it really take that long going the traditional route?"

He nodded. "Absolutely. New York moves very differently. They only have so many slots per month available. Our book would have to be scheduled for one of those slots, which would also require editorial and the art department being lined up. It could be a year away from when we sign the contract. Or longer."

"I hadn't realized that. Seems a long time to wait for a book that's already written."

"It would be. So if we did it ourselves, we'd control the release. And like I already mentioned, going indie means we'd make a larger share of the profits, too."

"We'd have to pay for everything ourselves up front, though."

"True. But I think we could do it for about fifteen hundred dollars."

She narrowed her eyes and smiled. "You've researched this."

"I work for a newspaper. Researching is in my blood."

"You already have some editors and cover artists in mind, don't you?"

He smirked. "Maybe I do."

She chuckled. "All right, go on. What else?"

"We'd retain the rights to everything. Which means digital books, print books, audio, television, film, foreign rights, merchandising—"

"Hang on. Are you saying we'd produce all of those things ourselves?" She'd never considered how many media variations of a book there could be.

"Not necessarily. Digital and print, sure. Audio... maybe. But we could sell those rights, too. If the offer was good. Same thing with foreign rights, which could be decent for the thriller genre. And if a movie producer ever came knocking, we could easily land an agent to handle things. Or just get a good entertainment attorney."

"Wow," Margo breathed out. "That is a lot to think about."

"You know the television and movie stuff is a long shot. I mean, a really long shot. Audio and foreign rights? Not so much. Those could definitely happen."

"And we'd handle all of that?"

He nodded. "To some extent, yes."

"So, we'd become our own publishing company."

"Basically, that's it in a nutshell."

She went quiet, her head swirling with all the new information.

He moved closer. "I know it's a lot to take in. A lot to think about. But we could do it. And if things really got hectic, if we somehow ended up with a best seller on our hands and we needed help, we could hire an assistant."

Margo hadn't considered that. "Wait. You don't mean Dinah, do you?" Dinah had talked about looking for something to do part-time, even if it was just volunteering.

He made a face. "I love my sister, but I don't think she's remotely tech savvy enough to handle the kind of work we'd need help with. I'm talking about someone capable of doing social media, possibly handling reader emails, maybe even working on the production side of things and running ads."

She blinked at him. "Ads?"

"Ads are something else we should do if we self-publish. In fact, I've been working my way through an online course on Facebook and Amazon ads. It's not for the faint of heart, I'll tell you that much, but Marines don't back down just because something's hard."

She smiled. "You've put a lot into this."

"I have, but it doesn't mean I'm trying to influence you. I know you have your heart set on a contract with New York."

"It's true. But you've given me a lot to think about." She loved his excitement. And how willing he was to teach himself whatever he didn't know. There was something so endearing about that.

"Well, why don't you go sit down and think while I finish prepping breakfast. Then I'll be out to join you."

"There's nothing I can help with?"

He shook his head. "All I have to do is cut up some fruit. Go sit and be a woman of leisure."

"All right." She smiled and took her coffee to the table, which was already set for breakfast. The morning sun streamed in, making it look like a warm day outside, even though she knew it was probably in the fifties and would feel very chilly.

She sat and thought about everything he'd told her. Even if he said he wasn't trying to persuade her, she knew he wanted them to publish the book themselves. The part about being able to keep all the rights was a very interesting bit.

It never occurred to her that there would be other ways of making money from a book. It should have. She knew movies and television shows sometimes came from books. She'd listened to countless audiobooks. And the fact that books were translated into other languages was no surprise.

It was very possible that without a publisher's support, their book would die on the vine. That saddened her. They'd put a lot of work into *The Widow*. The thought that no one would read it, outside of the friends and family members who already had, made her feel bereft. It was a good story. It deserved an audience.

But she supposed that having a publisher behind them was no guarantee, either. How many books did a publisher put out in a year? How many of them achieved best-seller status? Probably not that many.

Conrad came to the table with his coffee and a

beautiful bowl of fruit salad. "Quiche should be done in about fifteen minutes."

"Sounds good."

He sat next to her. "Need more coffee?"

"Not yet, thank you." She touched the handle of her cup but didn't pick it up. "We submitted to three publishers, right?"

"Right. And we have four more smaller publishing houses to submit to if those all fall through."

Going with a small publishing house as a backup had been her idea. Conrad hadn't thought much of it, but he'd gone along all the same. "If those first three all reject the book, then I don't think we should bother with the other four."

His brows bent. "No?"

She shook her head. "If that's what happens, we'll go your route. We'll do it ourselves."

He smiled. "You mean that? I don't want you to compromise just because you think it'll make me happy."

"But it will, won't it? Publishing the book ourselves?"

"It would. I very much like the idea of keeping the rights and being in control of things."

Smiling, she leaned forward and kissed him. "In

a lot of ways, so do I. And I trust your instincts on this. You've never steered me wrong yet."

He exhaled. "I have no intention of doing so in the future, either."

She put her hand on his cheek. "I know you don't. Whatever happens, we're in this together."

"That's really the best part."

She nodded. "It really is."

Chapter Sixteen

Four thirty a.m. was early, especially after the wedding yesterday, but Claire didn't mind arriving half an hour earlier at the bakery than she was required to. There was just so much to do, so much to get ready for in preparation for what would be another busy day. And somehow, along with all her usual tasks, she had to find time to make the mayor's Christmas party cake, too.

Rosemary and Raul, her two best workers, arrived as scheduled. By then, Claire had muffins in the oven along with fresh batches of cookies made from frozen dough. That was a lifesaver, allowing her to just put the frozen, pre-portioned scoops on the baking sheets and pop them directly into the oven.

"Morning, Claire," Rosemary said.

"Morning," Claire answered, giving them both a nod. "I see there's a new batch of buttercream made up. Thank you to whoever did that.

Raul pointed at Rosemary. "She did it."

Rosemary, an older woman, smiled. "I had the time. And Raul told me about taking on the cake for the mayor's office."

"I probably shouldn't have, but..." Claire shrugged.

"It could mean a lot of good word of mouth," Rosemary said.

Claire nodded. "That's what I'm hoping."

Raul got his apron on. "How was the wedding yesterday?"

Claire smiled. "It was wonderful."

"Glad to hear that," Rosemary said.

"Thanks." Claire glanced at the muffin timer. They had seven more minutes. "Muffins and cookies are in, but we need more tins filled and a batch of sour orange pies. We've also got fruitcakes being picked up today and some yule logs to get done. In addition to all the usual stuff."

Rosemary nodded. "We'll get it done."

"I hope so," Claire said. "I know we could use more help. I really didn't anticipate us being this busy. That's my fault. If either of you know anyone capable of helping us out, don't hesitate to tell me. It would only be until after New Year's, but it would be great to have an extra set of hands. Even part-time."

Both Raul and Rosemary shook their heads.

"I know," Claire said. "I can't think of anyone, either."

They got to work, each of them focused on a particular task. The bakery opened at seven a.m., but Danny would arrive at six thirty to get the retail side of things ready. He'd make sure the cases were clean and the coffee was on, then he'd help restock those cases with all the things they were turning out.

Like the turnovers Rosemary was making. Guava, lemon, and cheese. Once they were done, she'd glaze them, then line them up neatly on trays. Those trays would go on the rolling cart, which Danny would wheel out front to fill the displays.

Raul was working on more cookies, mantecaditos, some of which would go into the tins of Christmas cookies, and some of which would go into the sales case. It was the same recipe Claire had developed prior to the bakery's opening. The only change was instead of multicolored sprinkles, these were getting Christmas sprinkles of red, white, and green.

Claire was making cake batter for the yule logs, which would be baked in jelly roll pans. That's all a yule log was—just basically a jelly roll, except the cakes would be filled with buttercream instead of jam and decorated to look like logs. Not all that hard, but they did require a little technique to get the rolling right.

After the trays of batter went into the oven, she started in on one of her all-time favorite Christmas cookies. They were a family favorite, too. Snowballs. Light, airy, and a little bit crumbly, the shortbread-adjacent cookies melted in the mouth.

It wouldn't be Christmas without them, which was why they were another cookie included in the retail tins along with the mantecaditos, gingerbread snowmen, and M&M cookies made with the holiday-colored M&Ms.

She creamed together large quantities of fresh butter, vanilla, and powdered sugar until fluffy, then added flour, finely chopped pecans, and salt. When that was all mixed, she scooped out small balls of the stiff batter using her smallest cookie scoop. The cookies went onto baking sheets, but they weren't done yet. She hand rolled each scoop to give it more of a spherical shape, then the trays went into the oven.

They baked fast, needing only eight minutes. She used that brief window of time to check on the work orders for the day and make sure she wasn't missing anything. Once that was done, she came back to the worktable and emptied a few pounds of powdered sugar onto a large stainless-steel tray.

The snowballs had to be rolled in powdered sugar while they were still warm so the sugar would adhere. There was no slacking on getting that done, either. Then they'd be put on racks to cool.

Before Claire knew it, Danny strolled into the kitchen. "Morning, all."

"Is it really six thirty already?" Claire wiped her brow with her forearm and looked at the big clock on the wall. It was actually six twenty. Danny was early.

"Almost," he said. "You guys look like you're really cooking."

She nodded, listening for the timer. Something had to be coming out of the oven soon. "We are. We have to be. There's just so much to be done."

"You'll be happy to know that Ivelisse is coming in to help out again up front today. It's her day off but she knows we need her here."

"That's great. Any chance she has a friend who can bake?"

"No, sorry. But maybe I can send Amy back here to help while we have Ivelisse up front."

"Maybe. Although I might spend more time teaching her what needs to be done than anything."

Danny sighed. "You might. We'll be better prepared next year, I promise."

"I've told myself that, too." The timer went off. "I need to get that."

"And I need to fill the cases."

He grabbed one of the rolling carts, laden with trays of goodies, and took it to the front of the shop.

She headed for the ovens, slipping on the big heatproof mitts and taking out another batch of cookies. Once those were on cooling racks, she started assembling the yule logs. All she was doing was filling them with vanilla buttercream, rolling them into logs, then crumb coating them with a thin layer of buttercream.

After that, the cakes were put on baking sheets, loaded onto another rolling cart and the whole thing wheeled into one of the walk-in refrigerators. Once the crumb coat had set, Raul would expertly frost and decorate them to look like real logs, finishing with a sprinkle of powdered sugar snow.

She found five minutes to go up front and refill her coffee cup. Danny and Amy were too busy to talk but she didn't have time for a chat anyway. She took her coffee back to the kitchen and tackled the next item on her list.

About an hour later, Danny stuck his head in. She looked up to let him know he had her attention.

"Two things," he said. "One, Ivelisse is here, so we're in good shape out front."

"Great," Claire said.

"Two, Dinah is here. Conrad's sister. She wants to talk to you."

Claire couldn't imagine about what, but she was up to her elbows in chocolate cake batter. "Can you send her back here? The only way I can talk to her is if it happens while I'm working."

"Sure, no problem."

A few moments later, Dinah came through the door. "Hi, Claire."

"Hi, Dinah. What can I do for you?" Claire was filling round cake pans on a scale so that she could be sure the same amount of batter went into each one.

"Well…" She looked around. "You seem awfully busy."

"We are, but I can talk and work at the same time."

"That's sort of why I'm here. I was wondering if you might need some part-time help?"

Claire stopped what she was doing. "Absolutely. Do you know someone who's looking?"

"Me. I am."

Claire blinked. "Do you have any experience working in a bakery?"

"No, but I've done all kinds of home baking. I used to bake for my father all the time. And church events, plus his meetings at the American Legion. I ran their cake auctions for the years my father was alive."

Claire's heart sank. Home baking wasn't the same as working in a commercial bakery. She'd figured that out for herself pretty quickly.

Dinah seemed to read her mind. "I know that's not the kind of experience you're looking for, but I'm a fast learner. I don't mind doing the grunt work like washing up, scrubbing pans, whatever."

"Really?"

Dinah smiled. "I've been doing it all my life without getting paid for it. Doing it as a job can't be much different."

She had a reasonable point. "When can you start?"

"Right now?"

Claire hadn't been expecting that. Maybe this was a genuine Christmas miracle. Maybe it wasn't.

Either way, she wasn't about to turn Dinah down. "You're hired."

Chapter Seventeen

*P*erms weren't Trina's favorite thing to do, but they were a part of the salon business, especially when you had older clients. Mrs. Williams was one of those older clients. She was also the mayor's mother-in-law.

There was no way Trina would have turned down the appointment.

She got Mrs. Williams' set done, applied the perm lotion, then set the timer. "Can I get you a drink or a magazine, Mrs. Williams?"

"No, I'm fine. You just go do whatever you need to do."

Trina smiled. "I'll only be ten minutes. Just going to take the pups out for a quick break." Her mom had taken them out earlier, but she was on the phone now. Besides, Trina was ready for a little fresh air herself.

Mrs. Williams put her hand on Trina's arm. "I heard about what you did for Renee Bronson. That was very kind of you. And very much in the Christmas spirit."

"We all have to help each other out, right?"

Mrs. Williams nodded. She had two cocker spaniels she spoiled like grandchildren. "We do. You go walk those babies. I'll be right here."

Trina rushed to the breakroom where Walter and Tinkerbell were. Walter was drinking water while Tinkerbell was napping in his bed. "Let's go, doggies. Time for a quick tinkle break."

She got their leashes on them and hustled them out the back door and straight to a patch of grass. Thankfully, that was all the encouragement they needed, and business was done without any further prompting from Trina.

She would have loved to let them walk a little, but perm solution wasn't something you wanted to forget about. She clucked her tongue at them to get them moving and walked them back inside.

She gave them each a doggy biscuit, then washed her hands and went back onto the floor. She glanced at the timer she'd set for Mrs. Williams' perm. Two minutes left. She would have loved to sit down, but there really wasn't time.

With a smile on her face, Trina went back to her station. "How are you doing?"

"Just fine. How are those dogs?"

"They're great." She checked one of the rods, unwrapping the hair to see how it was taking shape. It wasn't quite where Trina wanted it to be. She wrapped it back up. "They are certainly enjoying each other's company. I'm going to leave the solution on for two more minutes."

"Whatever you think is best. Maybe you should get Walter a friend."

Trina added two minutes to the timer, then straightened up her station a little. "I've thought about it, but Walter does pretty well on his own. Doesn't mean he and Tinkerbell won't have some playdates in the future, though."

"That's good."

When the timer went off, Trina checked another rod, unwrapping it to see how the hair was holding the curl. It looked good. "All right, Mrs. Williams, let's get you rinsed."

By the end of the day, Trina was tired and ready for an evening of doing nothing. The best part was, Miles was coming over to do nothing with her.

Although they really weren't doing nothing. They were taking the dogs for a walk on the beach, then Miles was making dinner. Nothing fancy, he'd said. Just a simple stir-fry.

That was fine with her. Any meal she didn't have to make herself was already delicious.

She and her mom said goodnight to Ginger, who'd be closing, and the second-shift stylists, then loaded the dogs into the car and drove home.

"You had a crazy day," her mom said.

Trina nodded. "That's for sure. I have to hire another stylist. And possibly a part-time reception-ist. We're both working too hard."

"It'll slow down after the holidays, though."

"Probably. But we've had a lot of new people in, too. That means word is spreading. That could mean we won't slow down as much as you think."

"That would be good for business. But you're only taking one day off a week. It should be two. You're going to burn yourself out."

"I've been thinking about that. What I think I'd like to do is start by taking a half of a day off."

"Only a half of a day?"

Trina nodded. "I don't think taking two full days is such a good idea. Not yet."

"Honey, you need some rest, you know. I under-stand you want to be at the salon all the time and you're concerned about how business is going and keeping clients happy, but you're human. And humans need downtime."

Trina sighed. "I know. But you're right that I feel a real responsibility for the salon."

"Ginger is a great assistant manager. The woman knows her stuff when it comes to the salon business."

"True." She glanced at her mom. "Are you saying that for a reason?"

Roxie shrugged. "I think you could give her a little more responsibility. Help take some of the weight off your shoulders."

"Maybe. I'll think about it." But she didn't want to think about it right now, so she changed the subject. "Did you hear from Ethan? How did the meeting with planning go?"

"It went great. He got the new stores approved. The building permits will be ready in January and then he'll break ground."

"That's exciting! Mimi must be thrilled. Three new shops. Wow!"

"And the best part is, as Ethan was leaving, one of the planning committee members stopped him to say they might know someone who'd be interested in renting one of the spaces."

"Already? That's very cool."

Roxie nodded. "One of those mailbox places that does mailings but also has P.O. boxes you can rent."

"That would be convenient to have nearby."

"It would."

Trina pulled into the driveway. Both Miles and Alex's cars were there. Miles was just getting out of his, grocery bags in hand. He smiled when he saw Trina's car approaching.

She parked, then she and her mom got the dogs out. Trina waved at Miles. "Hi, there."

"Hey," Miles said. He came over and gave her a kiss. "Hi, Mrs. Thompson."

"Hi, Miles. Need any help with groceries?"

He shook his head. "I've got it. Thanks. Besides, you guys have the dogs already."

They all started up the steps, Roxie leading the way with Tinkerbell in her arms, because her little legs couldn't do the steps very well. Roxie unlocked the door and as they went in, she put Tinkerbell down and headed for her bedroom. "I'm off to Ethan's as soon as I change. You two enjoy your evening. I'll probably be gone by the time you get back from walking the dogs."

"Have a nice night, Ma."

"You, too." Roxie handed Tinkerbell's leash to

Trina, then went into her bedroom and closed the door.

Trina took the dogs into the living room and Miles followed, going into the kitchen to put the groceries in the fridge until he was ready to cook. "You want to change or anything?"

Trina nodded. "I do. I'll just be a second."

"Take your time. No rush." He came out from the kitchen and crouched down on the floor, petting both dogs at the same time. "Your girlfriend is pretty cute, Walter."

Trina laughed. "Be right back."

She changed into leggings and a big sweatshirt with a T-shirt underneath. The walk would be quick, but it was bordering on chilly outside and the temperature would only drop more as the night got later. She added socks and sneakers, then rejoined Miles.

"Do you want Walter or Tinkerbell?"

"Doesn't matter." Tinkerbell was standing on his foot.

"You take Tinkerbell. I think she's already decided she likes you better than me."

"Is she okay on steps or should I carry her? Your mom carried her up."

"Probably better if you carry her down."

He scooped Tinkerbell into his arms. She immediately licked his face. He laughed. "All right, that's enough of that. You're going to make Walter jealous."

Trina turned toward the hall. "Bye, Ma."

They headed out the back sliders and down the steps, past the pool and out to the beach. Even though the sun had set, there was enough light to see by from all the houses that lined the beach. Even more than usual with all the Christmas lights people had out. There was a full moon rising, too.

They held hands as they walked the dogs, who seemed more reserved than usual.

"Maybe they don't like walking at night as much," Trina said.

Miles nodded. "Or they're just worn out from a long day already."

"Could be."

"I've missed you," he said.

"I've missed you, too. And I've been thinking about us getting married."

"Yeah?" He smiled.

She nodded. "If we're really going to do this, we need to start making plans."

"I couldn't agree more. And the sooner, the better."

For some reason, she hadn't been expecting that. "You mean it?"

"More than I've ever meant anything."

"So...how soon do you want to do it?"

"How soon can it happen? I have no clue about stuff like this. The only thing I ask is that we pick a date that works for my parents. It's not a big deal for them to drive over, we just need to be sure they can be here on the day we choose."

"Absolutely." She'd met Miles's parents twice now. They lived in Grayton Beach, a couple of hours away. They were very sweet people. His dad managed a medical supply company, and his mom was a nurse. It was no wonder Miles had become a paramedic.

"Good. If you tell me some dates, I'll let them know."

"I'll call Pastor Tim tomorrow and see how soon he can do the wedding. And when the church is available. Then we'll need to work out catering and music and all of that stuff."

"And your dress," Miles said.

Trina nodded. "And whatever you're going to wear." She grinned. "I would love to see you in a tux."

"Then I'll get one. That bridal shop in town

probably rents them. In fact, I think that's where I got my tux for prom. Or maybe it was Portman's. Now I'm not sure. Don't worry, I'll figure it out."

"What about our bridal party?"

"I'm going to ask Alex to be my best man. Do we need more than one person?"

"Not really. Nothing wrong with keeping things simple. I'll ask Kat to be my maid of honor." Trina let out a happy sigh. "We're really doing this, aren't we?"

He pulled her closer. "Yep. And I can't wait."

Chapter Eighteen

It was odd being alone in the beach house. Somehow the morning light made the place look even emptier. Kat stood at the kitchen counter, drinking her coffee and trying to wake up.

Her mom was already gone for the day. She was always gone early now. One of the requirements for running a bakery was getting there in time to make all the goodies before customers arrived.

Kat needed to get going soon herself. She only had a couple more days of work before Future Florida closed for the holidays, but those days would be busy ones.

Christmas brought out the giving side of people, which meant lots of donations were coming in daily. But the holidays also meant an increase in requests for help. Kat's desk was overflowing with the files of people in need.

She hoped to get through a lot of them today. She didn't like the thought of leaving the truly worthy without an answer over the holidays. That would make it hard to enjoy Christmas. For them, and for her.

With that in mind, she carried her coffee into the bathroom and cranked on the shower. She finished her coffee before the water got hot, already planning on another cup before she left.

Half an hour later, she was dressed and ready to go in khaki pants and a red and white sweater that felt Christmasy. She filled her travel mug with coffee and headed downstairs to her car.

Arlene, the receptionist, was just unlocking the front door as Kat walked up to the Future Florida office. "Morning, Kat."

"Morning, Arlene. You look festive." Arlene's blouse was patterned with wreaths and candy canes and her earrings were small bows, the kind that went on packages.

Arlene smiled. "I can't help myself."

"I love it. You're in the spirit."

Arlene opened the door, and they went in. Arlene flipped on the lights, illuminating the tall, skinny tree in the reception area. It had been decorated and hung with envelopes at the beginning of December. Each envelope held a specific request from a local family in need. Most of the needs could be fulfilled for less than a hundred dollars, although there were a few slightly more expensive ones on the tree.

The area's radio station had been giving Future Florida free publicity by mentioning the tree several times a day during their broadcasts. So far, more than half of the envelopes had been taken care of.

But there were still quite a few to go. And Christmas Eve was fast approaching.

Kat studied the tree. "Do you think we'll get all of these requests met?"

"It would be nice," Arlene said. She went behind the reception desk and turned on her computer. "But generally, we take care of any that don't."

"We do?" Kat looked at her.

Arlene nodded. "Usually by the 23rd, the remaining envelopes get taken down and the requests fulfilled. Wouldn't be very much in the Christmas spirit if we didn't."

Kat smiled. "No, it wouldn't be. And I'm glad to hear that. I love this place."

Arlene picked up her coffee cup. "So do I. It really does the heart good, doesn't it?"

"It does."

Arlene held up her cup. "Coffee?"

Kat had brought her travel mug in with her. "I still have half a cup. I think I'll get straight to work."

Arlene headed for the breakroom. "Well, there will be coffee when you're ready for it."

"Thanks."

Eloise came in. "Morning, Kat. How are you?"

"I'm good. I love that dress." Eloise ran the social media and public relations for Future Florida, and she was a sharp dresser. Today's red and black dress was no exception.

"Thanks," Eloise said. "Your sweater is super cute."

Kat smiled. "Ready for Christmas?"

"I am. I bought Sir Isaac Mewton a new cat condo."

Kat laughed. "And what's he getting you?"

"Probably a hairball and more unreasonable demands." Eloise smiled. "And yet, I love him anyway."

"He is pretty adorable." Kat opened the door that led back to the individual offices and held it for Eloise. Kat had only seen pictures of Sir Isaac

Mewton, but she'd heard a lot of stories about him. He was clearly a character.

"And he knows it," Eloise said as she came through.

"He's actually made me think about getting a cat. I'd love a dog, but I don't like the idea of leaving a dog home alone so much of the day. Cats do better by themselves, right?"

"A lot of them, yes." Eloise went down the hall to her office but stood outside the door. "Some cats need a buddy, though. They definitely don't need the same level of looking after that a dog does. It helps that they don't have to be walked or to go out to do their business."

Then she smiled. "And they are really good company. All pets are."

Kat nodded as she got her key out. "That's the part I like best. Having company."

Eloise unlocked her office door and pushed it open. "See you for lunch?"

"You bet." Kat went in, leaving her door open. She flicked the lights on.

She really liked her office. Especially with the way she'd decorated it. She had a couple of plants on the windowsill, some pictures of Alex and her family, and a really cool painting of a wave that she'd found at the thrift shop. It went perfectly with the surfboard wall clock she'd painted, which hung right above the painting.

She put her purse in her desk drawer, set her coffee down, then settled into her chair and fired up her laptop.

The stack of files waiting to be read through looked like it had grown overnight. She sighed just staring at it. There had to be a hundred in that pile, but she was determined to get through as many of them as she could.

Arlene walked by, stopping at Kat's door. "Coffee's made." Her gaze went to the files. "You want any help with those? I know it's your job but maybe I could do a quick read through and try to weed out the obvious grifters?"

It *was* Kat's job. Didn't feel right to ask anyone else for help with it. "That's kind of you to offer. Let me see how many I can get through by lunch and I'll let you know."

"Okay. Sounds good."

Kat went through her usual morning routine of checking emails, then dove straight into the files.

Some of them were hard to read. Heart-wrenching stories of people with terminal diseases, families in need for various reasons, businesses on the verge of collapse, all of them with desperate requests for help.

In the time Kat had been with Future Florida, reading through these files had never gotten easier. But she had learned to deal with her feelings toward them in a healthier way.

Now that it was Christmastime, that ability seemed to be harder to come by. Her heart broke for so many of them, but unlike the early days of her work with the charity, she knew that many of them could be helped.

She didn't want to shortchange any of the requests by not spending an appropriate amount of time on them, but she also had a lot of files to get through. Fortunately, she'd learned to pretty quickly trust her gut in separating the grifters from those who truly needed assistance.

By lunch, she'd gotten through nearly half of the pile. Not surprisingly, half of the ones she'd gone through hadn't registered as legitimate to her. Apparently, Christmas brought out the con artists in full force.

It was possible she'd gotten more cynical working here, but she also believed her instincts had been honed by the job. She took the stack of questionable requests out to Arlene. "Is your offer of help still available?"

"Sure," Arlene said. "You want me to read through those?"

"I already have. What I want is your opinion on whether or not these are scammers."

Arlene's penciled brows went up. "All of them?"

Kat nodded. "I know. It's a lot. But all of these gave me that feeling."

Arlene pursed her lips. "Like they were trying to pull a fast one?"

"That's the feeling."

"Honey, I raised three boys. I know pretty well when I'm being sold a story." She rolled her eyes and laughed, then held out her hands. "I'll give them the onceover."

"Thanks." Kat passed the files to her and started back to her office. She glanced at the tree again and stopped. "Is it my imagination or are there fewer envelopes on there now than there were this morning?"

Arlene nodded. "Two ladies from the Diamond Beach Women's Association came in and took care of five of them."

"Wow, that's amazing."

Arlene gestured to the cards in front of her. "I was just finishing up the thank-you cards for them.

I'll bring them into the conference room later for everyone to sign." That was their standard practice, to have everyone in the office sign the thank-you notes that went out.

"Perfect. And thanks again for the help with the files."

"You got it."

Kat went back to her office. She had half an hour before her lunch break, and she was determined to get through another handful of files.

If she could help it, there were going to be as many happy families in Florida as possible this Christmas.

Chapter Nineteen

"Y ou're such a good girl," Willie cooed as she put Snowy in the carrier to take her to the vet. Willie was glad about that, too. She'd been a little worried that Snowy might try to resist. Thankfully, she hadn't.

Willie closed the carrier door, then went into Miguel's office. He was on the computer. Probably ordering the special paper needed to print out their trip photos. "I'm leaving for the vet now."

He looked up. "If you give me a minute, I'll come with you."

"It's all right, I can do it."

"You're sure? I don't mind."

"Nope, I've got it. I'll come back to drop her off, then I'm going to the craft shop to look for a nice photo album. If I can't find one there, I'll order one. Are you getting the paper?"

"I am. All ordered. Anything you need me to do around the house?"

"There's a load of whites that need washing."

He nodded. "I can do that."

"Thanks."

"How about I go with you to the craft store, but we have lunch at the café first?"

She smiled. "Okay. Sounds good. Back in a bit."

She grabbed her purse along with Snowy's file from the rescue, then picked up Snowy in her carrier and went out to the garage where her golf cart was. She put Snowy on the front seat with her and used a bungee cord to secure the carrier to the frame of the seat.

Snowy meowed, a sound that seemed very unhappy to Willie.

"Don't worry, my girl. I won't go fast. You'll be just fine, you'll see." Willie opened the garage door and climbed behind the wheel. She secured her purse and the files before putting the cart into reverse and carefully backing out. Golf cart in Neutral, she shut the garage door.

She put her own seatbelt on, then her sunglasses. "All right, Snowy girl, here we go."

She drove with more caution than she usually did, having such precious cargo on board. It took her a few minutes longer than it normally would have to get to the shopping area, but that was fine. She'd left early on purpose.

Snowy had meowed once more, but then seemed interested in watching what was going on around her after that.

"Such a good girl you are," Willie said. She pulled into the parking lot and found a spot near the vet's office.

Truth was, Willie was a bit nervous about taking Snowy in. She'd fallen hopelessly in love with the little cat in just a few days. She couldn't imagine what she'd do if there was anything wrong with her.

Not that Willie had any reason to think that. Snowy had come from a reliable rescue. And she wasn't acting sick or odd in any way. But Willie couldn't help herself. It was human nature to imagine the worst, she supposed.

With her purse over her arm, and Snowy's file tucked under that same arm, Willie carried Snowy into Westside Animal Hospital and went straight to the reception desk. "Willie Rojas with Snowy."

The young man in scrubs behind the counter nodded at her then tapped the touch pad in front of him. "Yes, ma'am, I have you checked in. We'll be with you in just a few minutes."

"Thank you." Willie took a seat on the opposite side of the waiting room, across from a man with a large dog.

The dog looked nice enough, but Snowy didn't need any additional stress.

Willie put the carrier on the seat next to her and peeked in. "How are you doing, my girl?"

Snowy was laying down on the folded towel Willie had tucked into the carrier to make it more comfortable. She didn't look the least bit bothered. Which wasn't how Willie felt at all.

A young woman in scrubs came out from the back. She had a tablet in her hand. "Snowy Rojas?"

Willie picked up the carrier and stood. "That's us."

The young woman smiled. "Right this way."

They went through a door and down a bright, antiseptic hallway lined with more doors, each one with a frosted glass window. The young woman stopped at Room 3 and opened the door. "I'm Penny, your vet tech for this visit."

"Hi, Penny." Willie went in and put the carrier on the stainless-steel table. She set the file down next to it.

Penny shut the door as she came in. "You're Willie Rojas?"

"I am, and this is my cat, Princess Snowball. Snowy for short." Willie smiled. "She was an early Christmas present from my husband."

"Isn't that sweet?" Penny set the tablet on the nearby counter, then washed her hands. "What's going on with Snowy today?"

"Nothing, really. I just thought it would be a good idea to get her in for a checkup and get her into your system."

"It's a great idea," Penny said. "Do you know where she came from? A breeder? Pet shop?"

"Family Friends Rescue," Willie answered. "I brought the file they gave me for her. It has the record of what shots she's had so far. And she has an appointment soon to get spayed."

"Very good. They're a great rescue." Penny brought over a long scale that looked a little like the kind used to weigh babies. She set it on the table, then opened the carrier and looked inside. "Hi, there, Snowy. Aren't you pretty?"

Penny reached in and extracted Snowy with both hands. Snowy looked nervous, eyes big, her gaze darting around.

"It's okay, baby," Willie said softly. She felt bad. Snowy was here because of her.

Penny put her on the scale. "Four pounds even. She's just a baby, isn't she?"

"She is. I just want to make sure she's healthy, too."

The tech took Snowy's temperature, an indignity to be sure, but Snowy didn't fuss. Penny looked at the thermometer. "Temp is normal. All right, the vet will be in shortly."

Penny left but returned a few minutes later with the doctor. He was a tall, dark-skinned man with a nice smile and kind eyes. "Hello, Mrs. Rojas. I'm Dr. Sharma. How are you today?"

"I'm good, thank you."

"And this is Snowy?"

"It is."

"She's a beautiful cat."

"Thank you."

"Any issues? Anything wrong that you're aware of?"

"No, nothing. Just a checkup to get her set up with the office here. I just got her. She was a present from my husband."

"What a lovely gift. She's eating and drinking okay? No issues using the litter box?"

"She's eating and drinking just fine. No problems

using the litter box, either. Plays a lot, sleeps a lot. Seems very normal to me."

"Excellent." He did a quick examination, looking at Snowy's eyes, ears, and teeth, listening to her heart, feeling her limbs, and inspecting her coat. He nodded. "She appears to be a very healthy young cat. We can certainly do bloodwork, if you like. That's entirely up to you. I don't think it's necessary at this time, however."

"If that means she doesn't have to get stuck, I'm all for that."

Dr. Sharma smiled. "It was a pleasure to meet you and Snowy. Thank you for choosing us as your veterinarian."

Wasn't like she'd had a lot of choice. Westside Animal Hospital was the only option in Dunes West. But she liked the place. "You'll see us again. Hopefully not too soon, though, but for Snowy's follow-up after she gets fixed. The rescue's doing that, but we'll be here for her follow-up. Thank you."

"We'll see you then. Penny will check you out. Have a good day. Bye, Willie. Bye, Snowy."

"Bye," Willie said.

He left, leaving her with Penny, who whipped out a little credit card reading machine. "I'll have your total for you in just a second."

Willie opened the door of the carrier, but Snowy didn't wait for help to get in. She went right through and curled up inside. "Ready to go home, baby?"

Snowy looked at her and meowed.

Willie smiled. "I know. There's no place like home, is there?"

She closed the carrier and got her credit card out of her purse, breathing a sigh of relief that her new baby was in good health.

Now she really had everything she wanted for Christmas.

Chapter Twenty

Jules stretched her arms and legs out as far as they would go and didn't hit a wall on either side. She grinned as she stared up at the ceiling. She'd definitely made the right decision to get everyone their own hotel room for the night.

The tour bus was great and far swankier than most RVs, but nothing compared to a full-size bed, a full-size shower, and the complete privacy of having your own room.

Even if she was sharing with Toby.

She sat up and looked at him. He was sprawled on the room's sofa on his back, feet in the air, snoring. She shook her head. He'd probably be doing the same thing if they were still on the bus. "Silly thing."

Finding a decent hotel that would take dogs wasn't that hard. She wasn't sure this one actually did, but sometimes being a bit of a celebrity had perks. When it came to looking after Toby and Shiloh, Jules wasn't above using that celebrity status.

Being in a hotel room meant it was easier for her to accomplish a few other things, too. Like the Christmas surprise she had planned for her band.

Right now, however, she was going down to the gym for a workout, then having a long, hot shower. After that, she was joining Jesse and the band members at the hotel's restaurant for a nice, leisurely dinner. She'd booked the private room so they could eat undisturbed.

Maybe not something that had been completely necessary, but she knew they could be a little rowdy, too. Plus, the possibility existed that she might be recognized. Crazy how that was happening more and more these days.

It would be a long while before she got used to that.

She changed into some workout clothes, stuck her earbuds in, then laced up her sneakers. The other perk to getting a hotel meant being able to have laundry done. She grabbed her phone, kissed Toby on the head, and headed for the hotel gym, the room key stuck in the interior pocket of her exercise leggings.

She grinned when she saw Jesse on the treadmill. She used her key to gain access to the room, then wiggled her fingers at him.

He took one earbud out. "You inspired me."

"Well, hey, points for both of us then." She climbed onto the treadmill next to him. "I needed this. I don't know about the rest of you, but—"

"You mean the workout or the hotel room?"

"Both. But the hotel room more than the workout."

He nodded. "The tour bus is great, but—"

"It's not home. I know." She started jogging slowly. "I think I forgot a little of that. It's been so long since I've toured. You tend to gloss over the not-so-fun stuff and focus on the good."

"I am looking forward to sleeping in a bed where my feet don't touch the wall."

She laughed. "I'm sorry about that. They can only make those bunks so big."

"I get it. And it's not a big deal. Just being on tour with you makes up for any inconvenience. But I'd be lying if I said I wasn't excited about sleeping in a king-size bed tonight."

"I get it. How's Shiloh?" They'd gotten adjoining rooms but had yet to open the doors to connect the two. Jules was a little concerned that the dogs would turn one of the beds into their own bed if left alone.

"When I left, she was still sniffing everything. Toby, too?"

"Are you kidding? He's passed out on the couch. He never misses an opportunity to nap."

"He lives the life."

"Yes, he does."

"It was really nice of you to spring for the hotel."

Jules smiled. Even he didn't know about the surprise she had planned. "The album is doing amazingly well. Even with the percentage that's going to Future Florida, there is more than enough to take care of some extras like this."

"The video paid off." He was smiling.

She nodded. "Yes, it did. It has nearly four million views. Four million!"

"I know," he said calmly. "I check it almost every day."

"You do not."

He laughed. "Yes, I do. I feel a lot of responsibility for that video."

"It wouldn't have happened without you." He'd actually footed the deposit himself so that the video could be made as quickly as possible. It was a completely selfless act that had really shown her just how much he loved her.

He shrugged. "It wouldn't have happened without your song or Cash and Sierra's script."

"True. But you were the key ingredient." She winked at him. "You're kind of the key ingredient in a lot of things these days." Like her happiness. Her sense of peace. Her ability to get through hard days. Her enjoyment of the good ones.

"I feel the same way about you."

She cranked the speed up on the treadmill a few notches. "I'm going to burn as many calories as I can now, because I plan to have a giant steak for dinner. I might even eat a baked potato. Fully loaded."

"Now you're just talking crazy."

She cranked up the speed again and ran as fast as she could go for a few minutes. Then she got off, lifted some weights, did some core work, and finally stretched. Jesse left a few minutes before she did, but they agreed to walk down to dinner together at seven.

The elevator seemed like a blessing as she went back upstairs. Maybe she'd overdone it a little with the running, but it was good to be worn out like that. It was a different kind of worn out than coming off stage. Hard to explain, but it was a calmer sort of tired.

She was always so wired when she was done with a show. Now she was just ready for a shower.

Thankfully, the water was plenty hot, and the pressure was strong. She also didn't need to worry about using it all up. She took her time, letting it beat on her like a mini-massage. She washed her hair, exfoliated, and shaved. All the stuff she normally raced through on the bus she now took her time with.

Made her miss home. A little. But she wouldn't have missed this tour for anything. Her career was in a totally different place because of the new album, and the tour was cementing that spot for her.

She got out of the shower, her fingertips wrinkled from being in so long. She wrapped up in the hotel's big fluffy white towels and went into the room. Toby had gotten up to eat. She'd set his food and water bowls out on an extra bathmat provided for just that reason.

"Nice place, huh, Tobes?"

He was too busy chowing down to answer.

No matter how nice the hotel's restaurant was, she wasn't getting dressed up. Jeans, a T-shirt, and boots, with a little makeup and minimal hair. Her skin needed the rest from all the stage makeup and her hair could probably use a break from all the products, too.

She picked out the jeans and T-shirt she planned to wear, then went back to the bathroom to dry her hair. She slathered on moisturizer then. Being on the tour bus seemed to dry her skin out. Maybe from the recycled air. Not that the hotel was probably much different.

Once her hair was dry, she dabbed on a little concealer, flicked mascara over her lashes, then swiped on some tinted lip balm. As an afterthought, she dotted some of that lip balm on her cheeks and used it like a cream blush.

That was enough makeup for the night.

She went back out and dressed. When she was done, she opened her side of the adjoining doors and knocked on Jesse's.

He opened his. "Ready?"

"I am. You look nice." He did, too. Jeans and a button-down shirt. Shiloh appeared next to him, tail wagging and tongue out.

"I might be a little overdressed, huh?"

"No, you look great. Don't change. Unless you want to. Up to you."

"I'll stay the way I am."

She couldn't have asked for more. "I guess I don't need a purse. Just my room key. I can put the bill on the room."

"Perfect." He was smiling in a funny way.

"What?"

He shook his head. "You look different without all the stage makeup, which I know you have to wear. But I sort of feel like I'm about to spend an evening with your younger sister."

She laughed. "Is that a good thing or a bad thing?"

"As long as it's still you, it's always a good thing."

She grabbed her room key off the dresser and stuck it in her back pocket, then put her phone in the other one. "Should we leave the doors open for the dogs?"

He glanced down at Shiloh. "Will you and Toby behave yourselves?"

Shiloh sat down and lifted her paw.

Jesse laughed. "That's very cute, but you're not getting another treat right now. I just gave you one."

"She's working you."

"Oh, I'm aware." He rolled his eyes. "I say leave the doors open. Maybe they'll just have a nap."

"Anything's possible."

They went down to dinner, going out through

the door on his side. Shiloh had already disappeared into Jules's room, and she swore she could hear the two dogs wrestling. Didn't take long for them to get into it.

At the restaurant, which was all decked out for Christmas, they were ushered straight back to the private room. Gold and silver ornaments hung from the ceiling, sending shimmering dabs of light all over the room. Rita and Bobby were there, and Cash and Sierra came in as Jules and Jesse were sitting down. Frankie, the banjo player, came in right after them.

"This is a great place," Bobby said.

"It is," Frankie agreed.

"I'll say," Sierra said. "That shower was so nice."

Jules nodded. "Yes, it was. If not for being hungry, I might still be in there."

"I took a nap." Rita laughed. "And it's not going to stop me from sleeping tonight, either. That bed is comfortable." She quickly made eye contact with Jules. "Which isn't to say the bus isn't nice. It is."

"I get it," Jules said. "Why do you think we're here? There are only so many nights on the bus a person can take."

The rest of the band joined them, as did Chuck,

their bus driver. Menus were passed out and glasses of water filled as drink orders were taken.

Once everyone had a glass in front of them, Jules lifted hers. "Thank you all for being a part of this tour. I am grateful to each and every one of you."

Cash lifted his glass a little higher. "It wouldn't have happened without you, Mom."

She smiled. "Here's to all of you. And Merry Christmas!"

They all said it back to her, then sipped their drinks. Everyone looked so happy.

Under the table, Jesse took her hand and smiled at her. She smiled back. She was definitely still missing her family, but the folks around her made up for a lot of that.

Chapter Twenty-one

"What do you say?" Roxie asked her daughter. They were headed home after another crazy day at the salon. "I know you've had a long day, but we could just take a quick look. And tonight's one of the few nights they're open late."

"I don't know," Trina said. "What am I going to do with Walter and Tinkerbell?"

"We'll run them home, then go. Classic Closet is only a few minutes away from the house." Roxie really wanted to go look at wedding dresses. "It might be a super quick trip. They might have nothing."

"Yeah, but it's still Classic Closet." Trina laughed. "It's never a quick trip."

"We could eat at that noodle place across the street."

"Siam House?" Still smiling, Trina sighed. "Okay. You talked me into it."

A few minutes later, they had the dogs dropped off at the house and they were headed to Classic Closet.

"Do you have any idea what kind of dress you want?" Roxie asked. "What kind of style you might like?"

"Not really. I think I was sort of just going to try stuff on and see what looked good."

"That works."

The big thrift shop wasn't as busy as Roxie thought it would be. The later hours were only on weekends and only for the holidays. Roxie was happy to take advantage of them. She gestured toward the women's section. "I don't really know where the wedding dresses would be, but they should be over there."

"If they have any."

"I'm sure I've seen some here."

They headed in that direction. Didn't take long to find the rack of white gowns. Most of them were in clear garment bags.

"Hard to tell what they look like in those bags," Trina said. "You really have to use your imagination."

"You do," Roxie agreed. "Don't forget, we can get the dress altered, too. Shortened, taken in, maybe let out, sleeves changed. There's all sorts of things a good seamstress can do."

"I'll try to remember that. Oh, this is pretty." Trina hauled out a dress that had a lot of sparkle on it.

Roxie nodded. "That looks like you."

"I'm definitely trying this one on."

"Get a couple. If you're going to the trouble of trying on one, you might as well try on a few."

Trina nodded and went back to digging.

Roxie worked her way through from the other end of the rack. She was three dresses in when she found something she liked, a dress that surprised her. It wasn't something she would have thought she'd like. It was a simple gown, without any decoration, but it had a kind of glamour to it. Like something an old-time Hollywood actress might wear.

She was almost afraid to show it to Trina, thinking her daughter might not like it because it was so plain. "I found one to try on."

"Just one?" Trina gave her a look.

Roxie laughed. "Right. I'll find at least one more."

By the time she had her second dress picked out,

a strapless number with some lace and crystals, Trina had four dresses selected.

They headed off to the dressing rooms to try them on.

Roxie saved the dress she liked the best for last, trying on the strapless one first. As it turned out, it was tea length, reaching about mid-calf. It was very sweet. A sort of matte satin with some lace appliques enhanced with sequins and crystals.

She got it zipped up, then pulled the curtain back just enough to see out. "Trina? Do you have one on yet?"

"Just about." A moment later, Trina pulled her curtain back and stepped out. "What do you think?"

Roxie nodded at the cap-sleeved lace gown. It had an empire waist accented with a slim ribbon belt. The lace was highlighted with seed pearls, sequins, and tiny rhinestones. "I'm going to be honest."

Trina nodded as she looked at herself in the mirror. She turned to get a better look at the back. "I want you to be."

"It's very pretty. But it looks like a nightgown. A fancy one, but still a nightgown."

Trina snorted. "It kind of does, doesn't it?" She shook her head. "This high-waisted look reminds me of the gowns the girls wore in that movie, *Sense and Sensibility*." She wrinkled her nose. "It's not me."

Then she looked at her mother. "Why are you still in the dressing room? Don't you have a dress on?"

"I do." Roxie stepped out.

"Hey, that's pretty. *Really* pretty."

"Don't you think it looks sort of...casual?"

Trina tipped her head to one side. "Now that you've mentioned it, yes. But not in a bad way. If you're having a more casual wedding in the afternoon. On the beach. Which I know you're not, but if that was the kind of wedding you were having, it would be perfect."

"Right."

Trina got a funny look on her face as she studied the dress her mother had on. "I actually think I'd like to try that on."

"You would?"

She nodded. "It's so feminine. And it's got a kind of retro vibe that I really like. We aren't doing a beach wedding, either, but we still want to keep it casual. That dress might be perfect for me."

"Give me a second and I'll hand it out to you," Roxie said as she slipped back into the dressing room. She unzipped the dress and carefully handed it through the curtain. "Here you go."

"Thanks, Ma."

Roxie secured the curtain and unzipped the garment bag on the other dress. She lifted the bottom part of the dress out to see the full length of it. The gown was crafted from thick, luxurious satin that had a silvery sheen to it like moonlight.

She examined the entire dress to see if there was anything wrong with it, trying to figure out why it had been donated. There wasn't a snag or a blemish anywhere. It didn't even appear to have been worn. She looked inside the dress and found a tag.

That seemed to confirm her guess that the gown had never actually been down an aisle.

The tag bore the name of a shop she didn't know and a price of thirty-four hundred dollars. She read it twice to be sure. Her heart beat faster at the thought of having such an expensive dress in her hands.

Who on Earth would donate such a thing? Had it belonged to a bride who'd never made it to the altar? That was a sad thought. But Roxie could understand how an engagement gone wrong would make the bride want to get rid of the dress. If that was the case, the dress would be a big white reminder of a broken promise.

Kind of sad to think that someone else's misfortune might be Roxie's great bargain, but then again, if she could make a happy memory with the dress, that seemed all right. Like she was finally giving the dress the ending it was meant for.

Or maybe she just read too many romance novels.

Smiling, she carefully slipped the dress on. It had thin straps that held up a cowl neckline and was fitted through the waist until about mid-hip, where the fabric flared out, ending with a small train.

Roxie stared at herself in the mirror. It was the most beautiful thing she'd ever worn, even if it was a little big in a few places. The sheen of the satin made her skin look luminous, even in the florescent lighting of the store.

The sizing was fixable. She'd told Trina as much.

"Ma, are you coming out?" Trina asked. "I have the dress on. The one you gave me."

Roxie nodded at her reflection. "Coming." She turned to see the back as best she could. It was so pretty. Could she really get married in a dress like this? She wasn't exactly the elegant glamour girl, and that's who this dress belonged on.

But she loved it. She loved it more than any dress she'd ever owned.

She stepped out of the dressing room and Trina gasped.

"Ma, where did you get that dress? You look like a movie star. One of the really big ones from the old days."

"I just found it on the rack. I don't think it's ever been worn, because it still has the tag in it."

The tea-length strapless dress fit Trina beautifully. Roxie could easily imagine it for a more casual wedding. It was young and pretty and very much Trina. "That looks so much better on you. It's really lovely on you. And it really would be perfect for a casual wedding."

Trina pointed at her mother. "Hang on, I'm not done talking about this dress you have on. You look amazing. How much is it?"

Roxie knew how much it *had* been, but not how much Classic Closet was selling it for. She checked the garment bag in the dressing room. The tag attached to the hanger said three hundred dollars and had a red dot on it.

"Three hundred, which seems like a pretty good buy, considering the original price was thirty-four hundred."

"Holy cow, that was an expensive dress. What color dot is on the tag?"

"Red."

Trina grinned. "Then it's only a hundred and fifty. Red and green dots are half off. Christmas special."

"Really?" She could easily afford the dress and the cost of having it altered. "Tell me the truth. Do you think I can pull this dress off? It's not exactly my usual look. It's very sophisticated and elegant."

"Ma, I've never seen you look more beautiful. You can totally pull that off. I'm already imagining ways to do your hair. Seriously, if you don't buy that dress, you're crazy. Wait until Ethan sees you in that. He might pass out."

Roxie smiled and glanced at herself in the mirror again. Then she turned and focused on her daughter. "What about you? That dress is so good on you. Do you like it?"

Trina nodded. "I do. Very much. It actually could be the one. But I have a few more to try on and since I brought them in, I might as well. Please tell me you're buying that dress."

Roxie smoothed her hands down the cool satin and made her decision. "I am. This is my wedding dress."

Chapter Twenty-two

Conrad came in through the sliding doors that opened onto the lanai. He'd been out on the patio, the unscreened paved area just beyond the screened part of the lanai, grilling steaks for dinner. They kept the grill out there so the heat and smoke wouldn't be too close to the house. He had the platter of steaks in one hand and the long grill tongs in the other.

"Those smell great," Margo said. She'd made a simple Greek-style salad to go with the steaks and baked some potatoes. "Did you make all four steaks?"

"I did, so there's plenty. Where's Dinah?"

"In the bathroom. She should be right out. She brought a good bottle of red, too. And a box of assorted desserts from Claire's bakery."

"That was nice of her." Conrad set the plate of steaks on the table next to the big bowl of salad.

"Very nice. She seems really happy about something, too."

"Even better. I'm sure she'll tell us if it's worth sharing. What else can I do to help?"

"Open that bottle of wine. That's it."

Dinah rejoined them, still wearing the big smile she'd had when Margo greeted her at the front door. "Hi, Connie. How's married life treating you?"

He smiled. "Outstanding. How's life in Diamond Beach?"

A new sparkle lit Dinah's gaze. "Really, really good."

"Oh?"

"Hold on," Margo said. "Let's sit and get started on dinner before those steaks go cold. Dinah, I want to hear all about why things are so good while we eat."

"Works for me," Dinah said.

They took their seats. Conrad poured the wine while Margo selected a steak and Dinah took a baked potato. When their plates were full, Margo looked at Dinah. "All right, out with it. You're bursting to tell us something."

Dinah hadn't stopped smiling since she'd arrived. "I got a job."

"You did?" Conrad stopped in the middle of cutting his steak. "Where?"

"The dessert I brought is a hint."

Margo added a small pat of butter and a sprinkling of salt to her potato. "At Claire's bakery?"

Dinah nodded. "I'm a bakery assistant. Part-time. And to be honest, I'm not sure it'll go much beyond the holidays, but that's okay. I worked for a few hours today. I liked it a lot. That place really does some business."

Conrad looked confused. "You've always been a pretty good baker, but you don't have any experience working in a professional kitchen like that. How did you get the job? What are you going to be doing?"

"I think I got the job because I was in the right place at the right time. And I'll be doing a lot of menial tasks, but I don't mind that one bit. It means Claire and her bakers can concentrate on the more skilled jobs."

"So what kinds of tasks will you be doing?" Margo asked.

"Things like cleaning up. Loading and unloading the dishwasher. Scrubbing the bowls and things that are too big for the dishwasher. Wiping down the worktables. Getting ingredients together. I did some of that today, along with measuring out some ingredients and learning to make buttercream."

"Don't you already know how to do that?" Conrad asked.

Dinah laughed. "It's a lot different making ten pounds of buttercream instead of just enough to frost one cake."

"I bet it is," Margo said.

"And Claire, who is lovely, by the way, said once things slow down a bit, she can teach me to do more things, like crumb coat the cakes, frost cupcakes, and even make cookies."

"That doesn't sound like a temporary position," Conrad said.

Dinah's brow furrowed. "No, you're right, it doesn't." She smiled again. "Even better, because I really enjoyed it. I'm working there again tomorrow."

"That's wonderful." Margo knew what it was like to isolate oneself, something she and Dinah had both done during their lives. This job sounded like just the thing Dinah needed. What a kind thing for Claire to do. Margo was so appreciative of her daughter. "You look very happy."

"I am. It was nice to be around people. To feel

like I was contributing. Even better to know I was getting paid for it."

"That's fantastic," Conrad said. "I'm really pleased for you."

"So am I," Margo added. "And thank you for the kind words about Claire."

"You must be so proud of her," Dinah said. "She's amazing in that kitchen. She really knows what she's doing. I was very impressed."

"I am very proud of her. Of both my girls."

Conrad glanced at her. "Have you heard from Jules?"

Margo nodded. "She called me last night from the bathtub of the hotel she was staying in. We had a nice chat."

"I thought they were on a tour bus?" Dinah said.

"They are, but they had a little more time between venues, so Jules decided they needed a night in a hotel. In real beds, she said."

Conrad cut another bite of steak. "I don't imagine they have a tub on that bus, either."

Margo laughed softly. "No and she mentioned how nice it was to take advantage of the one at the hotel."

"The tour is going well then?"

She speared a cherry tomato half with her fork. "Very well, from what Jules told me."

"That's great news." He sighed. "I have some less-than-great news, unfortunately."

Margo set her fork down, instantly curious. "You do?"

He nodded. "We got an email from Spectrum Publishing. They rejected the book. Nicely. But it was a rejection, all the same."

"I'm so sorry," Dinah said. "They clearly have no taste. I read that book and it was fantastic."

Margo smiled. The rejection hurt but not as much as she'd imagined it would. She'd almost been expecting it. "Thank you, Dinah." She shrugged as she looked at Conrad. "It's not the result I was hoping for, obviously, but at least it's one less response we have to wait on."

She turned her attention to Dinah again. "We're going to self-publish the book if all three publishers reject it."

"You are?" Dinah shook her head. "You and Connie are so fearless. I envy that. I need to be more like the two of you."

Margo used the edge of her fork to cut a piece of baked potato. "I'd say moving here and starting a brand-new life was a pretty fearless endeavor."

"Agreed," Conrad said.

"You're right," Dinah said. "It was. But I had a lot of help and handholding from you two. And Margo, speaking of fearless, you also made over this entire house. That was a major project."

"It was, but your brother helped me a great deal." She reached out to touch his arm. "And when we self-publish this book, he's going to be helping me again. I couldn't do it without him."

"When?" Conrad said, smiling. "You make it sound like it's a foregone conclusion."

Margo ate the bite of potato. "If one publisher turned us down, there's a good chance the other two will as well. I've done a lot of thinking and I'm okay with the plan we discussed. There is a lot to be said for keeping control of the process and being in charge of our own schedule."

She glanced at Dinah. "Conrad was explaining to me that a traditional publisher could take a year or two to publish the book, whereas we could have it up for sale in a few months."

"That's a big difference," Dinah said. "Sort of seems like you could have Book One on sale and probably Book Two as well before the traditional publisher even made Book One available. Doesn't really make the traditional publishing route sound that appealing, if you ask me."

Margo narrowed her eyes. She hadn't thought about it that way. "When you put it in those terms, I have to agree with you."

Conrad just shook his head and ate his steak. "I'm keeping my mouth shut."

"I already know you want us to go independent," Margo said. "But Dinah makes a good point. Waiting on a publisher could actually be costing us money. Sales. Readership!"

Conrad's brows went up. "Are you saying you don't want to wait to see what the other publishers have to say?"

"I'm saying..." Margo thought a moment. She sat back as a new feeling swelled inside her. "I very much like being the captain of my own ship. Our own ship. If we fail, we fail. That could happen with a traditional publisher, too. There's no guarantee of success just because we have New York's stamp of approval. I still want to see what the other two publishers say, but I'm leaning more toward publishing the book ourselves."

For a moment, Conrad didn't react. Then a big smile spread across his face. "We'll do everything the right way, I promise. We'll even start our own publishing imprint and set it up as an LLC. We'll need a name, of course."

Margo frowned. "You seem pretty certain the other publishers are going to reject us."

"I just think we should be prepared. No point in leaving all the details to the last minute."

"So a name, hmm?"

He nodded.

Dinah finished a bite of steak. "How about Gulf Coast Press?"

Margo nodded. "I like that. I like it a lot. Conrad?"

"Works for me."

Margo flattened her hands on the table. "Looks like there's a pretty good chance we're going into the publishing business."

Chapter Twenty-three

Another day closer to Christmas, another early day at the bakery. But not extra early. Just regular early. Claire unlocked the back door of the shop, flipped on the lights, and took a deep breath. Today would be very busy, again. But not as busy as she'd thought it would be just a day ago.

Dinah was returning to help them out for a few hours, coming in at eight and working until noon to take care of all the small things so the rest of them could concentrate on baking and decorating.

For a woman who'd never worked in a big kitchen before, Dinah had caught on amazingly fast. Claire figured it was because she understood the basics of baking. And she was a fast learner who paid attention. Plus, Dinah had managed a household nearly all of her life. You didn't do that without learning how to adapt and overcome.

Claire hadn't had to tell her more than once how something was to be done and Dinah had understood it. The woman had potential. Her age was the only thing holding her back from working more hours, but Claire was grateful for the hours Dinah could work.

The extra hands had been such a big help yesterday that Claire had actually finished the cake for the mayor's Christmas party. It was sitting in the walk-in now, waiting to be picked up.

She'd expected to have to work at least one long night to make that happen, but as it turned out, not having to do all the cleanup made a big difference. Dinah had been helpful in other ways, too. The woman was sharp, organized, and paid attention.

Claire wished she had a dozen more like her.

And as Claire had told her mother via text last night, hiring Dinah had absolutely not been done out of pity or kindness, but sheer necessity. Her mom had thanked her all the same, but Claire felt like Dinah had done her the favor.

Claire got to work on a batch of muffin batter. These would be cranberry orange walnut, a special fall seasonal flavor. Raul and Rosemary came in as she was portioning the batter into paper-lined tins.

Raul started on cookies, Rosemary on turnovers.

There was a little small talk, but not much as they concentrated on the work before them. Not to mention, the bakery would be open soon and a lot of these treats had to be ready for their early morning customers.

They'd really need Dinah now that Rosemary was on her last day before the holidays. Tomorrow, she headed out to Texas to see her son and daughter-in-law for Christmas. Claire and Danny had known about the trip when they'd hired her.

Of course, neither of them had anticipated back in April how busy the bakery would be.

It was going to make things even tougher around here, but Raul had agreed to work extra hours so long as he could bring Louisa in with him. Claire cracked eggs into the big mixing bowl.

Would Dinah be willing to work a little longer? They had three more cakes to finish today. If Dinah could crumb coat them, that would be a big help. Crumb coating wasn't hard. It didn't even have to be that neat.

Claire checked the time. Might be too early to text. Definitely too early to call. She'd wait another half an hour. She got the muffins done and in the oven, then started a second batch of a popular year-round flavor, banana nut.

Once those were in the oven, she sent Dinah a text. *Would you be able to work a little longer today? Maybe an hour or so?*

Claire set her phone aside and went back to work, but it chimed with a notification shortly after she put it down. She went back to it and checked the screen. Dinah had answered.

I can work until 3:00, if you need me that long. Happy to help in whatever way I can.

Wow, that would be fantastic. Thank you so much.

Looking forward to it. Dinah finished with a smiley face emoji.

"Hey, gang," Claire said. "Dinah will be working with us a little longer today. I'm going to teach her to crumb coat cakes, but if there's anything else you think she'd be good at, let me know."

Rosemary looked up from the pastries she was making. "How about popcorn bars? We need more of those. And they're kind of easy."

"Good idea. That could be a perfect thing to get her started on."

Raul slid two trays of sugar cookies into the oven. Once cooled, those cookies would need to be decorated before heading to the retail side. "I could work with her on some basic decorating skills. If she could flood the cookies after I outline them, that would be a huge timesaver."

Flooding the cookies meant filling in the outlines with the same color icing. The outlines were the hard part, requiring a steady hand, even pressure on the piping bag, and some experience. Claire nodded. "That's not a bad idea, either, but I don't know if this is the right time to teach her that when we're so busy."

Raul nodded. "Good point."

Claire shrugged. "But if you want to show her how it's done, that's fine. I just don't want to lose time to teaching her. We can't afford that right now."

"I understand," he said. "I know today is Rosemary's last day until she gets back from vacation."

"Sorry," Rosemary said. "I feel bad about leaving you with all this work to do, but this will be my only chance to see my son and his family for a while."

Claire shook her head and smiled. "Do not feel bad. We'll be fine. Raul's going to work some extra hours and we have Dinah. We'll manage."

"Thanks," Rosemary said. "Now, I'm getting back to work. I'm going to do as much as I possibly can today."

"Which I appreciate." Claire got back to work herself.

In a matter of hours, Danny and Amy had arrived and the retail side of things was open for business.

Dinah showed up at quarter to eight. "I know I'm early. I can just sit somewhere until you're ready for me."

Claire laughed. "You don't need to do that. I can put you to work immediately, if that's all right with you."

Dinah smiled. "You betcha."

"Get an apron on and there are baking sheets and muffin tins to be washed, then I'm going to teach you to crumb coat a cake. After that, we're going to make popcorn bars." Thankfully, Danny had gone by the popcorn shop and picked up two big bags of popcorn, which he'd brought in with him this morning.

Dinah nodded enthusiastically. "That's exciting. I'll have that stuff washed in a jiffy."

Claire loved the eagerness and the willing attitude. She turned on the speakers so that the Christmas music playing in the front of the shop could be heard in the back and the four of them got into a new rhythm.

Dinah understood crumb coating already, having baked her share of cakes, and took to it with little instruction necessary. She got the three cakes on the job list for the day done in a reasonable amount of time, setting them in the walk-in to firm up.

"What's next, boss?"

With a smile, Claire took her through the steps of making popcorn bars. "Today, we're doing plain popcorn bars, but we're drizzling them with dark and white chocolate, and then, while the chocolate is still soft, sprinkling them with crushed candy canes and red and green Christmas sprinkles."

"Those sound really good," Dinah said. "I've never had a popcorn bar before. Is it like a bar cookie?"

"Not exactly," Claire said. "Go out front and get one. You should know what the food you're making tastes like."

Dinah went and did just that, coming back in while chewing a bite of the bar. "These are good. Like Rice Krispies treats but with popcorn. So clever."

Claire smiled. "Thank you." She rubbed her hands together. "Ready to make some?"

"I can't wait."

Just like the day before, Dinah caught on fast. Claire supervised her making a batch on her own; after that, she was ready to fly solo.

By lunchtime, Claire felt like she could breathe. She went up front to refill her coffee cup—half decaf this time—and to see if they needed anything. Danny was always on top of keeping the displays stocked, but it was an excuse to see him as well.

Amy was ringing up a customer. Danny was rearranging a tray of cookies. He smiled when he saw Claire. "How's it going back there?"

She exhaled and nodded as she finished filling her cup. "Really well. Dinah is heaven sent. She's already making popcorn bars on her own. And she crumb coated all three of the cakes on the job board today. I don't want to say we're ahead of schedule, but we are certainly not falling behind."

"That's fantastic. A real diamond in the rough, huh?"

"She really is. And she's agreed to work some more hours. That will probably change once we get through the holidays, but she's great."

"I'm glad to hear that. Does that mean you're going to keep her on?"

"That's my intention."

"Good with me."

"Did the mayor's office pick up his cake yet?" She glanced at the order fridge, which was where they stored orders that were ready to go. Danny had set it up around Thanksgiving when they realized how much take-out business they were going to do. It really helped free up space in the main walk-in.

"They just did. They were very happy. In fact, they put a ten-dollar bill in the tip jar."

"That was nice."

"It was."

Claire leaned over to look at the display cases. "Need anything out here?"

"Cookie tins are getting low again."

"We just refilled those this morning. I'm guessing sales of those will die down soon. People will be tired of Christmas cookies before much longer."

"Maybe. We'll see what happens."

Another customer came in. Claire tipped her head toward the kitchen. "I'm getting back to work."

"Me, too," Danny said. "See you later."

"You're driving tonight, right?"

He nodded. "I am."

She pushed through the kitchen door. Tonight was the mayor's big Christmas party. It was *the* party to be at in Diamond Beach.

She was looking forward to it. She just hoped she could stay awake.

Chapter Twenty-four

Trina had done more hair for tonight's party at the mayor's than anything else during her day at the salon. Two classic updos, one bouncy blowout, and one full head of beach waves with a hot iron. That last one had been Rebecca Griffin, the mayor's wife.

Becs was also the reason Trina and her mom were going to the party, although Roxie could have probably gone with Ethan and his parents anyway.

Now home, Trina still had her own hair to do and her mom's, but that was just fine. With her mom's help, they'd taken Walter and Tinkerbell for a quick walk, then come straight back to the house. That had given her a few minutes to sit on the couch and decompress.

Her mom was in the shower already, which was

where Trina needed to be. She finished her Diet Coke and headed into the bathroom.

But not before stopping by her closet to look at the pretty white dress hanging there. She smiled at the sight of her wedding dress. She'd never imagined she'd find it at the thrift shop, but her mom had found one, too.

The craziest thing was, both dresses were perfect.

Trina touched the fabric. The lace was softer than it looked, the small accents of seed pearls and crystals the exact amount of bling she liked. She planned on adding a sparkly belt to the dress along with a short veil. Anything too big wouldn't look right for a casual wedding.

She wished she could show the dress to Miles, but that would ruin the surprise of the day. She thought he'd like it very much.

Still smiling, she clipped her hair up and got into the shower. She was going to wear simple white flats with the wedding dress, some pretty white ones decorated with pearls and crystals. She'd seen some for sale online, but she was thinking she could probably make them herself with some supplies from Michael's craft store and a hot-glue gun.

Her mind turned to what she was wearing this

evening. She had two options—a red knit dress that had a little bit of glitter right in the fabric, or a red sequined sweater with a black pencil skirt. She was wearing black heels either way.

She'd found some shoe clips a while back at Classic Closet. Glittery red bows. She hadn't really known what she'd do with them when she bought them, but they'd been a great price and hard to resist, so she'd snapped them up. Now they'd be the perfect addition to her black velvet pumps to give them a touch of festiveness.

Maybe she'd do the pencil skirt and sweater. It was on the chilly side tonight and if she wore the red dress, she'd probably need a jacket or a coat.

She rinsed and got out, wrapping herself in a towel. Her hair didn't look half bad clipped up. Maybe she should put it up in a simple twist and go with that. She didn't wear her hair up very often, but the red sweater was off the shoulders and having her hair up would accent that fact.

She nodded at herself in the mirror. "Hair up it is." That was an easy solution, too. It wouldn't take much time. Certainly, a lot less than if she was curling it all or doing something more elaborate.

She got out her hair pins and hairspray and whipped her hair into the updo in a matter of minutes. It was a little messy, but it looked deliberate, and she was just fine with that. She freshened up her makeup, then got dressed in the sweater, which required a strapless bra, and the black pencil skirt.

She looked at herself in the mirror. It was a good outfit. The heels weren't going on until they were ready to leave.

She put her necessities into a shiny black patent leather evening bag, then leaned out her bedroom door. "Ma, are you ready for me to do your hair?"

"Yes, please," her mother called back.

"Okay. On my way." Trina grabbed her supplies and went next door to her mother's bedroom. "Wow, don't you look nice."

"Thanks." Her mom was in a body-skimming black dress with rhinestone trim all along the neckline. She wore dangling rhinestone earrings and a bracelet, and for her makeup she'd done a smokey eye and a red lip.

"Do you think this is all right for the mayor's party? It's not very Christmasy." She pointed at Trina's sequined sweater. "You look great. And Christmasy." Her mom put her hands on her hips and sighed. "Maybe I should change."

"Ma, you look like a million bucks. Don't

change." Trina looked around. Her mother's closet was still open. "What shoes are you wearing?"

"Just my black heels, I guess. Why?"

"I was thinking you could borrow my green crocodile pumps." They weren't real crocodile, just glossy leather printed to look that way. "You have that green evening bag too. That would be Christmasy."

Roxie nodded slowly, like she was thinking that through. "You know what? That's perfect. I'll do that. Thanks, honey."

"You're welcome. How do you want your hair?"

Her mom shrugged. "I don't have a clue, but yours looks nice and I know Ethan likes my hair up, but you're the professional. Whatever you think."

"Then let's do it up. Maybe a low knot with a few tendrils on one side so it's a little softer and sexier."

"I'm never going to argue with softer and sexier."

Doing her mom's hair took a little longer than doing her own, but it was still pretty quick. When she was done, Trina stepped back. "What do you think?"

Roxie turned her head side to side. "I love it. Thank you."

They put on their shoes, got their purses, said goodbye to the dogs and were out the door. Trina drove, and even though she'd been to Rebecca's house once before, she still put the address into her GPS. Tonight was not the night to get lost.

There were cars all up and down the streets leading to the mayor's house. More cars filled the driveway.

"Are we late?" Roxie asked.

"Only a couple of minutes. I thought it wasn't fashionable to arrive right on time." Trina ended up parking a block away. Not that long of a walk, but the heels they were wearing made it seem longer. "Maybe we should have taken an Uber."

"Maybe," her mom said.

The sound of music and laughter mingled with the hum of conversation as they approached the house. All the lights were on and lots of people were visible through the windows. The house had been beautifully, and no doubt professionally, decorated for Christmas.

They went up the walkway toward the house and the front door opened. Ethan smiled out at them. "At last, two of the best-looking women in Diamond Beach have arrived."

Trina and her mom both laughed.

His gaze coasted over Roxie. "Wow. You look fantastic."

"Thanks." Roxie greeted him with a kiss on the cheek. "How did you know we were here?"

"I've been watching for you out the window."

She patted his chest. "That was very sweet of you."

He lifted his chin slightly. "I'm a very sweet guy."

Trina snorted. "And humble, too."

He laughed. "Come in. My parents are here. So are Willie and Miguel and Claire and Danny. Honestly, I'm not sure who *isn't* here. Feels like all of Diamond Beach has arrived. The lanai is just as packed."

"Sounds like we're the last ones to arrive," Roxie said, giving Trina a look that was more amused than bothered.

"We'll do better next year," Trina said with a smile. And next year, maybe she'd be here with Miles.

"Please tell me there's food," her mom said to Ethan. "We didn't have a chance to eat dinner. We got home, walked the dogs, and got ready."

"Don't worry," Ethan said. "There's all kinds of food, drinks, and desserts. And you'll be happy to know I've taste-tested most of it, so I can give you a guided tour. I highly recommend the cocktail shrimp and the roast beef carving station."

"A carving station?" Trina was surprised. "This is fancy."

"Only the best for the mayor's party," Ethan responded. "Also, Claire made the cake, so you know you can't go wrong there."

Grinning, they let Ethan show them the way, following him through the throng of people that had gathered to celebrate, but also to see and be seen.

Trina was extra glad she'd stuck some business cards into her purse.

Chapter Twenty-five

K at would have been just fine skipping the mayor's Christmas party, but all of the other Future Florida employees were going, so she figured she'd better show up, too. She would have rather gone to the fire station to hang out with Alex, but the mayor's office made a point of inviting everyone at the charity.

Wouldn't do for the newest hire to not show up, so here she was. She'd worn a simple black dress with a little cropped red jacket and a red crystal necklace. She'd worn red flats, as well. She wasn't feeling the heels, although most of the women at the party had them on.

She stood with Eloise, who was dressed head to toe in soft winter white. White turtleneck, white wool pants, and white high-heeled boots. She looked like a movie star. Or at least like someone famous, but Eloise always had that look about her.

Suddenly, Kat smiled as she spotted something on Eloise's sweater. "Did you hug Sir Isaac Mewton before you left?"

Eloise made a funny face. "Yes. How did you know?" She glanced down. "Let me guess."

Kat picked a fine dark hair off Eloise's shoulder. "Don't worry. It was hardly noticeable."

"I did run the lint roller over myself before I left. He'd be proud I missed one, I'm sure." She lifted her glass of sparkling water and gestured across the crowd. "Tom and Molly are really making the rounds. But that's good. A lot of these people are regular donors. We want to keep it that way."

"For sure." Kat had already talked to her mom and Danny and to Arlene, who was here with her husband, Ned. Kat had also had a plate of food, a small slice of cake, and half a glass of champagne. Now she was just wondering how long she had to stay to fulfill her work obligations.

"You're bored, aren't you?"

Kat shook her head. "Not bored, exactly. Just...I don't know what to do with myself. I'm not really a mingler. And, in all honesty, I'd rather be at the firehouse hanging out with my fiancé." That word never got old.

Eloise smiled. "I get it. Not everyone loves a party."

"Do you?"

"I wouldn't say I love it, but I can see the value in this kind of networking." She gave Kat an understanding nod. "Do a loop or two around, say hi to a few people, make sure you thank the mayor or his wife for the invite, talk to Tom and Molly for a minute or two, and then you can duck out, duty done."

"Really? You think that would be okay?"

Eloise's gaze held cynical amusement. "There are enough people here to violate a fire code. I think you'd be fine to leave."

"Thank you."

Eloise nodded. "I see someone I need to talk to anyway. Have a good night. See you tomorrow."

"Same to you." Kat made her way into the crowd. It was slow going, but that was fine. She was inching closer to the buffet area when she ran into Trina, Roxie, and Ethan. "Hey, guys. How are you?"

Trina hugged her. "Hiya, sis. You look sharp."

"You look better." Kat smiled. "You all look great."

"I didn't know you were going to be here," Trina said.

Kat nodded. "Everyone from the office got invited, so we're all here."

"I did Rebecca's hair," Trina said.

"Rebecca?" Kat wasn't sure who that was.

Roxie leaned in and proudly said, "The mayor's wife."

"Get out of here!" Kat grinned. "Look at you and your celebrity clients."

Trina laughed. "She's the only one, I promise. But she has been good for business. She's sent a lot of her friends my way. Very grateful for that."

"I'm sure. Hey, we're still on for tomorrow night, right?"

Trina nodded. "You bet. I've got his present all wrapped and everything."

They were going to see Paulina and visit with Nico, their half-brother. "Yeah, I still need to do that. All right, I'm off to mingle a little bit, then I'm headed to the fire station to see Alex."

Trina frowned. "I wish I could go with you. Tell Miles I said hi."

Kat shrugged. "Why don't you come, too?"

Trina sighed. "I wish I could, but I feel like I should stay a while, since Rebecca invited me."

"I understand," Kat said. "Text me if you change your mind. I won't hear it in this crowd, but I'll check my phone before I leave and if you want to come along, I'll find you."

"Okay. Sounds good. Thanks."

Kat gave them a little wave and continued on her loop. It took her nearly thirty minutes to make the journey. Along the way, she talked to her mom and Danny again, saw Willie and Miguel, who she waved to, and then, finally, she found Tom and Molly, who were talking to the mayor.

They introduced her.

She shook his hand when he offered it. "Thank you so much for inviting all of us to your beautiful home. That was very kind of you."

He nodded and smiled. "We're glad you could come."

She touched Molly's elbow to get her attention. "Would you guys mind if I left early?" Even though Eloise had said it was all right, Kat wanted to be sure. She was still the new hire, still the low man on the totem pole. She didn't want to upset her bosses by going against protocol.

Molly shook her head. "Kat, it's nearly Christmas. We all have a million things going on. If you need to go, then go. No worries." She smiled. "We'll see you at the office tomorrow."

Kat nodded. "Bright and early. And thank you."

"Sure. Get home safe."

"You, too." Kat made her way to the door, where more people were coming in. She slipped outside and checked her phone. No text from Trina, so Kat walked to her car.

She took a few deep breaths of fresh air, amazed at how quiet it seemed in the neighborhood after being in the midst of all those people.

It was even quieter in her car. She drove to the firehouse with Christmas music playing, happy to be on her way to Alex. Happy to be able to surprise him with a visit. She wished she'd thought of bringing clothes to change into, but she'd only be there for an hour or two before she had to head home anyway.

The fire station looked just as festive as the mayor's house, with its giant wreath hung over the open garage and lights strung around the sign out front.

She parked and went in, finding the on-duty crew in the lounge. A few of the guys whistled as she came in, making her laugh. "All right, settle down."

Alex was up and at her side in seconds. "Wow,

you look great." He kissed her, earning them a few more teasing sounds.

"I came straight from the party."

"How was it?"

She took a breath. "Packed. Food was good. You could barely hear the music, though. I did my part. Showed up. Shook some hands. Made a little small talk. But now I'm here."

"You want anything to eat or drink? Larry made cottage pie for dinner. Looked like shepherd's pie to me but he said that would mean it had ground lamb in it and he made ours with ground beef, which makes it cottage pie." Alex shrugged. "Whatever. It was really good. And tonight's cookies are peanut butter."

"I ate at the party, but I'd take some water."

"Coming right up." He left her, but returned quickly with a bottle of water. They found a spot to sit on one of the loveseats and settled in.

He put his arm around her and she rested her head on his shoulder. "I missed you. It was weird being at that party without you. I kept thinking you were there. I mean, I knew you weren't. But I kept expecting to see you."

"Sorry I couldn't be there."

"No, it's okay. I knew you were at work. Maybe it

was just wishful thinking, imagining you were there." She smiled at him and straightened to see him better. "At least we get to hang out tomorrow night, right?"

"Right." He tipped his head. "You sure you don't mind coming here on Christmas Day to hang out with me? You wouldn't rather be with your family?"

"I'll be with them for most of the day. I'm not coming here until after dinner at Willie and Miguel's. If anything, I wish you were going to be with me."

"I know. Me, too. Next year. I promise."

"Next year will be very different." She glanced at her ring, already envisioning what next Christmas might look like.

"Yes, it will be." He tightened his arm around her.

She looked at him, the man she was going to grow old with, and wondered how much better life could get. "I can't wait."

Chapter Twenty-six

Willie kept a tight hold of Miguel's hand as they navigated the crowd to make their way out to the lanai, where they finally found some seats. It was cool out, but after the crush inside, the change in temperature felt nice.

She and Miguel both collapsed into the chairs that had been set around the lanai's perimeter. The pool was lit up but there were also plenty of Christmas lights strung around the top of the lanai, giving them more than enough light to see by.

And out here, she could actually hear the music being piped through the speakers. She exhaled. "This is better. I needed to sit down a while."

"It is," Miguel said. "I just wish we had drinks. That punch is very good."

Willie grinned. "It had so much rum in it I thought maybe you'd made it."

He laughed. "Almost."

A young woman sitting nearby got up. "I didn't mean to eavesdrop, but I'm going inside for a drink myself. I'd be happy to get you both a cup."

"That's very sweet of you, my girl," Willie said. "Thank you."

Miguel nodded. "Very kind."

"Be right back," she said, taking off.

"I love the Christmas spirit," Willie said. "I wish people were that way all year long."

"Some of them are," Miguel commented. "Especially in Diamond Beach. Don't you think people are friendly here?"

"They are," Willie said. "Not always the case in Dunes West."

He waved his hand at her words. "Just because Marti Powers accidentally bumped her shopping cart into our shopping cart doesn't mean she's a bad egg."

Willie pursed her lips. "Marti's widowed and on the prowl. She's got her eyes on you, mark my words. She has no place wearing a Christmas sweater that tight anyway. And those shiny red leggings she had on with it? Who does she think she's kidding in that getup? She's definitely on the naughty list."

Miguel snorted. "My love, there's not a woman

alive who could take me away from you. None of them compare."

She smiled at him. He always knew the sweetest things to say. "Just so you know, if she tries anything, I'll be forced to make an example out of her."

"Willie." Miguel tried for a stern look, but to Willie, it just made him cuter.

"Don't worry. It won't be anything that can be traced back to me. I'm smarter than that."

He rolled his eyes and muttered something in Spanish.

Just then, the young woman returned with their drinks. "Here you go." She handed them each a paper cup of green punch. A little sherbet floated at the top of the liquid. She lifted her own cup. "Merry Christmas."

"Merry Christmas," Willie and Miguel said in unison.

"Very kind," Miguel said again. "I'm Miguel Rojas and this is my wife, Willie."

The young woman nodded. "I know who you are, Mr. Rojas. Everybody knows who you are." She smiled. "I'm Emily Castellano. My dad is the principal of Diamond Beach High School. I'm here with him tonight because my mom had too much

Christmas shopping left to do. Gotta represent, right?"

She couldn't be a student, Willie thought. She was drinking the alcoholic punch. "Where do you work?"

"I'm a librarian."

"That's wonderful," Willie said. "I love the library. Although it's been a while since I've been."

"You should come tomorrow night, if you're not doing anything. We're showing *It's A Wonderful Life* in the large meeting room. It'll be on the big screen, too. And there will be Christmas cookies, popcorn, and soda. Probably candy canes as well." She laughed suddenly. "I don't imagine our popcorn would be up to your standards, though."

"It sounds wonderful," Miguel said. Then he laughed. "But I guess that movie would be. We'd love to come. Do you need us to bring anything? I could certainly contribute to the popcorn."

"Really? That would be great. Anything you want to bring is fine with us. The movie starts at six, but I'd suggest getting there early if you want good seats. And cookies. Those always run out first."

Willie nodded. "We'll see you then."

Emily smiled. "See you then." She headed back inside.

Willie leaned into Miguel. "Maybe we could supply a little more than popcorn."

"Such as?"

"More cookies. If they run out of those first, seems to me that's what they need more of. But we have to buy them. I don't want Danny or Claire just giving them to us for free."

"I'll let Danny know before we leave."

She patted Miguel's leg. "Thank you." She sipped her punch. There was definitely rum in it, but they'd taken an Uber here tonight, so it didn't matter how much they had to drink. Although, she didn't want to accidentally fall into the pool, either.

The last thing she wanted was to make a fool of herself and spend time on the naughty list with Marti. That dizzy old thing. Women over the age of eighty ought to keep their cleavage to themselves. It was like staring at two wrinkled peaches. The nerve.

Roxie and Ethan stepped outside.

Willie waved at them. "Over here, you two."

They smiled as they joined Willie and Miguel.

"Hi, Ma." Roxie kissed her mother's cheek, then Miguel's.

"Pull up some chairs," Miguel said.

"I've got it." Ethan handed his drink to Roxie, then carried two chairs over. "It's nice out here."

Roxie nodded as she sat. "It's a little stuffy inside. And a little loud."

"Most parties are," Willie said. "Food is good, though. Did you try those crab-stuffed mushrooms? Out of this world."

"I missed those," Roxie said. "But I think I ate my weight in cocktail shrimp." She grinned. "How's Snowy doing? Is she settling in?"

Willie smiled. "She's perfect. She had a very good report from the vet, too."

"I'm glad to hear that," Roxie said. "She's absolutely beautiful."

"Yes, she is," Willie agreed.

Ethan gestured to them. "You guys need anything? I can run in and get it."

Miguel held up his cup. "A lovely young woman named Emily just brought us these."

"That was nice," Ethan said.

Willie nodded. "Her father is the principal at the high school, but she's a librarian."

"At the high school?" Roxie asked.

"No, at the library in town. We're going to a movie there tomorrow night. *It's A Wonderful Life.* You two should come with us," Willie said. "It'll be fun."

"I'm game," Ethan said. "I've never seen that movie. Might as well see it on the big screen, right?"

Willie and Roxie looked at him in disbelief. Willie went the extra step and put her hand to her heart. "You've never seen the most famous Christmas movie ever?"

"Nope." He shook his head, laughing. "I know, I'm an uncultured reprobate."

Roxie patted his leg. "We'll fix that tomorrow night. And just in time, too. I can't marry an uncultured reprobate."

Willie snorted, then noticed Miguel making an odd face. "Don't tell me you haven't seen it, either."

He shrugged and looked guilty. "What can I say? I've led a busy life."

Willie pursed her lips and looked at Ethan, then back at Miguel. "You two. We're fixing things tomorrow night." She raised her brows. "And we're bringing cookies and popcorn."

Chapter Twenty-seven

*J*ules belted out the last line of the Brenda Lee classic, *Rocking Around The Christmas Tree*, then backed away from the mic and played the outro along with the band. They'd just added the song to their set list, since it seemed odd to be performing so close to Christmas and not do a seasonal tune.

They'd practiced it on the bus for a few days, but it was a song most of them knew really well. Tonight was its debut and the crowd had loved it. Made a great way to end the set, too.

She leaned in toward the mic again as the audience applauded. "Thank you so much. You've been an amazing audience. I hope you all have a wonderful, safe holiday and that you get everything your heart desires, but more than that, I hope you get to spend time with those you love the most."

She lifted her hand and gave a wave. "Merry Christmas and good night!"

With the applause still coming, she led the way off stage, the band right behind her.

As always, Jesse was there to greet her. "Another great show. I love your rendition of *Rocking Around The Christmas Tree*. Brenda Lee would be proud."

Jules smiled and wiped sweat off the back of her neck, then took her guitar off. "Thanks. She's still alive, you know."

"Brenda Lee?"

Jules nodded. "I met her once. We were in the same recording studio. It was very early on in my career. Sweet lady. A real inspiration."

"That is very cool." He took her guitar and handed it off to a roadie. "You know, you should really think about doing a Christmas album."

She put her hands on her hips. "I have."

He nodded. "I know. But I meant a new one. With your current popularity, it would be huge next year. And an easy way to follow up this album. Could you come up with a new Christmas song?"

"Probably." She laughed. "You're starting to sound like my agent." She narrowed her eyes. "Have you been talking to Billy?"

"No, but when is the last time you talked to him?"

She tried to remember. "It's been a minute. He usually calls when he gets my gift basket." She'd sent him an extra big one this year, in thanks for all his encouragement about *Dixie*. "Maybe I should check in with him in the morning. Do we have dinner plans?"

Jesse nodded. "As per the vote, we're eating at the Big Star Grill tonight." He grinned. "It has steak. And the band requested steak."

She shook her head. "They should have gotten it last night. It was really good at the hotel."

"I think that's why they voted for it tonight."

"Works for me. I could just about have a steak every night." The exertion of being on stage always made her want protein. "Any meet-and-greets?"

"Not tonight. Too short of a stop. We have an hour and forty-five for dinner, then we need to be on the road."

There'd be no comfy bed or soak in a tub tonight, but that was life on the road. "All right, then. Let's get moving."

They made the restaurant in fifteen minutes and were shown back to the private room. They got a few looks along the way. Jules had come to recognize when someone identified her, and she was pretty sure that had just happened at a table they'd passed. One of the women there stared at Jules the entire time she'd been in her line of sight.

No big deal, it happened. It was becoming more and more frequent, too. Jules didn't mind being recognized, but it was a bit unnerving. Mostly because she was left wondering if that person would approach her and what the interaction would be like.

She had no issue with fans. She loved her fans. They were the reason for her success, and she never wanted to take them for granted. But the more popular she got, the more the potential grew for some of those fans to become...overzealous.

Jesse put his hand on the small of her back. "That woman back there definitely knew who you were."

Jules gave a little nod. "I know. She looks harmless enough. She'll probably just want an autograph. It's no big deal."

"No, probably not. Just wanted to make sure you knew."

"I want to sit with my back to the wall. So I can see the door."

He nodded. "Good idea."

At least that way, no one could surprise her. It was weird having to think like that, but that was part and parcel with her rising fame.

Then a new thought came to her as they went into the private room. She took a seat near the wall. Jesse sat beside her. She leaned toward him. "Do you think I'm going to have to hire permanent security?"

"You mean besides what we already have at the shows?"

She nodded, then gave her attention to the server, who was taking their drink orders. She got sparkling water with lemon.

Jesse ordered a Diet Coke, but he could handle the caffeine. Once his order was in, he turned back to Jules. "Depends on how things progress, I suppose. You don't have any issues with fans now, but if some develop, more security wouldn't be a bad idea. Not necessarily permanent security. But in a case like this, maybe a guy who stays with us until we're back on the bus and traveling again. Then have someone at the next stop ready to be with you until the show."

She let out a soft sigh. "My life is getting more complicated."

"Unfortunately, fame has a price, and it's one

that has to be paid, regardless of whether you want to or not."

She smiled at him. "You're awfully philosophical."

He lifted his brows, his expression one of mock indignation. "Still waters run deep, I'll have you know. Also, I'm a man of many talents."

She laughed and picked up her menu. "Yes, you are." She perused the options as the topic of steak was discussed around her. It did make her want steak again, but the restaurant offered wild salmon, the only kind she liked to eat, and that was pretty tempting as well.

A soft voice suddenly interrupted her selection process. "Excuse me. Are you Julia Bloom?"

She looked up, unsurprised to see the woman she thought had recognized her earlier. The woman stood just slightly inside the private room, twisting her hands. Jules answered, "I am."

"I'm sorry to intrude, but I just had to talk to you. You, uh..." The woman seemed nervous. She swallowed, still wringing her hands together. "You changed my life. Saved it, really. Your music, I mean."

The words left Jules temporarily dumbstruck.

That wasn't what she'd been expecting to hear. "It did?"

The woman nodded, looking around at the rest of the group and inching back toward the door like she might bolt.

Jules got up and walked over to her. "How did the music save your life?"

"My husband, he was not a nice man, especially when he was drinking. I heard your song, *Dixie's Got Her Boots On*, and it inspired me to change my situation." The woman suddenly laughed. "I didn't kill him, though. Just packed myself and my daughter up and went to my sister's place."

"That must have taken a lot of courage."

"It did." Her smile was gone. "I'm divorcing him now. I just realized I didn't have to take his shoving me around and shouting all the time and all that. Anyway, thank you for the inspiration. You donating that money to help battered and abused women, that was big, too. Made me realize you cared. Somehow, that made a difference to me. Made me feel like I was worth something."

Jules's heart broke a little. "I'm so glad you're safe."

She sniffed. "Thanks. I realized that if someone

like you could care, then I ought to at least care about myself. It's hard, but my daughter will have a better life now. All because of you." There were tears shining in her eyes, but she had the defiant look of a survivor, too.

The words touched Jules right down to her soul, but she couldn't take the credit. She shook her head. "You did all the hard work. You got yourself and your daughter out of there. I'm proud of you. That took real strength. I'm humbled and honored to have played a small part in your life."

"It was more than a small part." The woman sniffed again, nodding a little. "My name's Donna, by the way. And I'm sorry to interrupt your meal, but I didn't think I'd ever have the chance to speak to you in person. I couldn't pass it up."

"It's wonderful to meet you, Donna. I'm so glad you came to talk to me." Jules smiled. "Would you like a picture together?"

Donna smiled. "I would love that."

Jules turned to see Jesse already behind her.

His brows went up as his gaze flicked to Donna. "Everything all right?"

Jules nodded. "Everything's good. Do you think you could grab me one of those meet-and-greet bags from the bus?"

He gave her a quick nod of understanding. "I'll be right back."

Jules got Sierra to take some photos on Donna's phone and one for Jules on her phone, then Jules introduced Donna to the rest of the group. By then, Jesse was back, gift bag in hand. He gave it to Jules.

She smiled and held it out to Donna. "Here you go. Some goodies for you."

"Thank you," Donna said. "That's so kind of you."

"Merry Christmas," Jules said.

Donna smiled and looked weepy again. "Merry Christmas. Could I hug you?"

Jules laughed. "You sure can."

Donna hugged her and Jules embraced her back, letting Donna be the one to break contact.

When she pulled away, Donna was sniffling, but looked happy. "I'm so grateful for you and your music but meeting you has been awesome. You're even better in person than I thought you'd be. Thanks for that."

"You're very welcome. Have a good night."

"You, too." Donna gave them all a little wave then went back to her table.

"Wow," Sierra said. "I heard what she was telling

you about how *Dixie* inspired her. That's major stuff."

Jules nodded. "It is. Sometimes you get emails or letters from people, telling you how your music got them through being depressed or helped them recover from something, but that was a new one for me."

"I bet you won't forget that one for a while, huh?"

Jules looked out into the dining room. She could just see Donna at her table, looking through the meet-and-greet bag and showing off the things inside to the people she was sitting with. "I'll *never* forget that one."

Chapter Twenty-eight

*R*oxie slipped off her heels as soon as she and Trina were back in the car. She leaned back and sighed in relief before putting on her seatbelt. "My puppies are barking."

Trina laughed as she put her belt on, too. "Why do you think I walked to the car barefoot?"

Roxie hadn't been willing to go that far. "I understand. I just didn't want to step in something. Also, it's chilly outside!"

Trina started the car and turned on the heat. Probably to warm up her toes. "Ma, people pick up after their dogs in this neighborhood. They have to or they probably get arrested."

Roxie smiled and shook her head. "Maybe, but the birds still go wherever they want. You'd better wash your feet when we get home."

"I will." Trina let out a happy sigh. "What a

fun night. That was the biggest adult party I've ever been to. They must have spent a fortune throwing it. I can't imagine what the alcohol cost. And they had bartenders! Talk about fancy."

"No expense spared, that's for sure," Roxie said. "I wonder if that party is considered a campaign expense."

"Maybe," Trina said. She found her way easily back to the main road, no GPS needed, amazing Roxie with her recall. "I wonder if I should throw a Christmas party at the salon next year."

"To bring in new customers?"

"I was thinking more to say thank you to the existing customers."

"That would be nice." Roxie looked at her daughter. "But you might be in a very different place next year."

Trina frowned. "Meaning what? I'm not going to move the salon."

"No, silly. I meant that you and Miles will be spending your first Christmas together as a married couple."

"That's true."

Roxie shrugged. "You might not want to have the responsibility of a Christmas party like that. Or you might want to have one at the beach house for your friends and family."

Trina cut her eyes at Roxie. "Are you angling for an invite?"

Roxie laughed. "Do I need to?"

Trina shook her head, clearly amused. "You're always welcome, Ma, you know that. I guess you'll be living at Ethan's by next Christmas."

Roxie looked out the window, admiring the lights and decorations. "Yep. Next year will be a lot different for both of us." She wondered if Trina would be pregnant by then. She and Miles had already talked about having kids.

Roxie adored the idea of a grandbaby to love on. She knew Willie would, too.

"For sure," Trina said. "I've loved us sharing a house, I really have. I miss Mimi and she hasn't even been gone two weeks. I'm a little sad that you're going to be leaving me, too, but I'm also very ready to start my life with Miles."

"I know how you feel. It'll be strange being at Ethan's, at least until I get used to it. I hope it's not too big of an adjustment for him. He's been on his own for a while."

"Do you get that impression from him? That you moving in is going to be hard for him to get used to?"

"Not exactly. He seems very ready for us to get married. He's already offered to make whatever changes I want. But men can be strange creatures." Roxie hadn't realized until that moment just how possible that might be. Ethan might think he was going to be fine with her moving in, but would he really be?

"You're right, they can be, but Ethan's not like that. He's crazy about you, Ma. I see how he looks at you. He was looking at you that way tonight. Like you're the center of his world. Like you're the source of his happiness."

"I don't know about all that."

"I do. I've seen it. He could not be more in love with you. You need to marry that man as soon as possible before he gets lovesick."

Roxie pursed her lips. "Now you're being silly again."

"I'm being serious."

"Well, I'm going to talk to the pastor on Sunday about his next available date. For him and the church."

"Good," Trina said. "Which reminds me, I need to talk to him, too. I was supposed to call him about a date, but we were so busy at the salon it completely slipped my mind." She let out a little groan. "I am not complaining about being busy, but it will be nice when things aren't quite so hectic."

"Don't worry. You can have your first pick of the dates."

Trina glanced at Roxie. "Actually, you and Ethan should get married first."

"Why?"

"Um, so you can move out before Miles moves in?"

"Oh. Right." Roxie laughed. "You're going to be my maid of honor, right?"

Trina smiled. "You bet. And are you still going to have Mimi as the flower girl? Because I love that idea."

"That's my plan. I want her to walk down the aisle with Miguel, who will have the rings."

"They are going to be adorable. Just make sure Mimi knows she has to leave her flask at home. I don't think the church guests would appreciate her spiking the punch without them knowing."

"No, they wouldn't, so good call. I need to talk to her and Miguel about that." The two of them definitely liked a little something extra in their drinks, but Roxie didn't think Pastor Tim would be very happy if the rest of the guests were accidentally tipsy.

"Do you have it all planned out? Your wedding?"

"There's not much to plan. I don't need a lot of fuss. Just Ethan and our families, Pastor Tim, and a little party afterwards."

"What about flowers and music and pictures?"

She nodded. "We'll have that. Don't freak out, but we've already talked about having Publix cater the meal. Sandwiches and salads, nothing fancy. A cake from Claire. Thomas to take the photos. A simple bouquet for me and a boutonniere for Ethan. And Ethan's going to do a playlist on his phone, which he'll connect to some Bluetooth speakers."

"Ma, really?"

"What's wrong with simple? This is a second wedding for both of us. Neither of us needs all the fanfare."

"I get that, and I love Publix, but sandwiches for a wedding reception?" She turned toward the beach house. "You could at least get that restaurant Mimi and Miguel had. That food was great, and it wasn't super expensive."

Roxie thought about that. A hot meal would be nicer. "I'll see what Ethan thinks. We did both enjoy that food."

They arrived at the beach house. Trina parked, turned the car off, then twisted to face her mother.

"Listen, it's your wedding. You do whatever makes you happy. But if you're keeping things simple because it's a second wedding and you think that's how it should be, I say that's not being fair to what you and Ethan have."

"What do you mean?"

Trina took a breath, looking like she was searching for words. "Second chances are kind of rare, right? I mean, not everyone gets them. You and Ethan finding each other? That's something special. If you want your wedding to be more than just a ceremony that makes it all legal, you have as much right as anyone else does."

Roxie was touched by her daughter's kind and thoughtful words. "Thank you, Trina. That's really sweet of you to say. I mean that. It gives me a lot to think about. In fact, I sort of wonder if Ethan and I have both been feeling like we shouldn't do too much because it isn't a first marriage."

"To that I say, who cares? You deserve a special day."

Roxie nodded. "You're right. We do. I don't think either of us wants anything over the top, but sandwiches might be a little *too* simple."

"I love you, Ma. I want you to have a day you can look back on and smile. I don't want you to skimp."

Roxie took Trina's hand. "Thank you, baby. I appreciate that. I really do. Now, we should probably get upstairs and walk those dogs."

"Yep. Let's go."

They both put their shoes back on but took the elevator.

Walter and Tinkerbell were excited to see them.

"Hang on," Trina said. "Let me put some sneakers on and we'll go take care of business, babies."

"I'll help," Roxie said.

Trina shook her head. "You relax. I'm not taking them for w-a-l-k. Just to do a tinkle."

"Okay. You want a cup of decaf? I was going to make one for myself."

"I'd love one. And then maybe a little trashy TV."

Roxie smiled. "Coming right up."

Trina changed into comfortable shoes, then got the dogs leashed and took them down in the elevator.

Roxie started a half-pot of decaf before calling Ethan.

"Hey. Miss me that fast, huh?"

She laughed. "Yes, I did, but that's not why I'm calling."

"What's up?"

"Trina said something to me on the way home that really struck a chord. I think we're short-changing ourselves on the wedding. Going too simple because we both think we're supposed to, because it's not our first go-round. I don't want us to look back and regret the day for any reason."

"I can get on board with that. What kind of changes do you want to make?"

"Well, maybe a hot catered meal instead of sandwiches from Publix? Maybe a few more flowers than just a bouquet and a boutonniere. Things like that."

"If it makes you happy, it makes me happy. I can afford it. Whatever you want is fine with me. Just so long as we have a dance as husband and wife. And Claire makes the cake."

Roxie smiled. "I can promise you both of those." She wasn't letting him pay for all of it, either. She had enough of her own money, especially with the sale of her house in Port Rosa now complete, to handle her share.

"Then let's get this wedding scheduled."

She laughed, then went serious again. "You sure you're going to be okay with me living in your house with you? It's not going to be weird having a woman in your space?"

"Having a random woman would be weird.

Having you here? That's going to be a dream come true. And it's going to be *our* space."

"Ethan, be serious."

"I am being serious. I wake up in the morning and wonder why you aren't already beside me. Moving-in day can't come soon enough. I love you, Rox."

Her heart swelled at his words. "I love you, too, sweetheart. Talk to you tomorrow, okay?"

"Okay."

She hung up, still smiling and more in love with Ethan than she had been two minutes ago. He was right. Moving-in day couldn't come soon enough.

Chapter Twenty-nine

*D*espite the early hour, Margo was up and in the office. She stared at the computer screen, reading the email one more time. She blinked to make sure she was awake and reading it correctly. She was. The response had come to the email address she shared with Conrad, one he'd set up for their writing ventures.

"That just confirms our plans," Margo said to herself. Then she muttered, "The very nerve of sending a rejection right before Christmas. Bah, humbug to you, sir."

Conrad was out for a jog, but she'd let him know when he got back.

She returned to the kitchen, taking her coffee cup with her. She refilled it, added some sugar and cream, then stood by the sink, drinking it and gazing out the window into the backyard.

Two rejections. One more publisher to go. She doubted that response would be any different. If the first two publishers didn't want their book, why would the last one?

It made her mad. And hurt. And frustrated. She understood rejection was a huge part of trying to get published, but that didn't make it any easier to take. It felt a little like someone had just said something disparaging about one of her daughters.

Logically, her book was not her child. But creating something, whether it was a life or a book, gave one a certain feeling of protectiveness over that something.

Being told their book wasn't right for the publisher meant nothing. What did that mean? Why wasn't it right? What would make it right? Didn't they know how infuriating such a non-answer was? How long would it have taken to add one sentence explaining the rejection?

But the publisher hadn't thought enough of their book to take any more time with it than they already had.

She exhaled at the annoyance of it all. Then she took another sip of her coffee and lifted her chin. She'd had enough. They'd nearly made the choice to self-publish. The rejection just pushed her over the edge. They would retain full control, which was a good thing. So why did the rejection bother her so much?

The front door opened, and Conrad came in. He was breathing a little hard and slightly red-faced from either the exertion or the brisk morning air, but he was smiling through the sheen of perspiration on his face.

"Good run?"

He nodded. "Very good. Now I'm ready for breakfast. And a shower. Not necessarily in that order."

"I'll start cooking while you shower." She turned back toward the kitchen.

"Everything okay?"

She frowned. "We got another rejection."

He frowned, too. "It doesn't feel good, does it?" He came over to her. "I'd hug you but I'm sweaty."

She sniffed. "I don't care."

He pulled her into his arms. "I'm sorry. Those idiots don't have a clue what they're passing up."

She leaned her forehead on his shoulder. "No, they don't." After a moment, she pulled back. "I realize the only people who've read the book have been family, but they can't all be lying to us, can they?"

"No. And I think we'd be able to tell if they were."

She nodded, a little mollified by that point. "Well, I thought I was tougher than this, but those rejections hurt. You're more used to it, I think, because of your time working for the newspaper, but it's very new for me. I don't want to go through it anymore. We'll just put the book out ourselves."

"Rejections, no matter how many you get, are never easy." He took hold of her shoulders and kissed her forehead. "You're sure about wanting to self-publish?"

She nodded. "I am. And it seems like it's going to be our only option, anyway."

"There are always more options. If you want to query our second-tier publishers, we can certainly—"

"No. I see no reason to do that." She gave him a quick smile, mostly to let him know she was all right. "After breakfast, let's pick a cover designer and research editors. I want to get moving on this."

He smiled. "You got it, Mrs. Ballard."

She laughed. "Go shower. Breakfast will be ready shortly."

He unzipped his windbreaker. "On my way."

She returned to the kitchen and got the eggs and

bacon out. She put four strips of bacon on the griddle, then scrambled four eggs while a pat of butter melted in the pan. Three slices of whole grain wheat bread went into the toaster, but she didn't push the lever down yet.

By the time he came out, she had the bacon crispy, the eggs scrambled, and the bread toasted. His two slices were buttered and spread with a fat dollop of locally made strawberry jam, picked up at the farmer's market. Her one slice had a smear of butter and a tiny bit of jam.

She brought their plates to the table where their coffee was waiting. "Here you go."

"You're spoiling me."

She smiled as she sat next to him. "Am I? Good. You should be spoiled. You're a wonderful man."

He drank his coffee. "Who clearly married above his station."

She smiled but gave him a look at the same time. "I don't know about that."

Breakfast lifted her spirits even more and afterwards, he helped her clean up, then they went into their shared office.

He fired up his laptop and moved it so they could both look at it. "There are three cover artists I like, but I want to see what you think of them."

One by one, he brought them up and they looked at the artist's pricing, their portfolio of work, and some premade covers that were also available.

It was a lot to take in, but by the third one, Margo had a favorite. "I like Creative Covers the best. Not only did they have a lot of thriller covers, but they've done covers for a couple authors whose books I've actually read. Not only that, but I had no idea those books were self-published."

"I like Creative Covers, too. They're also right in the middle pricing-wise."

"I'm good with that. Let's email them and see what their scheduling is like."

He nodded and moved the laptop back in front of him. He started filling out the online contact form. When he was done, he hit Send. "You know, we probably won't hear from them until after the holidays."

"That's all right. We haven't been through edits yet."

"No, but once we have a cover, we can put the book up for preorders. And we can start advertising it."

She took a deep breath. "It's all becoming very real, isn't it?"

"It is. You okay with that?"

She nodded, smiling. "Yes. But it's a very curious thing to think about our book being out there for anyone to read."

"I understand. The first time I had a piece in the *Gazette*, I questioned myself for days. And that was nothing as big as a book. If you don't want to do this..."

"No, I do." She nodded. "I definitely do. It's scary, but it's also exciting." She gave his arm a squeeze. "I'm profoundly glad we're doing this together. I'd never be able to do it by myself. You're so smart about all of this. I'm very impressed with all the research you've already done and the information you've gathered."

He smiled, clearly pleased. "I just wanted us to be ready. If that's what it came to."

"Well, it has. And I'm so thankful you were prepared." She'd been blessed with not only a wonderful husband, but a wonderful partner in this new venture.

He looked rather satisfied with himself. "Well, I am a Marine."

"Through and through." Whatever the new year brought them, they'd be together. Success or failure. Rise or fall. Didn't matter. Because she'd already won, and her prize was sitting right next to her.

Chapter Thirty

Tomorrow was Christmas Eve, meaning Claire only had one day to finish the last of the bakery's orders. Unfortunately, she was down a baker with Rosemary gone. At least she had Raul and Dinah.

She'd arrived on time today, which had been hard, considering she'd been up later than usual due to the mayor's party. It had been a fun evening, though. And she'd talked to a lot of people about the bakery, so spreading the word about the business was always a good thing.

Raul came in right as she was turning on the lights. Dinah wasn't scheduled to arrive for another hour and a half, having kindly agreed to an extra early start today to help out. By then, they'd be ready for some cleanup. There would be more tins to pack with cookies, too. Claire planned on having Dinah do those.

Claire had thought that by now, sales of the cookie tins would peter out, but they hadn't. Apparently, people wanted to eat Christmas cookies for as long as they could. Fine with her.

Today's work orders included two large boxes of assorted Christmas cookies, as well as three sour orange pies, a dozen assorted popcorn bars, and the last of the cakes.

There really was no end to the number of cookies the inhabitants of Diamond Beach could consume.

She wasn't complaining. Tomorrow would be a half day. They'd close at one p.m. and wouldn't reopen until the 27th. She and Danny had decided to take the day after Christmas off just to help them recover. They'd been going pretty hard at the bakery since it opened.

No regrets for doing that, but they needed a break.

And now that she'd hired Dinah, Claire was going to reassess the weekly schedule and see if maybe, just maybe, Claire could manage two days off in a row. Hopefully with Danny having one of those same days off, too.

She loved working with him and getting to see him every day, but she missed spending downtime with him. Having dinner together after an exhausting day of work just wasn't the same. Not now that they had a wedding to plan.

Claire needed to get muffins going. She started pulling ingredients. "Morning, Raul."

"Happy Christmas Eve Eve," he said with a smile. "I am so looking forward to some time off."

"So am I," Claire said.

Raul tied his apron on. "That reminds me, my sister will be dropping Louisa off on her way to work. A little before nine, probably."

Claire nodded. "Okay, no problem. Also, just so you know, now that we have Dinah, I'm going to rework the schedule for the new year. I know she's only part-time, but it means we have more flexibility. If there's any changes you'd like to see in your schedule, let me know. Rosemary can tell me hers when she gets back."

"Will do."

"I know it's probably something you need to think about, so you don't have to tell me immediately."

Raul began the turnover dough. "I'll let you know by the end of the day."

"That's fine."

"I'll need to talk to my sister first," he continued. "Having her help me with Louisa is amazing, but if there's a way I can make things easier for her, I'd like to do that."

"I don't blame you," Claire said. "I'm going to finish this batch of muffins, then start another one. But we need lots of Christmas cookies today."

Raul went over to the job board. He glanced over his shoulder at Claire. "Do you think Dinah could get those sour orange pies done?"

"Maybe."

"If she can, then I'll work on the cake," Raul said. "The blanks are done. It just needs to be assembled and iced."

"Have Dinah crumb coat when she gets in. Until then, work on cookies after the turnovers. She can do the popcorn bars, too."

"Will do, boss."

They got busy with their tasks, making the bakery hum with the sound of their efforts. Time passed quickly and before long, it was starting to get light outside.

Dinah and Danny arrived within minutes of each other. Danny got coffee going while Dinah worked with Raul on the cakes that needed to be assembled and crumb coated. Raul's sister dropped Louisa off a little while later and Claire helped Raul get her settled in the office before going back to work.

The hours sped by and Claire didn't even realize it was lunch until her stomach rumbled and she looked at the time. She was suddenly very hungry, which gave her an idea. "Hey, would anyone else like pizza for lunch? My treat."

Raul looked up and smiled. "That sounds great, boss. I know Louisa would be happy. She doesn't like mushrooms but she's okay with the rest of the toppings."

Claire nodded. "No mushrooms. Got it. What about you, Dinah? You good with pizza?"

She scraped the last of the popcorn bar mix into a tray, then set the bowl down and looked in Claire's direction. "I haven't had it in a while, so it sounds like a real treat. Any toppings are fine with me. Thank you. Would it be okay if I ordered a little salad, too? I'd pay for that myself, of course."

"That would be fine." Claire washed her hands. "I'll get Danny to order for us."

She went through the door to the retail side. Danny and Amy were working away and there was a short line of customers. She'd order the pizza herself. She checked in with Danny first, though. "I'm getting pizzas delivered from Gino's. My treat for everyone. You good with that?"

"You bet. I'm starving. Get something with meat, if that's all right."

"I'm planning on it."

He winked at her before helping the next customer.

"Amy?" Claire called out. "You good with pizza?"

"Yes, ma'am," she answered. "Thank you."

Claire went back to the office. Louisa was watching a movie on the tablet she'd brought with her. Something with animated puppies. "Would you like pizza for lunch?"

Louisa smiled and nodded, while hugging a stuffed dog that looked very much like the ones in the movie. "I love pizza."

"You have great taste." Claire called the pizza place across the street. She and Danny had ordered from them a few times, but always picked up the pizza to take home. She ordered a large cheese, a large meat lover's, and a large veggie, along with a family salad, which was supposed to feed six.

Unfortunately, they were too swamped to deliver, something the woman who was taking her order informed about. "I'm sorry. No one wants to cook today." She laughed. "We're an hour out on deliveries and you guys are right across the street, so..."

"No problem," Claire said. "I'll come get it when it's ready." The short break would be nice.

"How about I call you then?"

"That works for me. Thank you. See you in a bit."

"See you then!"

Claire hung up and immediately set aside one of the cookie tins Dinah had been filling. "I'm taking that to Gino's when I pick up the pizzas. It's quicker than having them delivered."

"That's really nice of you," Dinah said. "What do you want me to do once I'm done filling these?"

"You can take them out to the front and restock, then the popcorn bars can be cut and trayed for the front, too."

"I haven't been shown how to cut them yet."

"Then that will be our lesson for today." Claire smiled. It was good to be busy. Having all these orders and customers were exactly what they needed.

But she was very ready for some time off, too. Time with Danny and her family. Time to breathe, wind down, and celebrate a relaxed Christmas with everyone she loved. She was looking forward to the Christmas Eve candlelight service at church, too. It had been a while since she'd been to one of those and she couldn't wait to experience it again.

Because that's what Christmas was all about. Family. Being together. Appreciating the real meaning behind the season.

She helped Dinah carry the tins up front and together they restocked the small display table. After that, she showed Dinah how to use the cutting tool to measure out the bars and make them all the same size, and how to lay them out on the trays that went into the display case.

Her phone went off as they were doing that. She answered it. "Hello?"

"Hi, there, it's Kara from Gino's. Your pizzas are ready."

"I'm on my way."

It only took Claire a few minutes to drive across the street. She probably could have walked, but she thought the food would be safer in the back seat than with her carrying it. She parked and walked into the pizzeria, cookie tin in hand. Kara was behind the counter. Claire handed her the tin. "Here you go. These are for you guys from all of us at the bakery. Baked fresh this morning."

"Wow, thanks, that's awesome." Kara smiled. "We

don't get a lot of Christmas goodies in here. These will definitely get eaten."

"So will those pizzas."

Kara laughed. "Be right back with your order."

She returned with three large boxes and a Gino's shopping bag that held the salad, salad dressings, paper plates, and forks.

Claire whipped out her credit card, ran it through the reader on the counter, and nodded her thanks. "Have a wonderful Christmas."

"You, too." Kara glanced at the shopping bag. "There's an order of cheesy bread in there for you guys. On us."

"Thank you!"

"Merry Christmas," Kara said.

"You, too." Claire brought the pizza feast back to the bakery and set it up on one of the stainless-steel work tables. She went out front. There was only one customer at the counter, and she was still making up her mind. Claire caught Danny's gaze. "I'll take over here for a bit. You and Amy go eat."

He frowned. "You need to eat, too."

"I will. But right now, you both go."

"I'll bring you a slice," Danny said. "What kind?"

"Meat lover's," Claire answered. "Thanks."

He and Amy went back. Claire approached the

customer, who was now looking intently at the Christmas popcorn bars. "Those are as good as they look. Kids love them, too."

The woman looked up and nodded. "I'll take three of those and some of those gingerbread Santa cookies."

Claire smiled. "Coming right up."

Chapter Thirty-one

*O*nce again, Trina had only managed to eat half a sandwich for lunch. At this rate, she had to be losing weight. Not her goal, but her pants were definitely fitting looser these days. As she finished up a full foil and took her tools to the sink in the breakroom to wash, her mom came up to her.

"Honey, did you eat lunch?"

"I had half a sandwich. I'll live." Trina smiled at Walter, who looked very much like he was ready for a walk. Tinkerbell was sleeping in his bed, which they seemed to have no problem sharing these days.

"You need to eat. You're doing too much."

Trina scrubbed her tools free of the bleach mixture she'd just been using. "It's only for the rest of today and half of tomorrow."

"Closing at three is not really a half day. There aren't any appointments after one. You should close after that customer. It's not like you can take a major walk-in. We really need to be home. There are things to do. And the candlelight service to get ready for. And tonight you're going to see Nico. That's going to take up time."

"True." Trina put her clean tools on the drying rack. "You're right." She turned to face her mom, leaning on the counter to talk as she dried her hands. "We'll close after the last appointment tomorrow. I'll tell Amber to make a sign up and put it on the door."

Roxie shook her head. "You take the dogs out for a quick pee. I'll tell Amber."

"Thanks, Ma." As her mom headed back to reception, Trina grabbed the leashes and attached them to the dogs' collars. "Okay, little ones. Quick walk. Let's go."

She got them outside and took them to their favorite patch of grass. Both of them peed, then started sniffing around.

A couple of doors down, she saw Danny carrying trash bags out to the dumpster. She waved. "Merry Christmas!"

"Merry Christmas to you." He waved back.

She took the dogs in and went straight to her client, to check how the foils were processing.

The rest of the day sped by, which she was grateful for. She was excited to visit Nico and give him his Christmas present.

She and her mom locked up and went straight home. Trina ate a granola bar while she changed into jeans and a Christmas sweater, then she texted Kat. *Ready to go.*

Downstairs in 5 mins! Kat texted back.

Trina grabbed Nico's present off her dresser, then went out to the living room. In the kitchen, her mom was heating up some soup for dinner. "I'm going down to meet Kat. See you when I get back."

"Okay, honey. Have a good time. Tell Paulina I said hi. Don't forget, I'm going to the movie tonight with Ethan and Miguel and your grandmother at the library."

"Oh, that's right. Have fun." Trina wiggled her fingers at Walter and Tinkerbell, who were both on his blanket on the couch. "Bye, babies. I won't be gone too long."

She took the steps, arriving as Kat was getting out of the elevator, carrying her present. "Thanks for driving."

"Sure," Kat said. "You drove last time."

They put the gifts in the backseat, then got in. Kat strapped on her seatbelt. "How was your day?"

"Good. We managed to help quite a few families and individuals this week, so I'm happy. Feels good to work at a place like that." Kat laughed. "Feels even better to have tomorrow off."

"Must be nice. I have three appointments tomorrow. But after the last one, I'm closing up."

"Same with my mom. They're doing a half day at the bakery tomorrow. I feel for Alex and Miles, though. Both of them having to work on Christmas."

"I know. I wish they were off. But we're going to see them, right?"

Kat nodded. "Absolutely. My mom is bringing home any unsold goodies so we can take them to the station."

"That's really nice of her. I'm sure the guys will love that."

"Alex told me Larry's been making cookies for a couple of weeks now, so I'm not sure how enthusiastic they'll be about more sweets, but at least they'll have some different varieties to choose from."

It took about fifteen minutes to get to Paulina's condo complex. Kat parked, they grabbed their presents, and headed up.

Paulina opened the door right away, a big smile on her face. "Hello, Kat. Hello, Trina."

"Merry Christmas," Trina said. "How's our little man doing?"

"He's doing great." Paulina stepped aside so they could come in. Her condo was decorated for Christmas and there was a tree in the living room. Her mother, Elena, was sitting in her recliner, crocheting something.

Nico was on the floor, playing with blocks while *Rudolph the Red-Nosed Reindeer* played on the television, the sound down low.

Kat waved at Nico. "Hiya, baby brother. How are you?"

"Hi, Nico," Trina said. She held out her gift. "Look what we brought you from Santa." She glanced at Paulina. "Is it okay if he opens them now? Or would you rather he wait until Christmas?"

Smiling, Paulina shook her head. "No, he can open them now. You won't be here for Christmas, after all."

"Thanks," Trina said. "Your house looks great."

Kat chimed in. "It really does. Very Christmasy."

They smiled at Elena.

"How are you, Elena?" Trina asked.

"Good," Elena answered. "*Gracias. Feliz Navidad.*"

"Merry Christmas to you," Kat said. "What are you making?"

Elena held up her work so they could see it was a hat. She didn't speak much English and Trina didn't speak any Spanish, but she and Kat had picked up a few words just from visiting. Trina kept meaning to download one of those language apps so she could learn some more but she'd been so busy the thought never seemed to stick.

She and Kat sat down on the floor with Nico, who was dressed in an adorable outfit of green pants and a red, long-sleeved T-shirt with a decorated Christmas tree on the front.

Trina set her present next to her and clapped her hands, then held her arms out. "Hi, Nico. How are you? Can you give your sister a hug?"

Paulina came over and sat on the couch. "*Tus hermanas*," she said to him. "Your sisters."

Nico looked at his mother, then smiled at Kat and Trina. He got to his feet and, with open arms, walked straight into Trina's embrace.

"Merry Christmas, little brother." She hugged him and kissed his face, while inhaling the baby shampoo scent of his hair. What was it about the smell of babies that made her insides ache for one of her own? *Soon enough*, she thought.

Chapter Thirty-two

*N*ico toddled over to Kat next. She gave him loud raspberry kisses on his cheek, making him laugh. "Hi, sweet boy. Do you remember us? We're your sisters, Kat and Trina. Remember?"

"Kat," he said proudly. Then he touched Trina's shoulder. "Tweena."

Trina laughed. "Close enough, kiddo."

"You want to open your presents now?" Kat asked.

He plopped down onto the floor and looked at Paulina.

"Go ahead," she said. "You can open them."

"Chwismas!" Nico clapped his hands.

Kat snorted. "Doesn't take them long to learn that word, does it?"

"No, it doesn't," Paulina said.

Elena just smiled.

"His vocabulary sure is growing. Very impressive, Nico," Trina said. She nudged Kat. "Give him yours first,"

Kat handed him her gift, wrapped as best as she'd been able, considering it wasn't a typical shape and hadn't come in a box.

He tore into the wrapping, revealing a big stuffed purple dinosaur with red and yellow accents and a blue bowtie. His eyes went big. "Mama, Mama, dinosaw!"

"That's right," Paulina said. "That's a dinosaur. Bingo Brontosaurus." She smiled at him before looking at Kat. "Thank you, Kat. That's very nice. He loves that show."

"I'm glad," Kat said. "And thanks for the suggestion."

"You're welcome," Paulina said.

"Same here," Trina said. "I had no idea what to get him. Not for a fun gift. I could have bought him clothes all day. There's so much cute stuff!" She pushed her present toward him. "Okay, Nico. Open mine next."

Kat waited eagerly to see what he'd think. She and Trina had coordinated their gifts, all thanks to Paulina, obviously.

Her wrapping looked about the same as Kat's had. Nico made short work of it again, tearing it off with abandon to uncover a hot pink stuffed dinosaur with yellow and green accents and long eyelashes.

"Mama, Mama, da dinosaw."

"That's right," Paulina said. "That's Bonnie Brontosaurus. Bingo's wife."

Nico clapped, then held up Bingo and roared like a dinosaur, making them all laugh.

Elena said something in rapid Spanish that Kat couldn't understand. She looked at Paulina.

"My mother said those are perfect for him and that was a thoughtful gift. He loves that show and watches it over and over. Thank you both very much."

"You're welcome," Trina said. She picked up the girl dinosaur and made the stuffed animal kiss the boy dinosaur. Nico laughed.

Kat smiled, watching him. "We were happy to do it." She glanced at Paulina. "How are things?"

"Good," Paulina said. "I'm so glad you have both stayed in his life. I think it's very good for him to know his sisters."

"I think so, too," Kat agreed.

Now Trina was humming a silly tune and making the girl dinosaur dance, which Nico found hilarious. "I can't imagine having a brother and not being in his life. Thank you for being brave enough to find us."

Paulina smiled as she seemed to exhale in relief. Had she thought they might change their minds about keeping in touch with her and Nico? "Can I get either of you something to eat or drink?"

Kat shook her head. "Nothing for me, thanks. We don't want to take up too much of your time. We have things to do and I'm sure you do. Who isn't busy this time of year?"

Paulina nodded like that was true. "Trina, I thought you might bring Walter."

Trina shook her head. "Next time, I will. I'm actually watching a customer's dog while she's away for Christmas, so I have two dogs at home right now."

Paulina's brows went up. "How is Walter handling that?"

"Pretty well," Trina answered. "He and Tinker-bell get along great. Almost makes me wish I had another dog, but it's definitely more responsibility." She smiled sort of shyly. "And who knows? By this time next year, I'll be married and there could be a baby on the way."

Paulina gasped. "What did you say? Are you pregnant?"

Trina quickly shook her head, laughing. "No, no. I said there *could* be. Miles and I both want kids and we don't want to wait too long, so who knows? Don't worry, I'm going to send you an invite to the wedding."

"So am I," Kat said. "Nico will be too little still to be involved in the actual ceremony, but I want you both there."

"Thank you," Paulina said. "That is very kind. I look forward to it."

Kat and Trina played with Nico and his new dinosaurs for another few minutes, then Kat gently elbowed Trina after seeing Elena yawn. "We should get back."

Trina nodded. "Okay."

Kat and Trina both gave Nico kisses goodbye. Kat brushed her hands over his thick dark hair. He was such a beautiful child and every once in a while, she caught a glimpse of her late father in the way he held his mouth or raised his brows. "Merry Christmas, little brother. Love you."

"Kat!" Nico proudly exclaimed, patting her arms with his small hands.

She smiled, heart full even as a new longing took hold inside her. "That's right."

She and Trina got to their feet, said goodbye to Elena and Paulina, and left. It was chillier outside than it had been earlier.

Kat hugged her arms around herself. "I never thought we'd end up with a little brother." Or how much he'd make her want a child of her own.

"Me, either," Trina said. "You realize if we both have kids in the next couple of years, he'll probably be closer to them than to us. They'll basically grow up knowing each other."

Kat nodded, pushing the button on her key fob to unlock the doors. "In a way, that's pretty cool. I never, well, I guess *we* never had any cousins growing up. It would have been nice."

"It would have," Trina agreed.

They both got into the car. Kat started the engine and turned on the heat. "Kind of makes me want to have kids even sooner."

Trina put her seatbelt on. "I know what you mean. Not only would they have Nico, but they'd have each other." She smiled at Kat. "Isn't that something? You'll be living upstairs with Alex, I'll be living downstairs with Miles. Our kids will be more like siblings than we are. That's pretty cool, actually."

Kat smiled. "You're right. And it is cool. I never thought about that before. We're sisters, our future husbands are best friends, and our kids will be cousins. They'll also never want for someone to play with as long as we're both living at the beach house. That would be amazing. For all of us."

"Yeah, it will be," Trina said with a warm smile.

Kat pulled out of the lot and got them headed home. "You know, our dad did a lot wrong. But we've made it work out for us, haven't we?"

"We have." Trina wiped at her eyes. "I'm so glad about that. I'm glad about all of it, really. You sort of have to be if you're going to get a benefit from something like that, don't you think? Not saying we have to be all right with him being unfaithful to our mothers, but like you said, we've made it work. We've done more than make it work. We've used the situation to better our lives. That's more than a lot of people would have done. Don't you think?"

Kat nodded, giving it some thought. "I do. Lots of people would have let it destroy them. Our moms somehow didn't. I know it was hard on them, but they were strong enough to survive it."

"Strong enough to not let it define them," Trina added.

Kat lifted her chin slightly. "It's made us stronger, too. And it's really helped me understand who I am. Helped me figure out what I want from life. Alex helped with that, too, but Dad's unfaithfulness pushed me to find a new direction."

"Weird how such an awful thing turned out to be ultimately a good thing for all of us, isn't it?"

Kat nodded. "It is. I guess that's why I've been mostly able to forgive him." She glanced at Trina and smiled. "After all, I got you out of the deal."

Chapter Thirty-three

Snowy didn't need a jacket, because she was already wearing the most gorgeous fur coat Willie had ever seen or felt. Willie, however, *did* need a jacket and a hat. Diamond Beach was a beautiful place to live but whoever was in charge of the weather had gone overboard with the cold.

She'd even worn her jacket and hat to the movie last night, which had been all kinds of fun. They would definitely be going to the next one in the spring. Hopefully, it would be warmer then.

She couldn't complain too much about the weather, though. It was about to be Christmas. Nothing wrong with a little cool weather for the holiday.

She rubbed her hands together and thought about maybe wearing gloves. Did she even own gloves? She didn't think so.

Would it be weird to put socks on her hands? She made a face as she pondered that. She wasn't someone who shied away from weird, but that might be a bridge too far even for her. And she didn't need her neighbors thinking she was stranger than she already was.

Not only that, she might lose her grip on Snowy's leash if she had her hands covered like that.

Miguel came out from his office. "All ready?"

"Just need to get my jacket and hat. I wish I had gloves. It's chilly today."

"We don't have to stay out long." He kissed her cheek. "I don't want either of my girls getting cold."

Willie smiled. He'd started referring to her and Snowy as his "girls" and it was very cute. "We have to walk at least twenty minutes." She'd read in the Dunes West newsletter that twenty-minute walks were the minimum required to obtain the best bene-fits of the exercise.

"Fine with me. However long you want." He opened the coat closet, getting his coat out, which he draped over his arm. "Which jacket do you want?"

"The blue fleece one. And the blue hat."

He handed the hat to her, then helped her on with the coat. She zipped it up then tugged on the hat. It was going to mess up her hair, but if the cold wind got in her ears, she'd be miserable.

Once they were bundled up, she grabbed Snowy's leash off the hook inside the closet and went to get her. Snowy already had her harness on, so all Willie had to do was attach the leash to the little ring on the back. Willie found her sitting by the sliding doors that led out to the lanai.

Snowy meowed at her, a sweet, plaintive sound that generally resulted in Snowy getting what she wanted. In this case, going out onto the lanai to watch birds and squirrels and any other wildlife that might be around.

"I know you want to go out, but we're going out the front door. It's time for our walk, Snowy girl. It'll be even more exciting than the lanai, I promise." Willie clipped the leash on, then slipped her hand through the looped end so that part was around her wrist. She gripped the section of leash that went through her hand. "Come on, now."

Snowy peered longingly out through the door.

Willie clicked her tongue, regaining Snowy's attention. "This way, Snowy girl."

Snowy was smart and was quickly coming to realize that the leash meant outside time. She liked outside time, even though so far it had mostly been in the yard and a little bit down the sidewalk. She stood up and went along with Willie.

She walked the little cat back to Miguel and the front door. He had his coat on. He smiled when he saw them. "There they are."

He opened the front door and let Willie and Snowy go ahead of him, then closed it and locked it.

Probably an unnecessary precaution. The Preserve was a gated community and Dunes West had its own security that regularly patrolled the entire development. But better safe than sorry. Especially with all the presents they had under their tree.

Snowy trotted right down the walkway and into the yard. She went through her usual routine of sniffing the grass, scratching on a palm tree, and lifting her face into the sun. She was momentarily distracted by the decorative grasses swaying in the breeze.

"She loves being outside, doesn't she?" Willie said, watching her.

"Who doesn't?" Miguel said. "It's cold, but it's still a beautiful day. Blue skies and plenty of sun." He looked in both directions. "Which way?"

"We went left yesterday. Let's go right today."

"Excellent choice."

They walked to the end of their driveway and

turned right. Not only were the walks good for them, but they were getting to know their neighborhood better.

Willie unzipped her jacket a little. She was plenty warm, especially with the sun on her. Miguel walked next to the street, and she walked beside him near the houses, keeping Snowy away from the road.

It wasn't a heavily traveled road and the cars that did pass were keeping to the twenty-five mile an hour speed limit, but Willie preferred to be as safe as possible.

Occasionally, Snowy stopped to scratch or sniff something, but for the most part, she walked along with them like a dog would. It tickled Willie. Not only had she become a cat lady, but she'd become a cat lady who showed off.

She giggled.

"What's funny?" Miguel asked. "Tell me the joke."

"I'm the joke. I'm the crazy cat lady taking her cat for a walk where all the neighborhood can see and you know what?"

"What?"

"I couldn't care less." She grinned at him. "I love this cat and I love you and I'm as happy as can be."

Smiling, he offered her his arm. She looped hers through it.

He let out a contented sigh. "You know what I have realized?"

"What's that?"

"I will never get you a better gift than that cat. I hope you are fine with inferior gifts for the rest of your life, because there is no way I can top Snowy."

She laughed. "It's true. You won't be able to, but I'm okay with that. She's amazing. There's not a gift in the world that could compare."

"Not even diamonds?"

Willie snorted. "Not even diamonds."

Miguel looked proud. "I've saved myself a lot of money then."

They followed the sidewalk as the road made a soft bend through the neighborhood. Up ahead was another walker, a woman with a large black Labrador retriever.

"Uh-oh," Willie said. "This might not be good. Should I pick Snowy up? She might get spooked. Or should we just go back?"

"We could cross to the other side," Miguel said.

But even as the words were leaving his mouth, the woman with the dog did exactly that, checking both ways before she guided the Lab across the road.

She gave Willie and Miguel a smile and a wave. "Merry Christmas. Beautiful cat."

"Thank you. Merry Christmas to you," Miguel called back. Then, just to Willie, he said, "Crisis averted."

She was about to nod when a squirrel darted across the street. Snowy loved squirrels. She darted after the varmint, yanking Willie's arm. "Snowy!"

The squirrel went into someone's yard and Snowy gave chase. For a small cat, she had a tremendous amount of pull.

Willie ended up tripping over a flower bed and landing in the grass. Better there than on the driveway, but still. "Snowy! What's gotten into you?"

"Willie!" Miguel hurried over to her. "Are you hurt, my love?"

"Just my pride." She sighed as she managed to sit up. She probably had grass stains on her pants. "I'm fine. I had no idea four pounds of cat could pull that hard."

"Neither did I. I'm glad you kept hold of her."

"Me, too." Willie frowned at the little cat, who was now rolling around in the grass and looking innocent. The squirrel was apparently forgotten. Willie shook her head. "You naughty thing."

The front door of the house opened and a white-haired woman came out. "You all right there?"

Miguel gave Willie a hand up.

Willie nodded at the woman. "Yes. Sorry to be on your property. Our cat saw a squirrel and went crazy."

Smiling, the woman walked out toward them. She was in a thick pink bathrobe and fuzzy pink slippers. "Did you say cat? Oh, there she is. Look at her. How pretty. Hello, baby."

Miguel nodded. "That's Snowy."

Snowy continued to lay upside down in the grass, showing off her belly.

Willie could only roll her eyes at Snowy's display of cuteness. "My husband got her for me for Christmas. I'm Willie, by the way, and this is the man responsible for the cat, Miguel. We live a few houses down. Just moved in."

"Welcome to the neighborhood. I'm Agnes," the woman said. "Agnes Kemp. But my husband, Herschel, always called me Aggie." She glanced at them, but then went right back to watching Snowy. "Your cat is beautiful. How on Earth did you ever train her to walk on a leash?"

"We sort of still are," Willie said. "But the rescue got her started."

They talked a bit about Snowy and the rescue, but then the conversation turned to Christmas.

Aggie's smile faltered. "Well, I hope you have a nice one."

"You, too," Miguel said.

Aggie just shrugged. "I haven't had a nice Christmas since my Herschel passed. You get used to it after a while."

Willie doubted that was true. "But you'll be with family, won't you?" She knew it was a personal question that might not be well received, but she asked anyway.

Aggie shook her head. "Both my sisters passed years ago and my son works for a big firm in Japan. I only get to see him about once a year." She sighed. "You'd think you'd get used to a thing like that, but you really don't."

Willie felt for her. This was no time to be alone. And there was no reason for it. Not with her and Miguel just down the street. "Why don't you join us for Christmas?" Snowy wound around Willie's legs, looking for attention.

Miguel smiled and nodded. "Yes. We would love to have you."

Aggie stared at them. "That's kind of you, but—"

"No buts," Willie said. "No one should be alone

on Christmas." She scooped Snowy up and smiled at Aggie. "You're not going to tell Snowy no, are you?"

A stubborn smile cracked Aggie's face. She reached out and petted Snowy's head. "Well, when you put it like that..."

Chapter Thirty-four

Nashville wasn't exactly home, but it was a familiar enough place that Jules felt some comfort there.

The hotel she and her band were staying in, courtesy of the Grand Ole Opry, was very nice. But the Christmas decorations were making her miss home and her family more than she'd expected. Every strand of garland and every shiny ornament seemed to be a reminder that she wasn't home.

Carols played softly as she waited in line at the coffee shop, making her grow even more nostalgic. Claire and Kat would both send pictures from Christmas Eve and Christmas Day, of course, but it wasn't the same as being there.

Nothing was the same as being there.

Jesse sidled up to her and patted his jacket

pocket. "The drugstore across the street had the cough drops you like."

"Great. Thanks." She didn't like to run out of them, just in case her throat needed extra attention.

His eyes narrowed. "You okay? You look like you're somewhere else. And not in a good way."

She gave him a quick smile. "I was, sort of. Just thinking about my family."

He nodded and put his arm around her. "It's tough, huh?"

"It is. I'll be fine. Trust me, once we get to rehearsal, I'll be focused. But I can't escape Christmas right now and that's not helping."

"Why don't you go call your mom? Or Claire? Go talk to them. It might make you feel better."

She glanced at the line ahead of her.

"I'll get your coffee and bring it up to you."

"You're the best. Tall skinny latte with an extra espresso shot." She leaned up and kissed him. "Thank you. Talking to them sounds like exactly what I need."

She took off for her room. As soon as she got in, she took out her phone and called Claire.

But the phone just rang until it went to voice-mail. No doubt Claire was busy at the bakery.

Jules left a quick message. "Just checking in from

Nashville. Miss you all so much. Wish I could be there with you. Love you."

She sat on the bed, staring at her phone screen. Kat was probably busy, too, so even if Jules called her niece, chances were they wouldn't get to speak very long.

She tried her mom.

"Hello, sweetheart."

Jules smiled, exhaling at the comforting sound of her mother's voice. "Hi, Mom. How are you? How's Conrad?"

"We're both well, thank you. How's Nashville?"

"Good. Cold. And not home." Jules let out a sigh as the depth of missing home hit her. "I wish I was there with you guys."

"I know. We wish you were here, too, but we also understand that what you're doing is hugely important for your career. Not to mention all those people coming to your shows that you're bringing joy to."

Jules blinked at that idea. "I hadn't thought about that. I know you're right, of course, but..."

"It's always hard being away from home. Even harder this time of year. But think about how many other people must be feeling that way. Some of those people are probably in your audience, and your music is giving them a chance to be happy and be part of something. Whether you realize it or not, you're probably the Christmas magic some of those people have been craving."

Jules sniffed at the kind words. "How do you know just what to say? What I needed to hear?"

Her mom laughed. "Sweetheart, I've known you all your life. I have a pretty good idea of how you think and what you must be going through. You're a sensitive soul, Julia. You always have been. It's what makes you so good at what you do. So creative. But feeling things deeply isn't easy."

"No," Jules breathed out. "It isn't."

"You have Cash with you. And Jesse. And the rest of your band. They're all missing people just the same. Don't shut them out or ignore what they might be going through."

Jules took a deep breath. "You're completely right, of course. I don't know why I'm feeling this way."

"What way?"

"Like I'm missing out. No, that's not really it. I feel..." She sighed in frustration. "I don't know how to explain it, Mom. I just miss you guys. All of you. And I know I'm where I need to be, doing what I need to be doing, but you just got married and this is

Claire's first Christmas without Bryan, Kat's first Christmas without her dad, and I'm not there!"

Jules was aware her voice had risen, aware of the higher tone it had taken, but she couldn't help herself. "I should be there!"

"Julia," her mother said calmly. "Take a deep breath. This responsibility you feel? You can let it go, I promise you. None of us are upset with you. Do we miss you? Of course, we do. But you know what else?"

Jules was trying to breathe. Trying to take deep breaths and not cry. "What?"

"We are so very proud of you. As much as we'd like you to be here, we'd also love to be there with you. Cheering you on. Supporting you. Showing you just how amazing we think you are. Watching you shine on that stage."

Jules's shoulders dropped from where they'd tensed up. She lay back on the bed and stared up at the ceiling. "Thanks, Mom."

Her mom went on. "We will have a big celebration when you get back. I promise you. And we'll keep you in the loop as best we can about what's going on here. You won't miss too much. We're going to the candlelight service at church tonight for Christmas Eve, then Claire and Kat are coming here for Christmas morning breakfast. After that, we're all going to Willie and Miguel's for Christmas Day. Well, not all of us."

Jules sat up again. "Not all of you?"

"No. Kat and Trina are going to the firehouse, since Alex and Miles are on call that day. Although maybe they are going to dinner first. I'm not sure."

"Oh. That's too bad they can't all be with you."

"It's okay," Margo said softly. "Christmas is a wonderful day, but there's no right way to spend it. You and Cash and Jesse and Sierra will all be together. You'll have your band members, and Toby—"

"And Shiloh," Jules added.

"And Shiloh. You'll celebrate Christmas with them on the day, and you'll celebrate it with us when you get home. But in the meantime, don't you have a big show to get ready for?"

Jules nodded and smiled. "Grand Ole Opry tonight, Mom."

"That's amazing. I don't have enough words to tell you how proud of you I am. You've worked so hard for this."

Jules sniffed. "Thanks, Mom. Speaking of hard work, how's the writing business going?"

Her mom laughed. "It's...going. We've had two rejections so far."

"Oh, Mom. I'm so sorry. That sucks." Jules understood rejection. She'd certainly had enough of it when she'd been getting started in her career. "I read that book. Those publishers are dumb if they've turned it down."

"No, it's fine," her mother said. "Conrad and I have made the decision to start our own publishing company and put the book out ourselves."

"Get out of here. You're going indie? That is so cutting edge. Wow. I'm impressed."

"*You're* impressed with *me*?" There was a smile in her mother's voice.

"You bet I am," Jules said. "That's a big undertaking. I bet you kill it. The book was so good. I couldn't put it down. Those publishers who turned you down are going to be so sorry."

Her mom laughed. "I'm not going to argue that. Thank you for your kind words. It is a lot to do, a lot to get right, but this way we'll be in control of all of it. Sink or swim, it's up to us."

"Well, the minute it's up for sale, you let me know."

"I will."

"You promise?"

"I do. And I'll go one better. I'll tell you when it's up for preorder."

"Yes, please. The moment it's live." Jules planned to share it on her social media. Hopefully, her audience would give her mom and Conrad a few sales.

A soft knock on the door caught her attention. Jesse with her coffee, no doubt. She got up and opened the door, smiling at him. "Thanks for talking to me, Mom. I feel better. Still miss you guys, but I don't feel so guilty about it now."

Jesse held up her coffee. Jules nodded at him, holding up her finger to indicate she just needed another minute.

"Good," her mom said. "You shouldn't. You have nothing to feel guilty about. I love you. Have a fantastic show tonight."

"Thanks, Mom. I love you, too." Jules took her coffee from Jesse's hand. "And I will."

Chapter Thirty-five

Roxie finished sweeping the salon. Trina wasn't quite done with her client, but Roxie could add those little bits of hair to the pile in a minute. Amber had already left, as had most of the stylists. Only Ginger and Trina remained, and Ginger was minutes away from heading out herself.

Roxie checked the retail shelves to see what needed to be restocked. She'd made up some gift baskets of shampoo, conditioner, and a brush, and was happy to see how well they'd sold. Easy gift options were always good, apparently. Next year, she'd create a broader range. More baskets, with more variety, and maybe some specifically aimed at men.

She noted the things that needed to be replaced and went to the stock shelves in the back room to get them. She smiled at the dogs, lounging in their bed. "Almost time to go home, babies."

Ginger came in with her used towels and dropped them in the hamper. "I'm all done, and Margie is checked out. Anything you want me to do before I leave?"

Roxie shook her head. "Just have a wonderful Christmas."

Ginger smiled and gave Roxie a hug. "You, too."

As Ginger left, Roxie gathered the items for the shelves. There wasn't time to run a load of towels, but those would keep until they reopened after Christmas.

Trina was blowing out and styling her client's hair now, so it wouldn't be much longer.

Roxie restocked the shelves. She was eager to get home, eager to get ready for the candlelight service, and eager to see Ethan. This might be her first Christmas without Bryan, but it was also her first Christmas *with* Ethan.

The man who'd helped put her heart back together. The man who'd shown her that love really could mean having someone's full attention. And that she alone was enough.

She'd worked very hard at coming up with the

perfect gift for him. Something that would show him just how much he meant to her and how excited she was about them starting a new life together. It hadn't been easy, but after a lot of thought, she'd found just the thing.

She stared out the salon windows, lost in thought. She really hoped he liked it as much as she thought he would.

The soft, mechanical sounds of the printer spitting out a receipt brought her back to Earth. She turned, smiling as Trina's customer left. "Bye," Roxie said. "Merry Christmas."

When the door closed, Roxie locked it. She and Trina seemed to both simultaneously breathe a sigh of relief. Roxie headed for the back room. "Let's get the dogs and get home."

They walked through the door of the beach house twenty minutes later, having made sure the dogs did their business before bringing them upstairs.

Roxie went into her room to change as Trina did the same. Roxie put on jeans and a T-shirt. Tonight, for church, she'd wear black slacks with a white blouse and a red blazer.

Right now, she was going to make them a quick

late lunch to get them through the service. Nothing fancy, just heating up the leftovers from a previous dinner of chicken and rice casserole. After eating, Trina would be taking the dogs out for a long walk to wear them out.

Roxie was going to have a nap. Working at the salon meant being on her feet a lot, and that wore her out a bit. She didn't want to be yawning during the service, which wasn't until seven.

Most nights, by seven p.m., she was in pajamas and looking forward to bed in a couple of hours.

They ate, Trina took the dogs out, then Roxie had her nap. After that, she did some much-needed laundry, wrapped a few presents in her room, and did a quick spot clean of the beach house. Not the most exciting Christmas Eve activity, but it needed to be done and tomorrow for Christmas, they'd be at Willie's all day.

By six, they were getting ready for church. Trina wore a red turtleneck with dark jeans and flats. Roxie added a sparkly pin to her jacket, a wreath dotted with multicolored ornaments made of colored rhinestones. It was ancient, having been Willie's once upon a time.

They left at six thirty, knowing they'd have to be there early to get good seats, even though they planned to sit with Ethan and his parents. Wouldn't be fair to make them hold the seats for too long.

The church was bustling when they arrived. Lots of people hugging each other and smiling and wishing each other Merry Christmas. Everyone festively dressed, and the church was lit almost entirely by candlelight and the Christmas lights that had been strung along the knee wall that defined the choir loft.

Wreaths decorated each window and garlands lined the sills. Off to one side of the dais was a small Christmas tree, decorated in white lights, paper stars, and little angel ornaments that the children's Sunday school class had made.

More greenery filled the altar table and on either side of the big church Bible were two tall white tapers. They were lit and the flames flickered in the air currents.

"It's so pretty," Trina breathed.

Roxie nodded as she took it all in. "It's beautiful." It had been so long since she'd attended church regularly. That had changed since moving to Diamond Beach. Now she wasn't just attending, she was a part of this church.

"It's really something, isn't it?" Ethan said softly beside her.

She turned. "Hi."

"Hi." He smiled in a way that made her feel like it was only for her. "You look beautiful. Merry Christmas."

"Merry Christmas. You look pretty handsome yourself, too."

They took their seats with his parents. Trina joined them. Margo, Conrad, and his sister Dinah sat in the row behind them, and before long, those three were joined by Danny, Claire, and Kat.

Willie and Miguel came in and sat next to Trina.

Pastor Tim took his place behind the podium. He welcomed everyone and as he did that, the adult choir filtered in. The music director, Mr. Williams, led the choir and the congregation in singing *Joy To The World* and *Hark, The Herald Angels Sing*.

After that, Pastor Tim and Mr. Williams sat down and the children's choir came on stage, adorable and fidgety with the excitement of Christmas. They were all dressed in white shirts and black pants or skirts. The boys had red ties and the girls had red hair bows. Miss Landon, their director, got them organized, then crouched in front of them on the floor and gave them a nod. She raised her hands to get them started.

They sang *Away In A Manger*, charming everyone

with their antics and sincerity, and bringing lots of smiles to the audience. One little boy sat down and refused to sing, making everyone laugh despite his stubbornness.

When the children had been ushered back to their parents, Pastor Tim returned to the podium. He read the Christmas story from Luke, his voice conveying just the right amount of seriousness and wonder.

As he spoke, Roxie listened intently. She could feel herself absorbing the happiness and contentment of the moment. She was deeply blessed to be surrounded by all those she considered family at this very special time of year.

She reached to her sides and took Trina's hand in one of hers and Ethan's in the other. She gave them each a quick glance accompanied by a smile. She loved them both so very much.

She held their hands until Pastor Tim asked them all to stand. Ushers passed out baskets of little white candles pushed through a small circle of white card stock to collect any wax drips.

Everyone took one, then handed the basket to the person beside them.

When the small candles had been distributed, Pastor Tim used one of the candles from the altar in front of the podium to light the candle of the person closest to him in the front two rows. Those people lit the candles of their neighbors and so the flame was shared, moving through the auditorium, building the glow of light until everyone held a lit candle.

Mr. Williams stepped back to the podium and led the congregation in an a capella version of *Silent Night*.

It was so beautiful and sweet that Roxie's emotions nearly got the best of her.

When the song ended, Pastor Tim stood in front of the altar, smiling at all of them. "Thank you so much for coming out tonight. I've been blessed by your presence. I hope you've been blessed by being here. I pray you all have a wonderful Christmas, and that the new year brings you more blessings and peace."

Soft murmurs went through the congregation, words of agreement and a few amens.

"Let me dismiss us with prayer." He prayed over them and then the church lights came up a little.

Candles were blown out and all around them, people wished each other Merry Christmas.

Roxie leaned in toward Ethan. "That was..." She shook her head, unable to find words that really did justice to the service. "Just beautiful. I loved it."

He nodded. "It was special, huh? Really puts you in the right frame of mind. And heart. This is all that really matters, isn't it? Being with those you love. Recognizing what's truly important."

She couldn't have agreed more.

Chapter Thirty-six

Margo hadn't made Christmas breakfast in a very long time. Not since the girls were in their late teens or early twenties. After they'd both gotten married, Christmas had alternated between their houses, until Julia's divorce from Lars. Then Christmas had become Claire's domain, so for the last couple of decades, Margo had spent the holiday at her eldest daughter's house.

She pulled all the necessary ingredients for breakfast from the refrigerator. Eggs, bacon, sausage, butter, milk, heavy cream, red and green bell peppers, and mushrooms.

The sad thing about those years spent at Claire's was that Margo had never truly felt comfortable there.

All because of Bryan, of course. Claire had

always made Margo feel welcome, but Bryan had never been one of her favorite people. Margo hadn't even wanted Claire to marry Bryan, but she'd kept her opinions to herself. Even so, there had been a palpable tension between her and Bryan when he'd been around that not even Christmas could resolve.

Her feelings toward him never changed and when it came to holidays, it had only intensified. Regardless of which holiday was upon them, he'd always, inevitably, found a reason to miss part of it. Christmas was no exception. Didn't matter if it was Christmas Eve or Christmas Day, he'd mysteriously have to be somewhere else. For the last two years before his death, he'd missed the entirety of both those days.

She knew why now. He'd had another wife. He'd had *two* other wives. But Paulina had most likely had Bryan all to herself the last two years. Margo chalked that up to Paulina's pregnancy.

It was understandable that Bryan would have wanted to spend time with her since she was pregnant, but it didn't excuse his behavior.

Nothing would. Just like nothing would change how Margo felt about him. Not now. Not ever. Margo huffed out a breath at that thought. Her frustration with him might remain with her for the rest of her life, but it no longer mattered. He was gone.

That freed her from having to pretend that his actions were fine. That it was okay that his work, which had always been his excuse, came first. This year, no one had to go along with that. They could celebrate as a family, unencumbered by the tension his absence created.

She got out bread for toast, potatoes that would become home fries, and all the ingredients necessary to make pancakes.

She didn't even mind that after breakfast they'd be spending the rest of the day at Willie and Miguel's. She was looking forward to it, actually. She hadn't seen their new house yet and Willie had become a friend. More than that, really. She had Willie to thank for Conrad, in a way.

Margo unwrapped the bulk sausage and got it browning in a pan along with some diced onion and peppers.

Miguel would soon be Claire's father-in-law, as well, so there would be a lot more shared celebrations in the future. Margo smiled thinking about it.

Amazing that Bryan's philandering ways had led to so many new connections. And so many genuinely good people. People who were becoming friends and were soon to be her extended family.

The doorbell rang. Probably Dinah, who'd offered to come over early and help with the food preparation.

Conrad called out, "I'll get it."

"Thanks." Margo went to work dicing potatoes and getting them into a pan where a knob of bacon fat was melting. She added the other half of a diced onion, then sprinkled the veggies with seasoning salt and some black pepper.

Dinah came in carrying a big bowl of fruit salad, her contribution. "Merry Christmas."

Margo smiled. "Merry Christmas. Thank you for coming over to help. I certainly appreciate it."

Dinah put the bowl on the counter. "Thank you for letting me be a part of today."

Margo started slicing mushrooms. She threw them in with the sausage as she got them cut. "Of course. You're family."

"That's kind of you to say. But I know this is a big day and..." She shrugged.

Margo understood. Dinah thought Margo wouldn't want her there because it was Margo's family coming over and Dinah and Margo had had a rocky start. But that was behind them. *Well* behind them.

"Dinah, it's Christmas. I am very happy to have you here." Margo hesitated. "I'm really happy you're a part of my life, too."

"You really mean that, don't you?"

Margo nodded and went back to slicing. "I do."

"Thank you," Dinah said softly. "I'm so glad you're part of my life as well. And my brother's. Especially my brother's. You've made him so happy."

"He does the same for me."

"Which is why you're so well suited. What can I do to help?"

Margo looked around. "There are eggs to be cracked, pancakes to make, toast, too, but that probably shouldn't get made until everyone's started to arrive." She assessed the workload. "How about you crack the eggs so I can get this casserole in the oven, then you can start on making the pancake batter?"

Dinah nodded. "Do you have a recipe for me to follow?"

"I do. I'll get it out for you in just a moment."

As they worked, Conrad came in to get everything he needed to set the table. Before he did that, however, he told Alexa to play classic Christmas music. As the familiar tunes started up, they applied themselves to their tasks.

Margo moved with precision and was amazed to see Dinah doing very much the same. She was efficient and hardworking, and Margo began to understand why Claire was so pleased with her work at the bakery.

It wasn't long until the breakfast casserole was in the oven, the home fries were browning nicely, and they had pancakes going on the griddle. As the pancakes were done, Margo and Dinah added them to a cookie sheet in the oven, which had been programmed to a low temp to keep the pancakes warm.

The table was set. Conrad filled a pitcher with ice water and another with orange juice. "What about coffee?" he asked.

Margo nodded. "I got the carafe out. We should make a pot, fill the carafe, then make another pot. I imagine we'll go through a lot of it."

"I'll get it done," Conrad said.

"What about me?" Dinah said. "You've got the pancakes under control. Maybe there's something else I can do?"

"We'll need butter and syrup on the table," Margo answered. "Salt and pepper, too." She glanced at her husband. "Unless you did that already, Conrad?"

He was measuring grounds into the coffee maker. "Not yet."

"I'll take care of it," Dinah said.

As she finished speaking, the doorbell rang.

"Want me to get that?" Dinah asked.

Margo had pancakes to flip. "Yes, thank you."

Dinah wiped her hands and went out to the foyer. Margo listened closely and soon heard the voices of Claire, Kat, and Danny.

She smiled and called out, "Merry Christmas!"

Claire came into the kitchen carrying a sour orange pie. "Merry Christmas, Mom. Brought a little dessert. I realize dessert after breakfast isn't really a thing, but it's Christmas, so we have an excuse."

"We do."

Claire leaned in and kissed Margo on the cheek. "Thanks for doing this."

"Happy to," Margo said.

Claire put the pie in the refrigerator. "Can I help?"

Margo shook her head. "Dinah's been lending a hand and we're pretty close to being done. Just go sit and relax."

Kat came in. "Merry Christmas, Grandma.

Breakfast smells so good. I'm starving. When do we eat?"

"Soon," Margo answered with a smile. "I promise."

The doorbell chimed again.

Dinah took the spatula from Margo's hand. "Go on. I'll finish these up and get the toast going."

"All right, thank you." She went out to the foyer, smiling at Danny, who was standing with Conrad by the sliders out to the lanai. They seemed to be talking about landscaping.

She answered the door, finding a young man obscured by a giant potted poinsettia. "Hello?"

The poinsettia moved to one side and Alex smiled at her. "Morning, Mrs. Ballard. I hope you don't mind me showing up uninvited."

"Oh, don't be silly. You are always invited to this house." He and a few of his friends from the fire station, Miles included, had helped her when she'd moved into the house. They'd moved boxes and furniture and all for the price of lunch.

He grinned and held out the poinsettia. "Thanks. This is for you."

"What a lovely gift. It's beautiful, thank you. I thought you had to work today?"

"I do, but not until later. Figured I'd surprise Kat."

Margo nodded with approval. "Well, you go right on in and do that."

As he went into the living room, she set the plant down by the front door. It added a nice touch of Christmas cheer.

She followed him into the living room to the sounds of Kat's happy exclamations.

Still smiling, Margo looked at Conrad. "We need to set another place."

He nodded but came over to her and put his arm around her. "This is nice, isn't it?"

"It's very nice." The house was filled with family and friends, Christmas music, the aroma of good food, and happiness. Not only that, but she had the most wonderful man at her side. The same could be said for her daughter and granddaughter.

Yes, some of her family were missing, but she knew they'd be here if they could. She'd talk to them all later.

She hadn't had a Christmas quite this good in a long time. It was a very good day and it had only begun.

She smiled up at Conrad. "Actually, it's better than nice. It's just about perfect."

Chapter Thirty-seven

Claire had eaten too much, but it was Christmas, and everything had all been so good. If you couldn't indulge on Christmas Day, then when could you? She couldn't very well turn down a piece of her own pie, either.

It had been a while since she'd tasted it and she was happy to know it was just as delicious as it was supposed to be.

After breakfast, she helped her mom and Dinah carry dishes into the kitchen, but once she'd had the table cleared, they'd shooed her out and told her to go relax. She didn't have to be told twice.

Now she was sitting on the lanai with Danny and everyone else, lounging and letting their meal settle while they enjoyed the lull in activity. The day had started off a little on the chilly side but had warmed up as the sun had risen in the cloudless sky. The weather had turned downright balmy.

"It's really something, isn't it?" she said.

"What is?" Danny asked.

"Celebrating Christmas like this. Outside under a gorgeous blue sky, sun bright and shining, the subtle hint of salt and sea in the air." She glanced over at him. "In most parts of the country, they're dealing with freezing temperatures and lots of snow. I know some people enjoy that, and I don't mind visiting it, but this right here? This feels pretty perfect to me."

He smiled and took her hand. "Feels pretty perfect to me, too."

Her phone vibrated. She took it out of her pocket and answered the incoming call with a smile on her face. As soon as she did, Jules and Cash appeared on her screen. "Hi, there. Merry Christmas! How are you guys? Where are you guys? Still in Nashville?"

Jules nodded. "We are. Merry Christmas. You're at Mom's?"

"Yep. Just finished our breakfast and now we're sitting out on the lanai, trying to digest all the food we ate. Trying to stay awake, too, although some of us are losing that battle."

Jules laughed. "I want to hear all about it, but

first I want a tour of Mom's house. I haven't seen it yet."

"Oh, right." Claire got up. "Hang on, I'll take you guys into the kitchen, and you can say Merry Christmas to her."

She carried the phone in, showing Jules the dining room and living room as she did. "And this, as you can see, is the kitchen. Say hi to Mom and Dinah."

"Hi, Mom and Dinah," Jules called out.

Cash followed with, "Merry Christmas, Grandma and Aunt Dinah."

Margo and Dinah both turned to look at the screen. Margo smiled. Dinah clasped her hands in front of her chest. "Merry Christmas to all of you," she said.

Margo gave them a wave. "Hello, Cash. Hello, Julia. How are things going? We miss you."

"Things are going very well," Jules answered. "We miss you, too. I wish we could be there with you, but we will be next year. The show last night was really special."

Claire couldn't really see the screen, since she was holding it toward her mom. "If you don't mind, Mom, Jules wants a tour of the house."

Her mom nodded. "Go on, show it to her. We

have a little more to do in here, then I'll be free to talk. Probably by the time you're done with the tour."

"Thanks, Mom," Jules said. "What I've seen so far looks great. You must be so happy to be in."

"I am." Margo smiled. "Happier to see you, though. Both of you."

Her eyes got a little misty and she went back to the leftovers she was putting away.

Claire faced the screen again. "Come on, I'll show you the bedrooms and the office."

When the tour was over, Claire brought the phone back out to the living room. Her mom was still in the kitchen, but she was just wiping down the counters. "Here, Mom. Take the phone and chat with Jules."

"Thank you, Claire."

Claire looked at the screen. "Handing you over to Mom now. I'll talk to you later. Love you both."

"Love you, too," Jules said.

Cash made a heart with his hands. "Love you, Aunt Claire."

Claire gave the phone to her mother and went back outside. No one had moved. She took her seat next to Danny, sighing as she sat down. "I wish Jules and Cash could have been here, but what an exciting thing they're doing. Christmas Eve spent performing at the Grand Ole Opry. How amazing is that?"

"Very," Danny said. His legs were kicked out in front of him, ankles crossed, the rest of him slumped in the chair. His eyes were heavy and he looked like he could drift off in a matter of minutes.

She laughed softly. "Are you going to make it? We still have your dad's house and a big Christmas dinner to get through."

He nodded but there was no conviction in it. "Yep. Might just shut my eyes for a few."

She looked around. Conrad was either about to be asleep or already there, his interlaced fingers steepled over his ribcage, rising and falling with each breath. Kat and Alex, sitting side by side in the loveseat, seemed equally drowsy.

Maybe a nap wasn't such a bad idea. But any minute now, her mother was going to open the door and return Claire's phone, probably waking everyone up.

With a sigh, Claire got up and went back inside.

She found her mother sitting on the couch, dabbing at her eyes with a tissue, still chatting with Jules and Cash. Sierra was in the picture, too, now. Dinah had yet to come out of the kitchen, the sounds of her puttering around barely audible over the Christmas music playing softly in the background.

"What's wrong, Mom?"

Margo looked up and shook her head. She smiled. "Nothing. Here." She handed Claire's phone back to her.

Claire didn't quite understand. "What's going on?"

Jules had a smile on her face like the Cheshire Cat's. She looked at Cash and Sierra. "Tell her yourself."

Cash put his arm around Sierra. "We're engaged, Aunt Claire."

Claire sucked in a breath. "You are?"

Sierra, nodding, flashed her hand for the camera. A very respectable diamond glittered on her ring finger.

Claire felt a little misty herself. "Congratulations, you two. That is such wonderful news."

"Thank you," Sierra said.

Cash nodded. "Thanks, Aunt Claire. Will you make our cake? We're going to get married right there in Diamond Beach next fall."

Claire wiped the corner of her right eye before a tear escaped. "I would be honored."

What a special Christmas this had turned out to be.

Chapter Thirty-eight

Trina stood at her grandmother's kitchen sink, peeling potatoes and thoroughly enjoying her Christmas day. She was also enjoying the delicious smells that had begun to waft from the top oven, where the turkey was roasting. Soon, the ham would be going into the bottom oven.

Walter and Tinkerbell were out on the lanai, basking in the last of the sun's warmth. Snowy was out there, too, but she was on one of the chairs and the dogs were ignoring her. Or she was ignoring the dogs. Either way, they didn't seem to mind each other.

Which was good, because they'd have to come inside at some point. It would definitely cool down again after sunset, which was why they were eating in the dining room. Even with the propane heaters, it would be a little too chilly outside to be enjoyable.

From her spot at the sink, Trina could also see into the living room and the gorgeous tree Mimi had set up. She'd hired a company to come in and do it, and the tree looked straight out of a magazine.

The color scheme was silver, turquoise, and pink and it glittered like it had come directly from Vegas. A place where it would probably fit in perfectly.

Trina smiled. Or at the hair salon.

Her mom was helping Mimi set the table in the dining room. They were going to have a full house today, although Trina would be leaving right after dinner to go see Miles at the fire station. Kat, who'd be coming over with her mom and Danny, would be going with Trina.

Next year, Trina thought, things would be different. Really different. Not only would she and Miles be married, but so would Kat and Alex. She smiled thinking about it. By next Christmas, she hoped the guys would be able to have the day off.

If not, she supposed she and Kat would be at the fire station again. It wasn't a big deal. But it would be nice to be able to celebrate with everyone together at least once.

She peeled the last potato and rinsed it, then placed it on the cutting board and cut them all into chunks. Those went into the salted water in the big pot on the stove. They were going to become some very delicious mashed potatoes in an hour or so.

She dried her hands, then went into the dining room to see how things were going. She found her mom and Mimi standing at the end of the table, staring at the centerpiece, which was a big, low floral arrangement of white lilies, pink roses, and little green and pink berries, along with some evergreen filler and some thin, curly sticks covered in gold glitter.

Set into the flowers were three white taper candles. Those would be lit right before dinner. Mimi had ordered the centerpiece from the florist in the Dunes West shopping center.

Mimi threw her hands into the air. "Trina, my girl, help us out. Your mom thinks we should move the centerpiece to the server and put the food on the table when it's time to eat."

Mimi cut her eyes at Roxie. "*I* think we should leave the centerpiece where it is and put the food on the server. It's called a server for a reason, after all."

Trina didn't usually like to get into the middle of things when it came to her mom and grandmother, but this was easy to solve. "Mimi, it's your house. If you want to wear the centerpiece on your head and call yourself the Queen of Christmas, it's your prerogative."

Willie laughed. "That's my girl. On the table it goes."

Roxie smirked and shook her head, obviously amused by the whole thing. "She's right, Ma. It's your house. Whatever you want to do is fine with me."

Willie grinned. "I'm going to check on Miguel. I'll meet you in the kitchen."

Roxie came closer as Willie left. She kept her voice low. "My only concern with people having to get up to get more food is that it's easy for an accident to happen. Something could get spilled. I don't want that to happen in her new house."

Trina did some quick thinking. "Well, what if, when everyone's ready for seconds, you and I stand by the server and pass the dishes to the table. Then only you and I have to get up and we can make sure the platters go right back."

Roxie nodded. "That works. That's what we'll do. Good solution. Your grandmother can be a little stubborn sometimes."

Trina shot her mom a look. "Really? Just Mimi? No one else you know?"

Her mom narrowed her eyes in amusement. "It's not too late to end up on the naughty list, you know."

Trina shrugged. "Doesn't matter. I already have everything I want."

"Smarty pants." Her mom laughed and hugged her. "This is a great Christmas, isn't it?"

Trina hugged back, nodding. "One of the best ever."

They went into the kitchen to help with more food preparation, but they found Mimi sitting at the counter, having a glass of wine.

Roxie put her hands on her hips. "Ma, I thought there was more work to do."

"There is," Mimi said. "But it's for you two to do. I'm old. You can't expect me to be much help."

"Not when you're already drinking." Roxie laughed. "Where's Miguel?"

"Taking a nap so he can stay up tonight." Mimi looked at Trina. "Don't get old, my girl. It's too much maintenance."

"I'll do my best, Mimi." Trina went into the kitchen. "Just tell us what needs to be done and we'll do it."

She and her mom spent the next hour prepping the vegetable side dishes of honey glazed carrots and dilled green beans. They also measured out the ingredients for the biscuits they'd be baking once the turkey came out.

They also made stuffing, gravy, and started the potatoes cooking. They got the ham in the oven. Trina sliced up some cranberry sauce right out of the can. Maybe not the fanciest, but the slices of jellied relish were kind of a family tradition.

Mimi, now well into her second glass of wine, pointed to the fridge. "Trina, there's a container of fresh cranberry sauce in there. Get that out and put it in a nice dish. I picked it up at the Publix in the shopping center so anyone who doesn't like the canned stuff has an option. There's a bunch of pickled things in there, too, so you can make up a relish tray when you're done with that."

"On it, Mimi." Trina opened the fridge and found the cranberry sauce right away. There were containers of two kinds of olives, plus pickled asparagus, and those fancy pickles that were about the size of her pinky finger. She got all the containers out and set them on the island countertop.

"This is a lot of food, Ma." Roxie checked the potatoes, which had just come to a boil.

"We're having a lot of people over," Mimi answered. "Thankfully, Claire's bringing dessert.

Yule log and cookies. Mmm, I can't wait. This is going to be a good dinner."

The doorbell rang. Trina looked over at her grandmother. "You want me to get that?"

"No, I'll get it. Probably just a neighbor wishing us Merry Christmas." She slid off her stool and toddled toward the door. "Coming!"

Trina laughed softly. "She's not going to make it to dinner if she has any more wine."

"You're right," Roxie said. "She might not."

Willie came back a few moments later. "Trina, Roxie, meet my neighbor, Aggie Kemp. Aggie, these are my girls. My daughter and my granddaughter."

Aggie, purse clutched in front of her like a shield, nodded. "Hello, there."

"Hi," Trina said. "Merry Christmas."

"Merry Christmas," Roxie added.

"Aggie's having dinner with us," Willie announced.

"That's great," Trina said. "Would you like something to drink? Dinner's not for a little bit yet."

"Have a glass of wine with me, Aggie," Willie said. "What's your poison? Red or white?"

Aggie looked slightly unsure how to answer that.

Willie didn't let that stop her. "You want something else? A gin and tonic, maybe? My husband makes great rum drinks, too."

"Did I hear my name?" Miguel walked in.

"No." Willie shook her head. "But I said rum, which is almost the same thing."

Miguel laughed. "Who wants some Christmas punch? It's about time I whipped up a batch of that."

"Sounds good," Aggie said.

"None for me," Trina answered. "I have to drive to the fire station later." She inched closer to her mother. "No wonder Mimi wanted us to come early. She had no intention of cooking this meal, did she?"

Snorting softly, Roxie adjusted the heat on the potatoes so they wouldn't boil over. "Nope. I'm pretty sure this was her plan all along."

Trina just smiled. "I don't mind. It is Christmas, after all."

Brows lifted, her mom poked her in the shoulder. "Just remember that when it's time to clean up."

Chapter Thirty-nine

Kat hated that Alex had had to leave shortly after breakfast, but she took comfort in the fact that she'd be seeing him again after dinner. She would have preferred spending the whole day with him, but that was a sacrifice the fiancée of a fireman had to make.

She turned up the Christmas song on the radio. She'd made a last-minute decision to drive herself to Willie and Miguel's, with her mom and Danny in their own car. That way, she could drive herself to the firehouse after dinner.

It would just be easier for her, especially if Alex got called out while she was there. Not that she couldn't ride with Trina, but Trina had the dogs to deal with and she was probably going to run them back to the beach house before heading to the station.

At least, that's what Kat thought. Maybe she was planning on letting her mom take them back? Or maybe Trina was taking them with her. She had taken Walter to the firehouse once or twice. What was one more little dog?

Kat arrived at Willie and Miguel's after giving her name at the guard shack and being allowed through the gates. The Preserve was even nicer than the rest of Dunes West. It was easy to see this was a higher-end area, although Dunes West was pretty high-end already.

Willie and Miguel had definitely spent some money on their new residence. The house was beautiful *and* on the water. Kat couldn't wait to see the inside. She parked behind her mom and Danny in the driveway, then grabbed the bottle of wine she was bringing as a hostess gift and got out of the car.

She walked in with Danny and her mom. Danny was carrying a tin of cookies and her mom held a beautiful yule log cake that Kat knew had been especially made for this dinner. Her mom had done a special chocolate rum buttercream in honor of Miguel.

Danny knocked and Roxie came to the door to let them in. "Hello, there! I'm so glad you could all come."

Warm, savory aromas greeted them, and Kat thought it smelled exactly like Christmas should. Delicious, homey, and welcoming.

Roxie stepped aside to let them through. "Merry Christmas!"

After lots of Merry Christmases, Roxie led them through to the kitchen. Ivelisse, her husband and kids were already there. They were in the living room. There was also an older woman Kat didn't recognize. Roxie introduced her as Aggie, one of Willie's neighbors.

Aggie and Willie were sitting at the breakfast bar that separated the dining area of the kitchen from the working area. They each had a glass of something red over ice. A slice of orange mingled with the ice cubes. Miguel was outside on the lanai with Ethan. They each had glasses of the same thing.

Roxie pointed to the kitchen table, which held a pickle tray, a big assortment of cheese and crackers, plus bowls of nuts, M&Ms, and other snacky things, along with a big bowl of the red punch everyone seemed to be drinking. "If you want a little nibble before dinner, help yourself. Get some of Miguel's Christmas punch, too, but be warned. It's not for the faint-hearted."

Danny laughed. "My father doesn't know the meaning of the word restraint."

"No, he doesn't," Roxie agreed. "Make yourselves comfortable. I need to baste the turkey."

Danny looked at them. "Claire, Kat, would you like a glass?"

"Sure," Claire said. "I'm not driving and we're going to be here a while."

"Half a glass," Kat said. "I need to be able to drive to the fire station after dinner."

"Right," Danny said. "One glass and one half-glass coming up."

Kat figured with the food she'd be eating, any effects from the punch would be long gone by the time she had to get back in her car.

Trina came in from the lanai. "Hi, guys! I was just checking on the dogs." She gave Kat a hug. "I'm so glad you came. Are you driving with me to the station?"

"No, I'm going to drive myself. I figured you'd have a carful already with the dogs. Are you taking them?"

"I was going to. I thought the guys might like the extra company on Christmas."

Kat nodded. "They probably will." Danny

handed Kat her half-glass of punch. "Thanks." She lifted it to Trina. "Merry Christmas, sister."

"Merry Christmas! Be careful with that punch. You know Miguel made it, right?"

Kat took a sip. It was strong but delicious. "I do. And that's why I'm only having half a glass."

A timer went off in the kitchen. Trina glanced toward the oven. "I'd better check on the biscuits."

"Do you need help?"

"No, my mom and I got it. Thanks, though. Go enjoy yourself. Larry will probably rope us into helping in the kitchen tonight anyway." Trina went to the oven.

"True," Kat said.

Kat's grandmother, Conrad, and Dinah arrived. Kat said hello and chatted with them for a bit, but then she took her glass of punch out to the lanai. It had been a beautiful day and although some of the warmth still lingered, it was fading fast as the sun sank lower in the sky.

Walter came right up to her, tail wagging, tongue out. "Hi, puppers. Are you having a good Christmas?"

Tied around his neck was a red bandana printed with candy canes. A second little dog came over. The long hair on the top of her head was clipped back in a red bow. They looked very festive.

"You must be Tinkerbell," Kat said. "Are you Walter's girlfriend?"

Tinkerbell sat down right next to Walter, which seemed like confirmation to Kat. She laughed. "You two are *very* cute."

Miguel joined her. "They *are* very cute. Have you met Snowy? She's the cat I got Willie for Christmas."

"No, but I've heard about her."

Miguel pointed to one of the lounge chairs by the pool. The water in the pool was lit up with alternating red and green lights. "She's right over there if you want to say hi. She's very friendly. Not like a dog, but friendly for a cat."

Kat laughed. "I get it."

She walked over. Snowy was a gorgeous creature and she was sprawled on the lounge chair like she was Cleopatra awaiting her attendants. "Hi, there, pretty girl. Can I sit by you?"

Snowy flopped over and curled to one side, showing off her fluffy tummy.

That seemed pretty friendly to Kat. She sat down on the lounge chair and carefully stroked Snowy's belly. "Wow, you are so soft."

She'd never had a cat or a dog, but she'd been

around Toby and now Walter enough to know what a dog felt like. They weren't really soft like this. Was this how all cat fur felt?

Kat kept petting her and Snowy began to purr and knead her paws in the air. Kat heard the slider open, and more people come out, but she was too fascinated with Snowy to pay attention to them.

"What do you think of her?" Miguel asked.

Kat looked up. "She's beautiful. I can't believe how soft she is. Willie must be over the moon about her."

Miguel smiled. "Willie is very happy. We both are."

"You did good by bringing Snowy home. How did you know Willie would like her?"

He sat on the lounge chair next to hers. "I didn't. I took a chance. But that's what life is. You take one chance after the other. You don't know if it will work out until you do it." He shrugged. "So what else can we do but keep trying?"

She nodded. Very true words.

He looked at Snowy. "I got lucky with this one."

Kat nodded. "You sure did. One of my friends at work has a cat and she tells the best stories about him."

"This one," Miguel said with a shake of his head. "She is already making stories."

Kat scratched Snowy under the chin. "I always thought it would be nice to have a dog, but I work so much it wouldn't be fair, you know? But a cat is different. They don't mind being alone as much, do they?"

Miguel laughed. "I'm not sure Snowy would know if she was alone or not. She sleeps all day."

Kat smiled. "Maybe a cat wouldn't be such a bad idea. She's awfully sweet."

But what would Alex think?

Chapter Forty

Willie had never hosted a Christmas dinner attended by this many people. Heck, she'd never hosted any kind of dinner attended by this many people. It was pretty amazing. Made her feel good, all these folks wanting to be at her house. Her dining room table was packed. They'd had to add the extra leaf and some kitchen chairs to accommodate everyone.

Now, sixteen people sat elbow to elbow, but no one looked unhappy about it. Not even Aggie, who'd never met most of them until today. She'd been smiling for quite a while now. Miguel's Christmas punch might have contributed to the general good mood, but Willie had no doubt it was the magic of the season, too.

No one cared that they were tucked in tighter than canned sardines. They were just happy to be here. Happy that they were about to indulge in a delicious meal. Happy to be together.

Miguel sat at the head of the table, Danny at the other end. Willie was at Miguel's right hand, Ivelisse at his left. Willie touched his arm and gave him a little nod, letting him know it was time.

He stood. "Thank you all for coming. Willie and I are so happy you're here. Before we eat, I'd like to say a blessing for the food."

Lots of nods.

He reached out and took Willie's hand. He took Ivelisse's hand as well. Then everyone joined hands and bowed their heads.

Willie paused to watch everyone. They made such a beautiful scene with their heads bowed and hands joined. Like a painting for a Christmas card. Maybe not Norman Rockwell, but something close, and that gave her great pleasure. She'd never been part of that sort of family before, never anything quite this picture perfect, but apparently, she was now.

It really was a Christmas miracle. She bowed her head and Miguel began his prayer.

"Thank you, Lord, for this great day. For the celebration of your son's birth, and for all of these friends and family gathered in our home. Thank you for the hands who prepared this food. Let it nourish us. Thank you that we can all be together."

Willie nodded as the words resonated, her emotions high.

Miguel finished. "In your name, amen."

A chorus of simultaneous amens went up around the table.

Miguel remained standing, smiling at everyone. "Now, we eat. Danny, please carve the turkey. Ethan, if you could do the honors with the ham?"

Both men nodded and stood to do the jobs they'd been given. Trina and Roxie started passing the bowls of side dishes. Christmas music played merrily in the background. The three candles in the centerpiece were lit and casting soft, glowing light over everything. Willie was so happy she could have cried. She sniffed softly and tried to hold herself together.

Miguel's punch was probably contributing to how she was feeling but that didn't mean those emotions weren't real. Granted, she might have had a little more of it than she should have, but the food would soak up the excess soon enough.

It didn't take long for plates to get filled and soon everyone was busy lifting their forks to their mouths.

The food was very good, and the compliments followed, but Willie held her hands up.

She shook her head. "I appreciate all the kind words, but I had nothing to do with the preparation of this food. I'm not that good in the kitchen, as my husband can attest." A few amused snorts interrupted her. "All the credit for this meal goes to my beautiful daughter and granddaughter."

Roxie and Trina smiled.

Miguel cleared his throat. "I did make the punch."

Everyone laughed.

"We know, Dad," Danny said. "We tasted it."

Willie nodded. "You made a fine punch and what a tasty treat it is! But Roxie and Trina deserve all the praise for this meal. And a little to Publix, I suppose, for supplying the ingredients."

She sipped her punch before going on, enjoying having everyone's attention. "Claire and Danny have been gracious enough to bring dessert, so I can't take credit for any of that, either."

"All Claire," Danny said. "I'm just the eye candy who fills orders and rings people up."

Laughing, Claire shook her head. "I'd say he was wrong, but he's really not, so..." She shrugged.

"Mom!" Kat snorted.

Willie grinned, pleased that everyone was so at ease with each other.

The rest of the meal was just as lively and entertaining. Plates were refilled and laughter often made the Christmas carols in the background impossible to hear. Willie wouldn't have had it any other way. Her heart was full.

At least twice, Miguel took her hand and gave it a squeeze. His way of saying how happy he was. Even Aggie, who'd been a little reluctant to come, seemed to be having a great time.

Willie had made sure to seat her next to Conrad's sister, Dinah. The two seemed to be getting on famously. Willie was happy about that. Aggie certainly could use a few more friends. Dinah, too, maybe.

As the meal wound down, there were soft groans and unconvincing complaints of having eaten too much. Plates were pushed back, but no one left the table. Maybe they were all too comfortable. Or maybe no one wanted to be the first to leave.

While Willie was happy to sit there as long as folks wanted, she knew her job as hostess. Not only was the living room more comfortable and spacious, but the food needed to be put away. She stood. "There's plenty of room for everyone in the living room. Why don't you all go in and relax while this gets cleaned up? Then, in a little while, we'll have coffee and dessert. We have eggnog, too."

Danny put his hand on his stomach. "I couldn't eat another bite."

Claire pursed her lips. "We all know that's not true."

Miguel chuckled and wiped his mouth before setting his napkin next to his plate. "We can spread out in the living room a bit, too."

"I'll help clean up," Ivelisse said.

"So will I," Kat volunteered.

"I don't mind helping," Ethan said.

"Don't worry about it," Roxie said to him. "We've got this."

They shooed the men out and the young women got to work cleaning up. Willie hooked her arm through Aggie's. "Come on. You, too, Dinah. Let's go supervise the men. You never know what they'll get up to on their own."

Dinah nodded from her seat. "Be there in a second."

Aggie glanced back at the table. "Shouldn't we help, too?"

Willie shook her head. "At our age, we've earned the right not to help."

"Ma's right," Roxie said, a stack of plates in her hands. "You two go on and relax. We've got this."

Aggie shrugged, smiling. "If you insist."

Willie walked with her to the living room, where everyone was taking seats. Snowy had found a safe spot under the Christmas tree. Aggie paused them at the entrance.

She held fast to Willie's arm. "I'm so glad your little cat dragged you into my yard and we met." She swallowed. "I needed this. It's been so long since anyone cared what happened to me on any day of the year, let alone Christmas, and I..."

Aggie sniffed, her brown eyes lined with tears.

"Don't go doing that," Willie said. "Or I'll be crying right along with you. I'm so glad we met. You're welcome in this house anytime. I want you to know that. I mean it, too. You feel lonely or bored or whatever, you come knock on our door."

Aggie nodded and managed to say, "Thanks." She composed herself. "You're a good egg, Willie Rojas."

Willie grinned. "Well, I've certainly been called worse."

Aggie's gaze drifted into the living room and toward the Christmas tree. "I've been thinking about

Snowy. She's such a good companion for you, isn't she?"

"She's the best non-human company I've ever had."

"Do you think maybe next week, you and Miguel would take me to the same rescue? I think I'd like to see if there's a cat that I could adopt."

Willie sucked in a breath. "Oh, Aggie, that's a fantastic idea. We would love that. Of course, we'll take you. I'm sort of excited to see where she came from myself. I've never been there."

Aggie sniffed again. "Thank you."

Willie patted her arm. "How about a little more Christmas punch?"

Aggie laughed. "Only if you promise to walk me home."

Willie nodded. "It's a deal."

Chapter Forty-one

*J*ules relaxed in front of the white marble fireplace, sinking deeper into the navy leather couch and a little closer to Jesse. Shiloh and Toby, both full of turkey, were snoring on the white shag rug close enough to the flames to literally be hot dogs, but they didn't seem to mind the heat one bit.

Jesse kissed the side of her head. "This was a *really* nice thing of you to do."

She smiled. "I think that's the third time you've said that."

"Give me a minute, I'm sure I'll say it again."

She just sighed contentedly. The house she'd rented as a Christmas surprise for her band in Kansas City had not been cheap, but it was definitely worth it. Not only did they all have their own bedrooms, but the living room was more than big enough for them all to gather.

The house was not exactly decorated to her taste, but it was still beautiful with its clean, white walls and touches of white marble, stainless steel, and deep blue accents.

All that mattered was that everyone was happy. And they were.

After the show at the Grand Ole Opry, which she would never forget if she lived to be a hundred, she'd made everyone get back on the bus. That wasn't how they usually did things unless they had a show the next day, but she'd let Chuck, their tour bus driver, in on the surprise. He'd been more than happy to go along.

There had been some grumbling from the band, because they *didn't* have a show until the day after and they'd been expecting to go to a hotel and crash. Instead, Chuck had told everyone he was worried about holiday traffic, so he wanted to get started toward Kansas City, their next gig.

But the truth was, Jules had wanted everyone to be able to spend Christmas in a place that, while it wasn't home, felt more like a home than a hotel room. A place where they could all be together.

So she'd rented this big house and paid the

management extra to set up a Christmas tree and put a wreath on the door. She'd also paid them to stock the fridge with two complete heat-and-eat Christmas dinner packages.

The management had complied, mostly because she'd paid the fee, not because she was Julia Bloom, and so, here they were.

Because of that extra help, Jules and her band had been able to sit down to a real Christmas meal today. They'd had ham, turkey, and all the fixings, including pumpkin pie and chocolate cake. Even jugs of eggnog and local cider. The food had been great, but the fellowship had been sweeter. It had been so good, they'd eaten the meal twice. Once for lunch, and again as leftovers for dinner.

It was easily the biggest and best surprise she'd ever pulled off.

Her slide guitar player, Rita, was in the chair closest to the fire, knitting a baby blanket in pastel shades of blue and green for her daughter, who'd shared the happy news earlier that Rita was going to be a grandma to a little boy in late June.

Cash and Sierra were at the dining room table, putting together a puzzle they'd found in the closet. Jules had a feeling that any second they were going to announce they were missing pieces, but so far, not a word. Just the soft banter of two newly engaged lovebirds having a wonderful first Christmas together.

Jules understood the feeling.

Bobby, her fiddler, was stretched out in the recliner and most likely asleep, judging by the fact that his eyes were closed. He'd talked to his wife and boys earlier. Frankie, the banjo player, was on the loveseat, texting with his brother in Dallas.

The big-screen television over the mantel was on with the sound down, but *Miracle on 34th Street* was playing and there wasn't much sound needed. Classic movies were classics for a reason.

Toby got up, stretched, then lay down again, this time so he was back-to-back with Shiloh. The cuteness was almost too much.

Jesse hugged her closer. "Merry Christmas, Jules. This sure has been a good one. Never in my wildest dreams did I think I'd ever be backstage at the Grand Ole Opry watching my fiancée perform in front of a packed house. That was something I will never forget."

She nodded. "Me, either. Out of everything that's happened this year, I think it's my favorite memory."

"Even more than being on the cover of *Rebel Yell*?"

"Even more than that."

"Even more than being nominated for an American Music Award?"

She smiled. "Close, but even more than that."

He hesitated. "Even more than me asking you to marry me?"

She looked up at him. "No, not more than that."

He exhaled. "Good to know."

"I can't wait to marry you. And not just because Shiloh needs a mother."

He laughed and sank down beside her even more. "The feeling is mutual. Although maybe we shouldn't tell Toby that he's about to be related by marriage to his girlfriend."

"Agreed," Jules said.

"Well, I guess I should give this to you before Christmas is over." He shifted, reaching into his chest pocket, and pulled out a small black velvet box.

"Jesse, what have you done? We said no presents."

"*You* said no presents. I never agreed to that."

Knitting away, Rita laughed. "He's got you there, Jules."

"Don't you go being on his side." Jules smiled and

took the box. She opened it, revealing an incredible sapphire and diamond heart pendant. It glittered in the firelight, almost looking alive. Her mouth came open, but she had no breath and no words for a moment.

"Do you like it?" Jesse asked.

She nodded and swallowed. "It's gorgeous. And too much. But I love it. Thank you." She sat up. "Help me put it on."

Jesse took the necklace and attached the clasp while she lifted her hair. "Only the best for my bride-to-be. I was thinking it could be your something blue."

She touched the pendant where it lay around her neck. "It's perfect. It is definitely going to be my something blue."

She stood. "Don't go anywhere. I'll be right back."

Without waiting for his response, she ran upstairs to her room and got the present she'd bought for him despite saying no gifts. It had just been too hard to stick to. And she'd stumbled upon the perfect thing without really meaning to.

She ran back downstairs with the manila envelope in hand. "I didn't get a chance to wrap it, but you probably don't care about that, do you?"

"No." He took the envelope, shooting her a wary look. "Didn't we just have a talk about no gifts?"

"Yes, but I knew you wouldn't stick to it, so I had to get you something."

Rita laughed again. "You two. So made for each other."

He lifted the flap and pulled out the contents. He stared at it for a moment. "Is this...real?"

She nodded and sat down next to him again. "It is. There's a letter of authenticity included."

"Wow." The word came out on a long breath.

She'd never seen Jesse quite so serious before.

"What is it?" Rita asked.

Jesse turned the photo around. "An autographed picture of Johnny Cash. Can you believe it?"

"Dang, you two give good gifts." Rita shook her head. "Very nice."

He smiled at Jules. "I love it. I can't wait to frame it and hang it up in my office. Thank you."

"You're welcome. I always wanted a signed photo of the Man in Black." She winked at him. "Now I have one."

He laughed. "You're right, you do. What's mine is yours. Does that mean we're definitely going to live in my place after we're married?"

"It does. So long as that's still all right with you."

"It's perfect with me. I like that we're only a few houses away from your sister and Danny, and Kat, too."

Jules nodded. "Soon, they'll be married. So will Cash and Sierra. Before you know it, we'll all be married." She smiled into the fire before looking at him. "Things are good, aren't they? I mean, *really* good."

He nodded. "We are so blessed."

"We are more blessed than I ever imagined we could be. And something tells me this is just the beginning."

Chapter Forty-two

Roxie sat with Ethan out on the lanai near one of the propane heaters. With that radiating heat, plus her jacket, and Ethan's arm around her, she was plenty warm. She glanced his way. "You're not cold, are you?"

He shook his head. "Hard to be cold sitting next to the hottest woman in Diamond Beach."

She smirked. He was always so complimentary. Always building her up. She'd never had a man who made her feel so good about herself. "You're very kind. And very silly."

His brows lifted as he wiggled them. "And you're very beautiful. I have to compensate somehow."

"Ethan, you're one of the best-looking men in this town."

He tipped his head as if he was bowing to her. "High praise."

All she could do was smile and snuggle closer. If she loved him any harder, she'd burst. "It's so pretty here, isn't it?"

Many of the houses on the canal had gone the extra mile with their Christmas lights, decorating the back of their homes as well as the front. The lights reflected off the water, doubling them, and making the entire waterway seem like a Christmas wonderland.

It was magical. Seeing it by boat would have been amazing. Next year maybe. Her mom and Miguel were talking about getting one.

"We still haven't exchanged gifts, you know."

"I know," he answered. "You've been a little busy. We all have been. Want to do it now?"

All she had for him was a certificate for the cooking classes, but it was in her purse, so she definitely could. "Sure. I just need to run inside for a second."

"Me, too." He lifted his arm from around her shoulders. "Meet you back here in a few?"

"Yep."

They went inside together. Things had quieted down a bit with Kat, Trina, and the dogs gone. Ivelisse had taken her kids home, too. Roxie had made sure to send her with a large container of leftovers, which Ivelisse had been thankful for. There was no way Willie and Miguel could eat all of that.

Roxie would take some home herself, and send more with Danny and Claire, if they'd take them. She hated seeing food go to waste. Maybe Aggie would take some, too.

She peeked into the living room. Miguel, Willie, Danny, Claire, Margo, Dinah, Conrad, and Aggie were all still in there, talking. Some about the bakery, but also about the book that Conrad and Margo were writing.

She went back to the kitchen and got the certificate in its envelope from her purse. She'd stuck her purse away in a corner next to the fridge, so it wouldn't be in the way of all the food prep. She looked around for Ethan. She wasn't sure where he had gone after he'd walked through the kitchen. Out to his car, maybe?

She took the envelope back to the lanai and sat in her seat to wait for him. He came out about a minute after her, carrying a silver and white striped gift bag stuffed with silver-flecked tissue paper.

"Very fancy," she said.

"I can't take any credit for the way this looks. The girl at the store did it." He handed the bag over. "You go first."

"Okay." She took the bag. It had more weight than she expected. She pulled out the tissue and found a long, white box underneath.

Instinctively, she knew it was jewelry. She looked at him. "I hope you didn't spend a lot of money on me."

His eyes narrowed. "Not even married yet and already bossing me around?" His mouth quirked up in obvious amusement. "Woman, I make good money. Don't worry about what I spent. Besides, it's Christmas. And like I said, I can afford it."

She smiled. "You're right, I'm sorry. I'm just...I don't know. Too concerned about what things cost, because it used to matter a lot more." At least to Bryan.

Ethan put his hand on her leg. "I get it. And you don't need to apologize. Now, open your moderately expensive present."

Laughing, she took the box out and lifted the top. She inhaled. "Oh, Ethan." Inside lay a gold and diamond link bracelet that was prettier than anything she'd ever seen, outside of her engagement ring.

"You like it?"

"No, I love it. It's *so* elegant." To her, it looked like

it had cost a million bucks. "And it goes beautifully with my ring!"

He nodded. "Came from the same place. I saw it when I got your ring, and I knew then you should have it, too."

She couldn't believe it. "It's so sparkly." She fastened it around her wrist, making sure to secure the safety catch, then turned her wrist so it caught the light. "Look at all that glitter!"

"Last time I checked, you liked sparkly, glittery things."

"Still do. Love them, actually." She twisted toward him and took his face in her hands so she could give him a really big kiss. "You're the only non-sparkly, non-glittery thing I love."

"And for that, I am eternally grateful." He kissed her back.

"Also, I'm not calling you a liar, but there is no way that bracelet was *moderately* expensive." She smiled at him. Her wonderful, indulgent, generous fiancé. "But I don't care, because you said you can afford it and it's Christmas."

"That's right." He pulled her close, his soapy fresh scent surrounding her. "I just want to make you happy. Always."

"You do that without even trying. No gifts needed." She snuggled next to him. "I love you."

"I love you, too."

She knew her present for him couldn't compare to the bracelet on her wrist. Now she was a little reluctant to give it to him, but what else could she do? She handed him the envelope. "It's nothing like what you—"

"Uh-uh," Ethan said, shaking his head. "No comparisons. This isn't a competition. I don't care what you spent. I don't even want that to matter. I don't want things to work like that between us."

She nodded. "No, you're right. I don't, either."

"Did your gift come from the heart?"

"Yes."

He shrugged. "Then nothing else matters."

"Agreed." She still felt unsure. "I hope you like it."

He opened the envelope and took out the certificate. He held it closer to the light of the propane heater to read it better. After a moment, he looked at her. "You got us joint cooking classes?"

She couldn't read his expression or his tone. She lifted one shoulder hesitantly. "I thought it would be a fun thing to do together. Plus, it would give us some new dishes to make for dinner."

He shook his head. "This is so much better than that bracelet."

"What?" She laughed. "No, it isn't."

"Yes, it is. This is a *whole* series of classes. Five nights that we get to be together, learning a new thing, and obviously being the best-looking couple in the class. It's amazing. You're amazing. How did I get so lucky?"

She cut her eyes at him. "Do you really like it? Or are you just saying all of that for my benefit?"

"I love it. I can't wait to get started. And not just because I look so good in a chef's hat."

She chuckled at his silliness, her heart light that he was so pleased with her gift. "I don't think they give us chef hats to wear."

"So I have to bring my own?"

She threw her arms around his neck, noticing the glints of light her bracelet threw off. "Never change, Ethan. You make me so happy."

He embraced her. "It feels like my purpose in life. To love you and spoil you and support you in whatever you want to do. I've never had a relationship like this before where it felt like no matter how much I gave, I got more back."

He put a little space between them and looked into her eyes. "My life is much better with you in it."

"So is mine. And my mom's. And Trina's. You're such a big part of our family now, sweetheart. I can't imagine where we'd be without you. Certainly not where we are now."

He took her hands in his and looked at her engagement ring. "I never told you this, but right before I met you, I was thinking about moving away from Diamond Beach. There were so many memories here and most of them weren't good ones."

She held onto his hands and let him talk.

"Now I think about what I would have missed out on and..." He sighed. Then he smiled at her. "I guess I'm just trying to say thank you."

She smiled right back. "You're a good man, Ethan. I thank God for you a lot. And when I think that you're going to be my husband?" She inhaled deeply, trying not to cry. "I know that I'm blessed."

"We have so much to look forward to. It's been a long time since I've celebrated the new year. This year? I'm actually looking forward to it."

"So am I." She was looking forward to a lot of things these days. And all of them included Ethan.

Chapter Forty-three

It was almost nine when Margo and Conrad finally got home. They'd stopped to drop Dinah off. She'd talked nonstop on the ride back about what a nice evening she'd had and how she and Aggie were making plans to get together to play cards.

Margo was happy for her. Willie had done a good thing by seating the two women next to each other. It had been a wonderful Christmas. Still was, technically. But it had also been a long day. It was good to be home.

She put her purse on the table by the door as Conrad locked up. "If you don't mind, I'm going to get ready for bed, then that's exactly what I'm going to do."

He nodded. "Long day. Longer for you, because you made breakfast for everyone this morning."

She smiled. "Good day, though. And Dinah did help me."

He took her in his arms. "It was a very good day. One of the best Christmases I've had in a long time. Thank you for including Dinah in everything. That was...a big thing. Means a lot to me that you did that."

Margo rested her arms on his shoulders. "She's family. Why wouldn't I have included her?"

"For a lot of reasons. But you did. And I am grateful for that. I'm grateful you consider her family, too." He kissed her before letting her go. "I never thought I'd see the day that Dinah had a life of her own. A real life."

They walked into the bedroom together. Margo flipped on the light. "I have to admit, I was a little worried about her moving here."

"I know you were. I was, too. But getting that job at the bakery was huge. Whatever we got Claire for Christmas, it probably wasn't enough."

Margo chuckled. "We got her a gift certificate for the Brighton Arms spa. Enough that she can have at least two treatments."

His brows rose. "That sounds pretty good."

"It is, I promise." Giving Dinah the job had been

a big deal. Margo thought her daughter deserved some appreciation for that.

Conrad pulled off his Christmas sweater. "Dinah sure hit it off with Aggie. You think anything will come of that?"

"You're probably better equipped to answer that than I am. Is your sister in the habit of making dates she doesn't keep?"

"She's not in the habit of making dates at all, so it's hard to say. I hope she does, though."

Margo nodded as she slipped off her jewelry. "So do I. Aggie was a bit of a lost soul, wasn't she? Poor thing. I know what it's like to go through that feeling of limbo after your husband dies. It takes a while just to figure out who you are. A new friend can be a good thing."

"Well, Dinah could use a friend, too." Conrad changed into his pajamas. He patted his stomach, which was as trim as any man half his age. "I ate too much today, but I don't regret it. Every bite was delicious."

"I agree." She took off her black slacks and black and white striped sweater, replacing them with her nightgown and robe. "But I'm going to be careful with my choices the rest of the week."

She went into the bathroom to wash her face,

apply her eye cream and moisturizer, and brush her teeth.

He joined her, going to his sink. "Do you want to write tomorrow? Or did you have other plans?"

She shook her head, catching his gaze in the mirror. "I want to write. We need to make progress on the second book."

He smiled. "So do I. You up for a little TV in bed or do you want to go right to sleep?"

She'd actually been thinking about reading, but she doubted she'd get more than a paragraph or two in before she fell asleep. "A little television would be fine. Anything you want to watch. Even sports."

Laughing, he picked up his toothbrush. "Now I *know* it's Christmas."

Amused, she shook her head at him.

A few minutes later, they were both in bed, settling in and adjusting pillows. Conrad turned on the television and scrolled until he found his favorite sports commentary show.

Margo looked through Facebook, smiling at all the festive photos her friends had posted. Photographs of Christmas trees, table settings, gathered family and all kinds of food.

She hadn't posted any, but she had taken quite a few. She found a couple in her Gallery, some from the morning here at the house, and some from Willie's this evening. She added them to her account with the simple caption, *A wonderful Christmas with family and friends.*

It *had* been a wonderful Christmas. She'd talked to Fen right before they'd gone to Willie's, who'd told her she was going to be a great-grandmother, then Jules and Cash, and spent time with Claire and Kat.

But really, her family was so much bigger now. Danny would soon be her son-in-law, which meant Miguel and his family were about to be even closer. That meant Willie, too. And Willie's family.

What an odd, strange, amazing journey they'd all been on this year.

"Margo? You still awake?"

She nodded. "Just lost in thought. Sorry."

"Nothing to apologize for. Everything all right?"

She smiled at him. "Everything is perfect. I was just thinking about this past year and what a curious adventure it's been."

"You can say that again."

"In the beginning, I was furious with Bryan when I found out about Roxie, but now..." She stared at the television without really seeing the picture. "If it hadn't been for Willie pushing me to get back into the world, I never would have met you."

He grinned. "What did we get her for Christmas?"

"A cashmere scarf."

"Fancy."

"I had a coupon. It wasn't as expensive as you think."

He laughed. "I'm all right with whatever you spent. You have your own money anyway."

It was true. She did. So did he. But she also didn't mind him being in charge of the finances. He was excellent with them. Maybe even a little tighter than she was, which was probably a good thing.

She reached over and took his hand. "I'm looking forward to working on the new book, but I'm really looking forward to the challenge of getting *The Widow* published. It's scary. But exciting, too."

He held her hand, gazing into her eyes. "That's how I felt dating you."

She would have laughed, but she could tell he was being serious. "You were scared of dating me? You're not afraid of anything."

He nodded, his sports show forgotten. "It was because I knew you were someone special. But I also knew you weren't looking for a relationship. I kept thinking, here is this incredible woman and if I don't impress her, she's going to disappear from my life. My shot will be gone."

"Oh, Conrad. I don't know if that's true... although..." She sighed. "I wasn't in a great place when we first met. You're right that I wasn't looking for a relationship, either. But you were too special to ignore."

"Fortunately for me."

Her smile returned. "And then, before I knew it, I'd fallen in love with you."

"There was no getting rid of me then."

"By then, I didn't want to." Impulsively, she inched closer until she was touching him, and put her head on his shoulder. "Life is funny sometimes, isn't it?"

"Funny and wonderful and really, really good." He rested his cheek on the top of her head. "I thought I'd spend the rest of mine alone. And now, here I am, married to an outstanding woman with an incredible family, and we're about to publish a book."

She patted his chest before slipping her arm around him. "Next year will be interesting, won't it?"

"My darling, every day with you is interesting."

Chapter Forty-four

Trina laughed as the fire station crew tossed chew toys for Walter and Tinkerbell to play fetch with. Tinkerbell wasn't as good at the game as Walter was. She only returned the toy when she felt like it, which seemed to be every third or fourth time. Mostly she just ran around with the toy in her mouth.

Tinkerbell was also easily distracted by the guys who called her name, running over to them for pets and belly rubs. That was about the only way they could get the toy back to throw it again.

Kat stood next to Trina, a glass of punch in her hand. Unlike what Miguel had made, this one was non-alcoholic. Just Hawaiian punch, Sprite, and something else Larry, the station cook, had added in. Sherbert, maybe, Trina thought. Whatever he'd put in there, it was tasty.

"Bringing the dogs was a great idea," Kat said. "Although I bet they're both asleep before we go home. This has been a big day for them."

"That's for sure," Trina said. "For all of us, really." She smiled at her sister. How amazing was it that this Christmas she had a sister to hang out with? "Did you have a good day?"

Kat nodded. "I had a great day. Even with Dad not being here, it's been a good Christmas. Still is. You?"

"Same. So good. I do miss Dad, but he hadn't been around much for holidays these last few years anyway. I guess because of Paulina. That probably made this year easier, you know?"

"Yeah." Kat nodded. "I was thinking the same thing. I'm not mad, though. If anything, I feel for Nico. He'll never get to know his father."

"No, poor thing." She watched the guys playing with the dogs. What was it about dogs that brought the kid out in people? "I think it's helped, too, that I got to spend some time with Miles."

"Same. Seeing Alex has been just what I needed."

Just then, Miles, Alex, and a couple of the other guys came in from doing something with one of the trucks.

"Speaking of," Kat said. "I'm going to hang with him. Just like I'm sure you're going to be with that guy." Kat pointed to Miles as he walked toward them.

Trina nodded. "Yep. Have fun." Miles reached her side.

"You, too." Kat went toward Alex, who was waiting for her by the kitchen door.

"Hey," Miles said. "You want some cookies? Larry's making a fresh batch of chocolate chip. He does it every year for Christmas."

"Is that why Alex and Kat are headed into the kitchen?"

He nodded. "Yep. The cookies have to be made. We were going to help. Unless you don't want to."

She did, but she felt like she had a responsibility to the dogs, too. She glanced at them.

Miles obviously understood. "They'll be okay. The guys will watch them."

"I know, but Tinkerbell isn't even my dog."

Miles turned. "Ritter, keep an eye on Walter and Tinkerbell. Trina and I are going to help with the cookies. Anything happens to those dogs and you're cleaning the bathrooms for the next two weeks."

Ritter, a young man with a baby face that made him look even younger, nodded sharply. "Yes, sir."

Miles looked at Trina and smiled. "Rookie. The dogs will be fine."

"All right." She glanced at Ritter. "Thank you."

"Yes, ma'am."

She and Miles went into the kitchen. "He's very polite."

"He has to be. He's a rookie. He needs to dot every I and cross every T until he's proven himself."

Alex and Kat were at the counter, stirring batter in a big stainless-steel bowl. Ingredients were already on the counter. Larry was lining large cookie sheets with parchment paper.

He stopped to hand Miles another big bowl. "Here you go. We need another batch, just like the first."

Kat held up a three-ring binder. "We have the recipe. And all the measuring cups and spoons."

"Okay," Trina said. But baking wasn't really her thing. She didn't want to mess this up. Not when the whole station was going to be eating them. Suddenly, she understood how Ritter felt.

She and Miles read over the recipe before doing anything. Then they carefully measured ingredients and cracked eggs. He stirred everything together with a big wooden spoon. Finally, they were ready to add the chips.

While Trina was measuring out the exact amount, Kat and Alex's first batch had been scooped out on the cookie sheets and gone into the oven. The warm, chocolatey aroma had begun to waft through the kitchen.

"Boy, those smell good," Trina said, tipping the cup of chocolate chips into the bowl. "I can't believe with everything I ate today that I'm actually hungry for a cookie, but I am."

Miles mixed the chocolate bits in. "Good dinner at your grandma's?"

"Really good," Trina answered. "Would have been better with you there."

He smiled. "Next year. I promise."

The cookies didn't take long and soon the timer dinged that they were ready. Larry used his heat-proof mitts to take the trays out of the oven.

"Don't touch," he warned as he brought them to the counter. "These are plenty hot."

Despite telling them not to touch, he deftly slid the parchment paper and cookies off each sheet by grabbing an edge and pulling them onto cooling racks, freeing up the sheets for the next batch.

He put new parchment paper down before looking at Miles. "You think you and Trina can handle scooping out the cookies?"

Trina grabbed the scooper from Kat. It looked just like an ice cream scoop and might have been in a previous life. "We're ready."

"Have at it," Larry said. "Just space them out evenly."

She and Miles quickly filled the trays with nice, fat scoops of cookie dough, lining them up as neatly as possible.

As soon as the trays were full, Larry popped them back in the oven and set the timer. "All right, go on back out. I'll plate these up and get the milk out."

Trina laughed. "Milk and cookies?"

Larry nodded. "We stay up all night just like Santa does, so we deserve them, too."

She liked that idea. "You sure do."

A few minutes later, Larry came into the lounge. "Milk and cookies. Come and get 'em."

Trina was sitting with Miles. Walter and Tinker-bell were on the couch with them, fast asleep.

"I'll get us some," Miles said. "You stay with the dogs."

"Okay."

He returned shortly with two cups of milk and a plate of cookies balanced on top of one. "They're still warm."

"I hope we didn't forget anything in the recipe and we got it right." She glanced around. She had no idea which batch of cookies was theirs, but everyone who was eating them seemed to be reacting in a positive way. Not like the sugar had accidentally been replaced with salt or anything like that.

Miles carefully sat down and offered her the plate.

She took it so he could stop balancing it and set it on her lap.

Walter immediately woke up, his little nose twitching.

"Nope," Trina said. "Not for you, baby. Sorry. Chocolate's no good for you."

"It's good for me, though," Miles said. He took a bite of a cookie, nearly devouring half of it. After a couple of chews, he nodded. "We did good."

"How do you know those aren't Kat and Alex's cookies?"

"I don't. Well, one of us did good."

She smiled and grabbed a cookie, trying one for herself. He was right. They were good. Was there anything better than a warm chocolate chip cookie?

Larry stood in the kitchen door, eating one. He lifted it. "Nice work. Thanks for helping."

"You're welcome," Trina called out. She looked at

Miles. "This is a good life, isn't it? All these guys are really like your extended family."

"They are, in a lot of ways."

A new thought came to her. "Does that mean when I marry you, I'm really marrying all of them?"

He laughed. "Heck, no. I'm not sharing you with anyone." Cookies and milk gone, he set the cups and the plate on the floor and tugged her nearer. "I can't wait for that."

"Being married?"

He nodded.

"I know what you mean." For most of her life, she'd thought marriage might not be in the cards for her. Now, here she was, with a great guy, a new business, a puppy, and family she never knew she had.

That was why she hadn't needed anything for Christmas. She'd already gotten more than she could have dreamed of.

Chapter Forty-five

After tasting their handiwork, Kat and Alex went out into the garage where the trucks were to have a moment for themselves. As much as she loved hanging out with the whole crew, there were times she just wanted to be with him alone.

That wasn't really possible when they were at the firehouse, unless they found a spot away from everyone else.

The garage was as good as anyplace. The doors were up, letting in the chilly night air, but Kat didn't mind. She had a sweater on. And Alex was close by if she needed his arm around her.

They sat on the bumper of Engine 2 and stared out at the night. Beyond the lights of the station, stars were visible in the dark expanse of the evening sky.

"Pretty night," Kat said.

Alex nodded. "Before you, I used to come sit out here a lot and look at that sky. Never thought I'd do it with my future wife by my side."

She smiled. "Yeah?"

"Yeah." He winked at her.

"What did you do when you sat out here?"

He shrugged. "Just think. About life and stuff like that." He got a slightly embarrassed look on his face. "Sometimes about the waves I'd caught that day. How good the ride was. Or how I could have done better."

"Hey, I can totally see that. I think about that sometimes at work. It's a good distraction."

His expression morphed into something more serious. "I also used to think a lot about my future. If I'd be a firefighter forever or if I'd end up doing something different. If I'd ever find a good woman. If I'd get married, have kids, all those sorts of things. Didn't you think about that stuff, too?"

She shook her head. "Not really. I pretty much had all those answers already. Or at least I thought I did with Ray."

"Right."

"My life was pretty much mapped out for me." She let out a long exhale. "I'm so happy he was not my path."

"That makes two of us."

She slipped her arm through his. "There aren't enough words for me to tell you how grateful I am that you stopped to talk to me that day on the beach."

He smiled. "I'm more happy you talked back."

"I almost didn't."

He snorted. "Yeah, you made it pretty clear you weren't interested."

"Good thing you don't give up so easy."

"We were meant to be."

"I think so, too."

They sat quietly for a few moments. She thought about that first meeting on the beach. She'd still been reeling from the news that her father had had a second family and that she had a sister she'd never known about.

Alex had appeared almost out of nowhere, offering her a flyer about a sandcastle building contest. She hadn't intended to go, but Trina had kind of talked Kat into it and the next thing she knew, Alex was in her life.

"You've done so much for me," she said softly. "Thank you. You really did change my life for the better."

"I can say the same thing about you."

She pursed her lips. Other than being his girl-friend, she wasn't sure what she'd done to make his life better. "You can say it, but it's not really true."

"Yes, it is. I'm way happier now and that's because of you. I mean, I'm engaged to a girl who understands what it means to be involved with a fireman and doesn't mind. You were with me when I got injured, helped me when I needed it, and took amazing care of me. Plus, you like to surf. With me."

"All because you taught me."

"Yeah, but you did the hard work of learning and overcoming your fears about the water." He brushed a strand of hair out of her eyes. "You're something, Kat. You inspire me. You make me want to be a better man."

She was touched by his words. "Alex, you're already a great guy."

"Thanks. But watching you go after a new job and being unafraid of changing your life so drasti-cally, that was pretty cool. Who does that? Not a lot of people. But you not only did it, you did it fearlessly."

She laughed softly. "I hate to tell you this, but I had plenty of fears and plenty of doubts. It *was* scary."

"No doubt. But you still did it."

She hugged his arm. "You helped me with that."

"I did?"

She nodded. "You were my inspiration. I just saw the way you lived your life and that made me realize I wanted mine to be different. It had to be if I was ever going to be truly happy. And now I am."

He smiled. "I'm glad. I want you to be happy. I want us to be happy together."

"I don't think that's going to be a problem. Not that I think marriage will be easy. I know it takes work and commitment and all of that, but I'm ready. I was never ready to marry Ray, but I was ready to marry you a long time before you asked."

His smile grew bigger. "We're going to have such a good life."

"We are. About that..." She really wanted to talk to him about her new idea.

"What? If this is about me moving in with you at the beach house, you know I have no issues with that."

"I know. But this is about something else. About us getting a pet."

His eyes narrowed. "I thought you decided you weren't home enough to have a dog."

"I did. And that's still true. But how do you feel about maybe getting a cat? Hear me out. Willie,

Trina's grandmother, got a cat from her husband for Christmas."

Alex nodded. "Cool gift."

"Very. I met Snowy today. She's all white and so unbelievably beautiful, and she's, like, the coolest little animal ever. Very chill, loves hanging out and getting pets and belly rubs. And so, *so* soft."

"Cats are cool. Larry has a cat. Big Head Fred."

Kat started laughing so hard she almost fell off the bumper. "Big Head Fred? I've never heard Larry talk about him."

"Oh, trust me. Just ask him one question about Fred and you'll know everything you ever wanted to know about that cat or any other cat." Alex rolled his eyes good-naturedly. "He loves talking about him. And showing you pictures of him. But you should see him. Fred is a beast. He's some kind of coon cat."

"Maine Coon?"

"Yeah, that's it. He's huge. Like, twenty-two pounds or something."

"Wow, he might be bigger than Toby."

"He is," Alex said. "But he's all right. Just a big mush, really." He stared out at the night again. "Yeah, I could see getting a cat. They're easier to take care of than dogs. You don't have to walk them."

"Willie walks hers. On a leash. Like a dog."

Alex glanced at Kat. "Of course, she does."

"That is the Willie way." She leaned in again. "You're really okay with getting a cat? It's as much of a commitment as getting a dog. Litter boxes and all that."

"I'm a hundred percent okay with it. On one condition."

"Which is?"

"We pick the cat out together."

"Absolutely. I wouldn't want to do it any other way."

"Then let's go day after tomorrow. I'm off. There's got to be a rescue in town, right?"

Kat nodded right away. "There is. The one where Walter came from. Same place where Miguel got Snowy."

"Perfect. You want to go? Are you ready to adopt?"

She nodded. "I am." She couldn't stop smiling.

He was smiling, too. "Might be good practice for the future, huh?"

She knew what he meant. He was talking about having kids. "Yeah," she said softly, already thinking about what that would be like. She wrapped her hands around his arm and kissed his cheek. "Might be very good practice indeed."

Chapter Forty-six

Claire and Danny were almost the last to leave Miguel and Willie's. Roxie and Ethan were still there, but they'd said they were headed out shortly, too.

Danny drove them home. Claire spent most of the ride looking out the window at all the bright, cheery Christmas lights. They washed over the car in a kaleidoscope of colors. "Diamond Beach really goes all out for the holidays, doesn't it?"

"It does." He nodded. "Lots of Christmas lovers here. Pretty, don't you think?"

"Very," Claire agreed. "Anyone who doesn't like Christmas lights has something wrong with them."

He turned toward their houses. "Wouldn't be Christmas without them." He glanced at her. "Sleepy? It's late. At least for us."

"I should be." Claire didn't mind the late night.

The bakery was closed tomorrow. She could sleep in. Although she wasn't sure her body would let her. Her internal clock had been reprogrammed to wake her up early.

"But you're not?"

"No. Too wired from the day, I guess. Although, honestly, I just don't want it to end."

He pulled into the driveway of the beach house, parked, and turned off the engine. "It doesn't have to."

"No?"

"We could go for a walk on the beach. Make Christmas last a little longer."

"I love that idea. But I want to put on a hat." The last thing Claire wanted was to catch a cold.

"Smart move. I'll do that, too. And probably wear my heavier jacket."

"And I'm going to change into sneakers." She'd ruin her flats if she walked on the wet sand in them.

"So basically, we're changing then meeting back here?"

She laughed. "Yes. Five minutes." She opened her door, knowing he needed to move the car to his own driveway.

"Five minutes. I'll meet you by the pool. Your pool."

"You got it." She hopped out and went straight to the elevator while he started the car and went next door to his house.

Upstairs, she quickly changed into jeans, a sweatshirt with her coat over it, sneakers, and then added a hat that covered her ears. She thought about gloves, but it wasn't *that* cold, and she didn't want to miss out on holding Danny's hand. That would keep her warm enough.

Kat wasn't home yet, but Claire hadn't expected her to be. Young people, especially those who didn't have to get up before sunrise on a regular basis, didn't mind late nights. Claire went out the back sliders and down the spiral steps.

Danny was already there by the pool, waiting for her. He was in jeans, sneakers, and an old Army surplus peacoat that somehow looked like a designer label on him. "That was fast."

"I had good motivation." She joined him. "Ready?"

"Almost." He reached for her, drawing her in against his chest to kiss her. Then he wrapped his arms around her and held her close.

She rested her head against his, content to just be. When he finally let her go, she looked up at him. "What was all that about?"

His smile had the enigmatic look she'd come to understand was a sign of deep joy within him. "Just because I can." He held out his hand. "Ready to walk?"

"I am." She shook her head, smiling, and joined her hand with his.

"I have a flashlight in case we need it, but it seems brighter to me than usual out here. All the Christmas lights, maybe?"

"Maybe." People certainly hadn't held back with their decorating. Even the decks on the rear of the homes lining the beach were lit up with strands of lights. One had a big blow-up Santa waving at them. More than one had Christmas trees.

And in some strange Christmas coincidence, two had festive flamingos wearing Santa hats. Florida never disappointed.

They walked without saying anything at first, both content to just be in the moment. Claire loved the soft shushing of the waves and the salty tang in the air. It always gave her a sense of peace.

Finally, she spoke. "This is a privilege, you know."

"What is?" he asked.

"Being able to walk on the beach on Christmas Day. Or, more appropriately, Christmas Night."

"You're right, it is. Even more so because we get to do it with someone very special."

She smiled, although she wasn't sure he could see it. "That does make it better." They went another minute in silence. "Maybe we should do this every Christmas Night. Make it a new tradition. What do you think?"

"I like that," Danny said. "Having traditions is important." He hesitated. "Did you have a lot of those with Bryan?"

Claire snorted. "We were lucky if Bryan was home. These last few years, he wasn't. Not on Christmas Day. Too busy with work, which I now know was code for Paulina. You know, I love Christmas. Always have, but the last few years it's been hard to feel that way. Not this year. Not with you."

Danny pulled her toward him and put his arm around her. "I'm so sorry you had to go through all that. But then again, it brought you to me, so I'm not completely upset about it."

She laughed. "I know what you mean. But I'm not sure I would have survived as well as I did if not for you. You were definitely in the right place at the right time."

He snuck a quick kiss against her temple. "We both were. And you didn't just survive. You *thrived*.

Life is funny that way. It takes you through some awful valleys only to raise you up on glorious peaks and somehow, along the way, it shows you how much stronger you are than you realized."

She *was* stronger. She knew that. Despite what she'd been through, she'd come out the other side a better person. Better because of Danny, too.

"For the record," he said. "I hope this peak lasts for the rest of my life."

"Me, too." She exhaled. "I love my life in a way I never thought possible. I feel...unbelievably blessed. Not just because I have you, although you are a huge part of the reason. But because my entire family is in such a good place right now."

He nodded. "They are. Kat and Alex are great together. He's an exceptional young man, not the easiest thing to find these days."

"And she's got a great job. Then there's Jules, who has somehow become a bigger star than I think even she thought was possible. Well, not somehow. She's got more talent in her little finger than half the musicians on the radio these days."

"Cash is right there with her."

"Yes, he is. I'm very proud of both of them. And my other nephew, Fender, who is making his way in the world very nicely. I can't believe he's going to be a dad."

"Your mom and Conrad sure seem happy."

"They do. And they've written a book! My mom is going to be a published author. If that's not crazy, I don't know what is."

"How about the fact that you have single-handedly brought back a Florida tradition? People come from all over to try your sour orange pie."

"Okay, you're right, that is pretty crazy, too." She slid her hand into his and brought them to a stop. "How did all of this happen? How did I get here? Less than a year ago, my life exploded in a way I never thought I'd come back from and now..."

She shook her head as she stared up at him. "Do you believe in miracles? Because there's really no other explanation."

He smiled, wrapping his arms around. "I've always believed in miracles. I also always thought they happened to other people. Not me. Until I met you."

She nodded, understanding that feeling exactly. Life hadn't suddenly become perfect, but it was about as close as she'd ever experienced. "Yes, I feel that way, too. I guess I was meant to be here, in

Diamond Beach. So I could meet you. Because we were meant to be together."

"I couldn't agree with that more. And we're going to have a great life. The best kind. Nothing but happiness and blue skies and sunny days. Even when the skies aren't so blue or the days so sunny. You know what I mean?"

"I do." She smiled at his confidence, letting it flood her with a sweet sense of bliss. Easy to do, because she felt the same way. "You know what the best part is?"

"What's that?"

She leaned in to kiss him. "There is so much more to come."

Claire's Snowball Cookies

Ingredients

2 sticks or 1 cup salted butter, at room temperature

½ cup powdered sugar

1 ½ teaspoon vanilla extract

Dash of nutmeg

2 ¼ cups sifted all-purpose flour

1 cup very finely chopped pecans/pecan flour

½ cup powdered sugar reserved (more if needed)

Instructions

Preheat the oven to 350 degrees.

In a large bowl, whip the butter, first 1/2 cup of powdered sugar, and vanilla together with an electric mixer until smooth. Gradually mix in flour, and pecans, until thoroughly incorporated. Roll dough into ping pong ball sizes and place 2 inches apart onto parchment-lined baking sheets.

Bake until the bottoms are just golden brown but tops are still pale. Approximately 12 to 15 minutes.

Don't let the cookies get too brown!

Take the cookies out of the oven and let cool for a few minutes.

Once cool enough to handle but still very warm, roll the cookies in the reserved powdered sugar to coat, then transfer to wire racks to cool. Once cooled, roll cookies in the powdered sugar once more, if desired.

Want to know when Maggie's next book comes out?
Then don't forget to sign up for her newsletter at her
website!

Also, if you enjoyed the book, please recommend it to a
friend. Even better yet, leave a review and let others
know.

About Maggie:

Maggie Miller thinks time off is time best spent at the beach, probably because the beach is her happy place. The sound of the waves is her favorite background music, and the sand between her toes is the best massage she can think of.

When she's not at the beach, she's writing or reading or cooking for her family. All of that stuff called life. She hopes her readers enjoy her books and welcomes them to drop her a line and let her know what they think!

Maggie Online:

www.maggiemillerauthor.com
www.facebook.com/MaggieMillerAuthor

Made in United States
Orlando, FL
16 May 2024

46908274R00232